Vengeance Delayed

Lady Mary Mysteries, Book 2

Alyson Chase

ARE YOU SIGNED UP FOR DRAGONBLADE'S BLOG?

You'll get the latest news and information on exclusive giveaways, exclusive excerpts, coming releases, sales, free books, cover reveals and more.

Check out our complete list of authors, too!

No spam, no junk. That's a promise!

Sign Up Here

www.dragonbladepublishing.com

Dearest Reader;

Thank you for your support of a small press. At Dragonblade Publishing, we strive to bring you the highest quality Historical Romance from some of the best authors in the business. Without your support, there is no 'us', so we sincerely hope you adore these stories and find some new favorite authors along the way.

Happy Reading!

CEO, Dragonblade Publishing

Additional Dragonblade books by Author Alyson Chase

Lady Mary Mysteries
Envy Unchecked (Book 1)
Vengeance Delayed (Book 2)

Author's Note

Hello, dear reader. One of the things I love about writing historical fiction is all the research I get to do for the time period. I can see pictures of the clothing my characters would have worn and learn of the fascinating people and ideas that shaped the world I'm writing in. As a history lover, it's a blast.

But one of the things I hate about writing historical fiction is all the research I have to do. It's a paradox, I know. Checking every other word on etymonline.com to see if it was in usage yet. Making sure I don't mention door knobs (although according to my research, they are about to start being used in my time period). And most irritating of all, finding out that a perfect plot point can't be used because the knowledge or level of advancement in a science or industry didn't exist yet.

To that end, I must admit that sometimes I fudge things. Just a little. If my etymology research shows that a word wasn't known to be used until 1830, well, I might slip it in. My books are set around 1820, and that's close enough. And there is one thing I fudged in this book that I feel I should make you aware of. It isn't a large plot point, but I'd feel guilty just letting the misinformation slip by unnoted.

Lady Mary references the mental disorder of 'moral insanity' and the research on it by Phillipe Pinel. The term 'moral insanity' was actually coined by James Cowles Prichard in his 1835 work titled *Treatise on Insanity and Other Disorders Affecting the Mind*. This is fourteen years too late for my purposes. But Prichard was inspired by the work of Pinel, acknowledging his contributions to Prichard's own study of the field. And I really wanted to use the nifty term 'moral insanity.' So I attributed it to Pinel instead.

Even with all the tools of research at my disposal, I'm certain I still get some historical facts wrong. To err is human, and all that. Since this was an intentional misattribution, however, I hope this note will suffice by way of apology. For me, story is greater than strict historical accuracy. I hope you feel the same.

Chapter One

Lady Mary

Devon 1821

IT WAS A miserable night. For the hundredth time I was regretting accepting his invitation, familial obligation or naught, and I'd only been at his estate for two days.

Lightning blanched the faces of the guests in the sitting room, the rumble of thunder following like a slow-moving rock slide.

"I think the storm is moving away." Miss Walker turned up the wick on the oil lamp next to her chair, her voice brimming with more hope than confidence.

Our host, and, unfortunately, also my brother-in-law, rolled his eyes. "It has been coming on us, steadily closer, this entire evening. One would think a country mouse would be more familiar with such tempests."

My two days' acquaintance with the 'country mouse' had left me an unfavorable impression of her person, but I disliked my husband's brother even more. "Truly, Perrin, we are all feeling imprisoned by this weather, but it is no reason to act boorishly. I'm certain Miss Walker has better things to do with her time than study storm patterns."

The little I had learned about the woman made me wonder if this were true. Miss Charlotte Walker, a plain but agreeable looking woman in her thirties, was the nearest neighbor to the

Earl of Perrin. At least the nearest with any significant social standing. She was the only child of a sickly baron and apparently had never wed in order to take care of her father. She had proven a dull conversationalist and an atrocious partner at whist, but neither of those conditions earned an insult from her host.

"Oh, it's all right." Miss Walker tittered, the uncomely curls that framed her face jiggling. "I *should* know more about the natural world having lived in the country all my life. The earl is perfectly correct."

I ground my jaw. The woman was also insufferably ingratiating in her behavior to Perrin. I would have thought my brother-in-law would have liked her better for it.

"Well, I for one have never seen the like of this storm." Lord Havenstone stood and stretched. He was a baron from the north of the country who had apparently attended Eton with Lord Perrin. From our two days' acquaintance I'd learned he was subject to bursts of joviality which were quickly dampened by his wife. "Lady Havenstone and I had hoped to do some riding on your southern lands, but it looks to be raining the entire week of this house party."

His wife looked up at him from the settee. "The riding on our property isn't much different. Our estate is quite as large as Perrin's."

"Yes, but we don't have those lovely sea cliffs," Lord Havenstone said wistfully.

"My lord does have an impressive estate," Mr. Taylor agreed. If there were a contest between who could be more obsequious to my brother-in-law, I wasn't sure who would win, the neighbor Miss Walker, or Perrin's secretary, Jeremiah Taylor. Mr. Taylor had drawn up a chair next to another guest, Miss Smith, and when he wasn't paying the young lady compliments, he was doing everything in his power to bolster his employer's ego.

Not that it needed further bolstering.

"Shall I continue reading from where I left off last night?" Miss Smith lifted the Mary Shelley book from her lap. She tucked a strand of her light brown hair behind her ear. "It's a good story for a dark and stormy night."

"That will be a strong inducement for me to join your father in the billiards room." Mr. Bertram Withers shifted in his chair, a frown creasing his face. He'd arrived this morning and said little all day. He was of a stern, taciturn disposition, and I wondered at his accepting an invitation to anything so merry as a house party.

But Bertram had always had a core of kindness. He must feel the same sense of familial duty as I did. He was Perrin's brother-in-law, as well, his sister having married the earl. I wasn't quite sure what that made us, his sister's husband having been my husband's brother. No direct relation, certainly, but there was a connection. I rubbed my breastbone. One that had grown thin over the years.

There had been a time when we used to see each other often. Lord and Lady Perrin, Bertram and his wife, Martha, me and Cavindish. We'd come together for holidays. Enjoyed each other's company. Well, as much as our differing personalities would allow.

But then my Cavindish had died, much too young. At least he hadn't suffered through a protracted illness like Bertram's wife had. The last time I'd seen Martha, the pain had clouded her mind. And she'd grown so thin, had trouble feeding herself, and was too proud to want help.

And then Lady Perrin had left us not two years past, and from such a stupid cause. Falling off a ladder while tending one of her climbing vines in her garden.

One would have thought that as Bertram, Perrin, and I were all widowers and widow connected by family, our common grief would have brought us closer.

One would be wrong.

"Mr. Withers, that is most unjust." Mr. Taylor leaned closer to Miss Smith. "Miss Smith's readings are most compelling." He turned to her. "You speak so well, you know."

Miss Smith angled her body away from the secretary. "Yes,

I'd always heard that was one of my more admirable features. Some women can paint masterpieces. Others write works advocating for universal human rights. I can talk."

Mr. Taylor furrowed his forehead. "Uh…. Yes. Quite."

I smothered a snort.

Bertram removed a deck of playing cards from an inside coat pocket. He plucked a card from the top of the deck and rolled it between his fingers. "We could play a round or two of faro. I know Perrin is always eager for a chance to recoup some of his losses."

Perrin grunted, digging the knuckle of his thumb into his chest. "Not tonight." Another wave of thunder rattled the windows. "Damn this storm. Not only will it trap us all indoors together, but I fear it will keep my remaining guest away, and I had so wanted him to join us." He accompanied that last remark with a significant look to myself, one I wasn't sure how to interpret.

I frowned. Perrin and I had few acquaintances in common, and none that would make me uneasy. He was up to something, and not knowing what it was annoyed me.

Lady Havenstone cleared her throat. "Have you heard anything about Cook Clem, Lord Perrin? Is he recovering his strength?"

Everyone in the room leant forward to better hear Perrin's answer. A large inducement to travel to Perrin Manor had been the well-earned reputation of its chef. Perrin had discovered the man in some unknown village near the border of Wales and plucked him up. The meals at Perrin Manor were held in great acclaim. Cook Clem was a master in the kitchen.

The chef was not yet thirty. While Perrin Manor was a step up from some country hamlet, the nearest village of Modbury was hardly a lively metropolis. Tucked away in the remote southwest of England, it lacked the verve and vigor a young man might desire. I wondered if the chef had ever considered a move to London.

Perrin slapped his hand down on his thigh. "I wish everyone would stop pestering me about him. Clem has merely caught a chill in this dratted weather. He'll be back in the kitchen soon."

Like we were all a part of a collective bladder, the guests in the sitting room sagged back in their chairs, deflated. Soon wasn't soon enough.

"It isn't as though I don't miss his cooking, too," Perrin grumbled. He rubbed a stomach that had gradually expanded over the years. "The assistant cook's meals give me colic."

I looked heavenward. Dinner hadn't been that bad, merely completely lacking in flavor. But Perrin always found any opportunity to gripe about his situation. Though if I went this whole trip without tasting one meal from Clem, I feared I would match my brother-in-law's ill temper.

Lady Havenstone sat forward in her chair. She was a slender woman with a turned-up nose which gave her the appearance of disapproving of everything she saw. "I have a tonic that might help Cook Clem. When I catch a chill, it straightens me right out."

"He is being well taken care of," Perrin nearly shouted. He glared at the baroness.

Lady Havenstone glared back. If she had any tonics for the colic Perrin had mentioned, I noticed she didn't offer those to him for any relief.

An uncomfortable silence reigned, with only the heavy pelting of the rain sounding in the room.

After a moment, I raised one shoulder. "We could always—"

"No." Perrin sagged back in his chair. "We will not be entertaining another of *your* suggestions."

I glowered down at my boots. If more of my suggestions were entertained, this would be a much livelier party.

My scowl deepened when I examined the lace trim on the hem of my gown. The trim newly acquired to hide the small tears one of Perrin's beasts had inflicted upon my Mornine gown. There was no good food at this house party, a pesky animal was always underfoot, and I had to suffer through dull company. I never should have come. I lifted one boot to bring the lilac trim closer to the light. The needlework of Perrin's maids was excellent, however.

Miss Walker stood and went to the sideboard. She poured a glass of wine from Perrin's amber decanter and brought it to Perrin. "Being forced to remain indoors isn't such a bad thing when the company is good."

There existed another awkward moment.

"I don't know how you drink that rot," Bertram said, nodding at Perrin's glass. "You must have a stomach of iron."

"Wormwood is good for the digestion." Perrin took a large swallow as an example.

Miss Walker tugged on one of the poorly-cut curls that framed her face. Whichever maid had done that to Miss Walker's hair should be barred from ever holding another pair of shears. "Have you thought about refurbishing Perrin Manor, my lord?" She poured a drink of her own, a small glass of sherry. "My father and I recently repainted the first floor of our home. It makes such a difference. You should come by soon for supper and see."

"My paint colors are fine," Perrin said. He removed his handkerchief from his pocket and dabbed his forehead.

"Yes, but even rearranging things can make such a difference." Miss Walker pointed to a portrait above the mantel. It was of the Lady Perrin, commissioned soon after her marriage to the earl. She'd had the same dark eyes as her brother Bertram, but a much cheerier disposition. "I've always thought that picture would look so much better in a west facing room. The library perhaps."

A room Miss Walker most likely didn't enter, and therefore a place where she wouldn't have to see the portrait of Perrin's late wife. All of the neighbor woman's flutterings and flatterings toward Perrin, a most undeserving subject, led me to the conclusion that she desired to be the Lady Perrin. Reminders of the past countess could only be displeasing to Miss Walker.

I looked toward Miss Smith. That young lady's presence here must be a similar cross for Miss Walker to bear.

Perrin scowled. "What does the direction of a painting matter? No, it stays put. Besides"—Perrin gave me a sly look from the corner of his eye—"it's a good reminder of how fortunate I was in my marriage. I've always said a good wife makes or breaks a man. When disloyalty is found in a home, you can be sure the man is miserable."

And there it was again. A poisoned-tipped dart Perrin seemed to have aimed at me. One I couldn't understand. While our relationship had never been what one would call amiable, it had always been civil. He was my husband's brother. I respected that connection. I'd thought he did, as well. Ever since I'd arrived at Perrin Manor, however, I'd felt a sort of malice directed at me, almost as if....

My stomach cramped. No. That made no sense. There was no way he could know.

"Well, if my wife doesn't find it too disloyal, I think I will leave her and all of you to join Mr. Smith at billiards." Lord Havenstone ran his fingers over his wife's shoulder. "Be careful what you and the other ladies get up to, my love. On a night such as this, one never knows what sorts of monsters and ghosts will want to steal away fair ladies."

Frowning, she brushed his hand from her person. "Stop being foolish. The only monster here is the storm."

The casement doors that led to the back terrace whipped open, making everyone jump. Wind rushed inside, blowing out every candle. In the threshold, a figure loomed, black against a flare of lightning. It looked human in form but it was misshapen. Wrong.

The men jumped to their feet.

Miss Walker screamed.

Chapter Two

Lady Mary

"GOOD GRACIOUS." I pressed my hand to my thumping heart. "There's no need to scream down the rafters. It is only Mr. Evans."

The man in question ambled in sheepishly, clutching something to his chest, his shoulders curled around it. He shut the doors and the whirlwind sweeping about the room stilled. "I apologize for startling you. The wind took the doors from my hand, opening them harder than I would have liked."

Miss Walker pressed a hand to her chest. "Oh, goodness. My heart nearly stopped."

Mr. Taylor busied himself relighting the candles in the candelabra along the wall.

Perrin went to the sideboard and poured himself another glass of wormwood wine. "You look a disaster. And you're dripping all over my floors." He sniffed. "What were you doing out in the storm?" He went back to his chair and dropped onto it heavily.

"I thought I saw something moving out the window of the library." Mr. Evans held up the bundle he cradled. When the beast caught sight of me, it started to wriggle. "And I was right. Southey was caught out in the rain."

All the women in the room cooed: all except me. That dog had been underfoot ever since I'd arrived, putting tiny holes in my gowns and slippers and nearly sending me down a flight of stairs. The little black terrier might be a fetching-looking dog, and was undoubtedly proficient at his job as he'd left a dead mouse on my bedroom's doorstep, but frankly, I would have preferred the rodents.

"Well, don't let him—"

Mr. Evans bent and let Southey jump to the floor.

"—go." I watched with dread as the dog raced around the corner of a settee and headed straight for me. He made to jump onto my lap, but a cleverly placed elbow dissuaded him from that action. Instead, he stood in front of me and shook with all his might. It started with his head, the swinging to and fro moving down through his spine, until only his rear end vibrated. He sat back on his haunches and panted happily up at me.

Jaw clenched, I removed my spectacles and dried them with my handkerchief. There was nothing I could do for my gown.

I leveled a glare at the man who had brought the fur demon into the room. Mr. Henry Evans had been at Perrin Manor when I'd arrived. He was Perrin's attorney and here to draw up a marriage contract if the gossip of the servants could be trusted.

I looked to the woman on the other end of that contract.

Miss Katherine Smith had much to recommend herself to becoming the wife of an earl. Most significantly, a sizeable fortune. Her father was a wealthy man of business who had already successfully married off his two elder daughters to peers.

Not that the woman herself didn't have her own charms. A little shorter than my own five foot five inches, Miss Smith had honey-colored hair and a healthy figure. She couldn't have been older than five and twenty, but her large, brown eyes held the wariness of someone much older. Or perhaps what I saw was sadness.

That wariness was on display when Mr. Taylor again seated himself next to her, turning an unctuous smile her way, and she popped to her feet. I nodded. If she wanted to marry the earl, she couldn't let his secretary make cow eyes at her. Miss Smith went to the oil lamp on Perrin's right side and lengthened the wick, making the light flare.

Perrin flinched. "Turn that damn thing down."

Miss Smith blinked, but did as he asked. "As you wish," she replied, a hint of ice in her voice.

Perrin groped for her hand. "I apologize, my dear. It's been a long day."

Miss Smith smiled tightly while sliding her hand free. "Of course." She left Perrin's side and stood by me.

"Indeed, it has been a long day." Miss Walker rose and took Miss Smith's place by Perrin's side. "After calling for the servants to bring a hot bath for Mr. Evans, how about I direct them to set one up for you, as well? It will do you good on a night like this."

I blinked. Even for close neighbors, ordering a man's bath was a bit presumptuous. All Miss Walker needed was a chatelaine fastened to her waist and her image as mistress of the manor would be complete.

My brother-in-law must have felt the same and disapproved. Perrin pushed to standing. "I don't need anyone telling me what is good for me." Frowning, he tromped from the room, his shoulder bumping into the doorframe.

Miss Walker swallowed and looked down at her clasped hands.

"Well, a hot bath sounds good to me," Mr. Evans said kindly. "Chasing after dogs has left me drenched to the bone. I'll pop down to the kitchen to ask—"

"I'll do it." Miss Walker lifted her chin. "And ask someone to dry those puddles you've brought in." She strode from the room.

Southey watched her go before returning his attention to my new lace trim.

The attorney ran his hand up the back of his wet head. "Well, I guess I'll go clean up." He moved just as Miss Smith did, the two almost bumping into each other. He moved left just as she moved right. He went right as she stepped left.

Miss Smith stepped back, sighing heavily. "This won't do. 'And Benjamin, among the stars, beheld a dancing, and a glancing, such retreating and advancing—'"

"—'As, I ween, was never seen, in bloodiest battle since the day of Mars,'" Mr. Evans finished.

Miss Smith's eyebrows shot up. "You read modern poetry?"

Mr. Evans arched his own dark eyebrow. "I may not have attended Eton, Miss Smith, but even us lowly solicitors enjoy reading. In fact, it is what we are best trained to do."

Miss Smith crossed her arms over her chest. "Clearly. An Eton man would know to formally request a dance. And provide some music."

"Next time then." The attorney swept a magnificent leg, bowing deeply, with his arm extended to allow her to pass.

Miss Smith's lips twitched as she walked past him to the sideboard.

"Good evening," Mr. Evans said to the rest of us, and left the room, a trail of water following after him.

"Well, at least we've had some entertainment." Lady Havenstone pursed her lips. "And that Miss Walker seems awfully familiar with the household doings of Perrin Manor."

Her husband nudged her, and jerked his head toward Miss Smith. "I'm *sure* it's just the familiarity from living so close to Perrin Manor."

The lady colored. "Oh, yes, I'm certain you're right, of course."

"Don't be certain on my account." Miss Smith picked up a napkin and unfolded it. She returned to my chair and knelt beside Southey. "While I am only a guest in this house, Miss Walker can be as familiar as she wishes." She took a bit of this evening's dinner from the napkin, a chunk of overcooked chicken, and fed it to the dog.

Southey wolfed it down, not seeming to mind the inferior cooking.

Lady Havenstone scooted to the edge of her seat. "But aren't you to become the mistress of this house? Heed my warning, a neighbor like that will be trouble."

And if the baroness hadn't looked so gleeful at the idea of said trouble, her warning might have had greater effect.

Miss Smith finished feeding Southey and refolded the napkin. "Nothing is settled as yet." She rose to her feet. "I'm going to check on my father. The last time he played billiards, he broke his cue stick in anger." With a nod and a tight smile, she departed.

I shook my foot, dislodging Southey. The girl didn't seem as eager to wed an earl as I would have expected. But Perrin was over twice her age. I could see how that would be hard on a young woman.

Lady Havenstone sat back in her chair. "My advice was well-intended." She lifted her chin.

Lord Havenstone patted her shoulder before making his own exit. Mr. Taylor and Bertram began making their excuses until only I and Lady Havenstone remained.

"Well, this is the dreariest party I've ever attended." Lady Havenstone poked at the bowl of nuts next to her and picked out an almond. "Though we have days yet. It could become more lively."

"Yes." Or it could be a full week of tedium. I wondered how Jane, my lady's maid, was spending her time. She was bound to have better conversation than this. It was times like these that had me especially missing my club. The Minerva Club was never lacking in interesting conversation. I had just resolved to retire myself when Miss Smith hurried back in, dropping onto a settee.

Southey trotted over to her and sniffed her feet.

My eyebrows drew together. "Are you all right? You look quite flushed."

Miss Smith smiled tightly. "I'm quite well." She bent and picked up the dog, settling him on her lap.

Mr. Taylor strolled in, and Miss Smith tensed.

Ah. More unwanted advances from the secretary. That man

had more bollocks than brains if he made an avid pursuit of his employer's affianced. It almost made me respect the man.

Mr. Taylor wandered about the room, adjusting a picture, poking at the fire. When he came near my seat, he picked up the knife that lay on the side table. "You couldn't get anyone to join you in throwing practice, Lady Mary?" A smile curved his lips.

I looked sadly at the knife. It had a three-inch blade and a lovely mother-of-pearl handle. The balance was excellent, and from what I'd learned from the classes at my club, would have made an excellent throwing knife. "You heard Perrin. Not in his house. Maybe if the weather clears tomorrow…."

Mr. Taylor tossed it back on the table with a rattle. "Well, I suppose I will go to bed. Good evening, ladies." He might have bowed before he left the room; it might have been the curved set of his shoulders that made it appear so.

I tapped my fingers on the arm of my chair. Another week of this tedium would be untenable.

"Dash it all." Lady Havenstone stood. "I always say, when in doubt, eat. Instead of twiddling our thumbs, let's go see if any of the sweets remain in the dining room."

As the dining room was just next door, I had no objection. Lady Havenstone, Miss Smith, and I went through the adjoining doors, the dog trailing behind. With a stomach full of bite-sized tarts, even those of marginal quality, I found myself in a much better mood. It helped that Miss Smith doted on Southey, keeping his attentions, and his sharp little teeth, elsewhere. I was even amenable to Lady Havenstone's suggestion of reading aloud for the remainder of the evening.

"But let's not continue with *Frankenstein*," I said. "I'm in the mood for something cheerier. If we keep reading that book, we're liable to see specters and hear banshees and all manner of horrors while we're lying in our beds."

The horrors didn't wait until we were snug abed. A woman's scream tore through our cheerful reading. We ignored the crashing sound from the adjoining sitting room and ran out into the main hall, to the source of the yelling. A maid and two footmen were clustered together at the base of the stairs leading up to the first floor.

I hurried toward them as people drifted from other parts of the house to investigate the noise, as well. I paused next to the young maid, wrapping my arm around her shaking shoulders.

Because there, at the foot of the staircase, lay Lord Perrin. His eyes stared vacantly at the ceiling. A knife with a mother-of-pearl handle stuck out from his chest.

Chapter Three

Henry

THE SCENE WAS grotesque, the brutal image an insult to the sanctity of life. The body left for all and sundry to see was a further insult. Henry Evans hadn't particularly liked Lord Perrin, but no one deserved such.

Henry came down the steps, rubbing a towel to his hair, still damp from his bath. He perused the faces of those crowded about the body. Shock was the dominant emotion. Miss Walker had started weeping, her sobs grating in the otherwise hushed silence. Mr. Smith, still holding a cue stick in his hand from his game in the billiards room, looked more intrigued than shocked. His daughter, the lovely Miss Smith, looked ill.

And frightened.

Henry stepped carefully around the body and realized, as Perrin's attorney, he held the most authority right now. It would fall to him to organize matters. And the first step was removing the women from this gruesome scene.

"Please, we've all had a terrible shock," he said. "If you could go to the sitting room. I'm sure we could all do with something hot to drink to settle the nerves." He started herding the group away from the body with small presses of his palm on the backs of gapers.

One woman stepped away from his prodding hands and walked closer to the body. "I recognize that knife." Lady Mary tilted her head, a small frown pinching her face. "And stabbed in the chest without any indication that he attempted to fight back. Interesting."

Henry cupped her elbow. "You can tell the magistrate all about the knife when he arrives." He tried drawing her away, but she was surprisingly adept at escaping his grip for a woman of her age.

Ignoring her for the moment, Henry turned to one of the footmen. "Can you find a blanket to cover his body?"

The young man nodded and trotted off.

Henry went to the butler, a short but plump man who hadn't moved except to blink since seeing Perrin's body. Henry rested a hand on his shoulder and squeezed lightly. "Can you send someone to fetch the nearest magistrate?"

The butler pointed a shaking finger at the body. "My lord was the magistrate for this county, but there's a constable in Modbury. We could send for him. He should know what to do."

A constable for a village of not even two thousand souls? Henry didn't hold out much hope in the experience of the local constable when it came to murder, but as he had no other ideas, he nodded. "Send for him at once."

Looking relieved at having a task, the butler nodded and scurried off. Henry turned to the remaining servants. "If you could serve coffee and tea to the guests and then join us in the sitting room, I think that would be most appropriate. I don't want anyone alone at the moment."

They nodded and set off, leaving only Lord Perrin's body in the hall. And Lady Mary.

The earl's sister-in-law had a presence much larger than her physical size. She was most likely half a foot shorter than he, with the snowy white hair and faded blue eyes of one who had seen quite a few years. But she held her spine ramrod straight and had an air of independence Henry was willing to bet caused consternation in her relations.

"My lady, I know this is distressing, but I feel it best that we join the others." He held out his arm, indicating the direction of the sitting room. "The proper authorities will take the situation in hand."

The woman snorted and pushed her spectacles higher up her nose. "Your faith in our justice system is stronger than mine, but perhaps you've never known an innocent person who was arrested." She circled the body. "Does something about this seem amiss?"

Henry shook his head. "Aside from the intentional taking of a life?"

"Yes, aside from that." She bent, stretching her hand toward the knife handle, and Henry hurried forward.

He grabbed her wrist. "We cannot disturb the body before the constable arrives." Nor after. Why anyone would want to touch a dead body, much less a lady of quality, was a question he didn't want to ponder.

"Of course, you're right." Lady Mary stepped aside as a footman appeared with a heavy wool blanket.

Henry took one end, the footman the other, and they gently draped the cloth over Perrin. The bulge from the knife under the shroud almost made the tableau more obscene, if that were possible.

"Now, the sitting room, my lady?" When Henry guided her out of the hall, this time, she allowed it.

The rear sitting room was spacious, taking up half the length of Perrin Manor's back wall. With all the guests and all the servants crowding into it, however, it felt stifling. Tea and coffee had been distributed, along with stronger spirits, and clusters of people hovered in small groups speaking in hushed tones. Instead of joining her fellow guests, Lady Mary headed straight for a group of maids, leaning in to whisper something in her lady's maid's ear.

"Bloody hell." Lord Havenstone lifted one foot to peer at the bottom of his boot. "I've stepped in something and tracked it on the rug."

Henry frowned. Everyone had experienced a great shock, but that was little excuse for poor language in front of women.

A maid stepped forward, clasping her hands. "I'm sorry, my lord. When I heard the scream, I dropped a glass of wine I was clearing. I'll get something to clean it up."

"Oh, wait until morning for any cleaning." Lady Mary squeezed her maid's arm, then found the nearest chair to drop into. "After such a nasty business, no one should have to clean. Everyone, avoid that wet spot near the sideboard."

"Is everyone here?" Henry looked to the butler.

"Yes. Well, everyone except Cook Clem. He still remains abed." There was a round of forlorn sighs before the butler continued. Perrin's famed chef had been a draw to many of the guests for accepting his invitation, Henry knew. His illness and temporary replacement with a less experienced cook had been much lamented. "But the stable master and all his men are here, along with every other servant."

"Where's the dog?" Lady Mary looked at her ankles, as though expecting the terrier to appear at any moment.

"We put him in a room with food and a warm bed." The butler scratched his head. "We didn't want him getting in-to…well, with the body there, we didn't want…."

Henry nodded. "Quite right. For those who might yet be unaware, Lord Perrin's body was found at the bottom of the main staircase with a knife in his chest." Henry rubbed his own chest. It must have hurt, Perrin's death. Did he not have time to cry out in pain?

"Who found him?" Lady Mary asked.

A red-haired maid raised her hand. "I did. Me and Bob, 'ere. We were going upstairs to check on that one leak, see if the bucket needed emptying. But we didn't 'ave nothing to do with the lord's death."

The butler drew his shoulders back. "Of course not, Marie.

No one would think you had."

Henry was silent. He wouldn't have thought anyone here could have done such a thing, but obviously, he'd been wrong. Someone had.

"I can't believe he's gone." Mr. Taylor wiped his brow with his handkerchief. "He was always so good to me."

That Henry found difficult to believe. Lord Perrin had treated Henry, a solicitor, with barely disguised contempt. And attorneys were a step above personal secretaries in the hierarchy of society. But perhaps Perrin had treated the man who worked with him day to day better.

Or perhaps the shock of sudden death had erased some of Taylor's more unpleasant memories of the earl.

"And an even better neighbor." Miss Walker dabbed at her eyes. "Always so generous."

A bark of laughter burst from Mr. Smith's lips, his bushy eyebrows quivering. He had the grace to look embarrassed at his lack of decorum. "I'm sorry. I believe one shouldn't speak ill of the dead, but that doesn't mean one has to lionize them, either. Not when it isn't warranted."

In my dealings with Miss Katherine Smith's father, I had no problem believing that the man only spoke his mind. He'd been most vocal in his objections when he'd learned of the change in terms in the marriage contract. Perrin's office had nearly shaken from the oaths and insults Mr. Smith had shouted. He'd made Lord Perrin quite aware what he thought of him in life. Why should he stop in death?

"Here, here." Mr. Bertram Withers, Perrin's brother-in-law, raised his glass. "Not everyone is deserving of tears."

"How can you say that?" Miss Walker daubed a handkerchief under her eyes. "He was the best of men."

Lady Havenstone, seated near Miss Walker, leaned over and patted the woman's knee. "I'm sure he'll be greatly missed."

"Not everyone will miss him." Lady Mary leaned back and stared at the ceiling. A lock of her white hair escaped their pins.

"Somebody stabbed him."

That set off another round of tears from Miss Walker and several female servants. Miss Smith, Henry noted, the victim's intended, remained dry-eyed. The marriage had seemed more a business arrangement than love match, and a business arrangement that showed all the signs of crumbling. Henry wouldn't blame the woman for feeling some relief. He dragged his gaze from her face when Lady Mary continued speaking.

"There wouldn't have been much time," the lady said. "After Mr. Taylor picked up the knife, it wasn't more than ten minutes that we'd left this room unoccupied for the killer to pick it up and use it."

All eyes swung to the secretary. "Yes, I picked it up. It was just lying on that side table. But I put it back down. You saw me put it back down, Lady Mary."

"Yes, I saw." She tapped her lips with her knuckle. "Anyone could have come back in to grab it."

"This is all good information that the authorities will want to hear." Henry rubbed the back of his neck. All things considered, he wished he were back in the storm chasing dogs. "Perhaps we should wait for the constable to arrive before we speculate."

"That won't be happening for a while, I'm afraid." A man stepped into the sitting room, the bottom of his legs and his collar dripping wet. He gave a slight shake to his head, water droplets flying.

Lady Mary sucked in a breath and sat up straight at the man's entrance. Her eyes narrowed. "Mr. Ryder. What are you doing here?"

The man dipped his head, a smile curving his lips. He was tall and lean, his light-brown hair threaded through with silver and white. "I was invited." His face went serious once more. "And I'm afraid I'm the last person who will arrive here until the rain stops. The road is washed out. My carriage driver and I had to walk the last mile."

A footman stepped up beside him. "He's right. I tried riding for Modbury, but turned around when I met Mr. Ryder here. I was risking a broken leg on my horse trying to ride through the muck. We'll have to wait for the sun to dry things out a bit before getting help."

The muscles in Henry's back knotted. Their host had been murdered and ingress and egress from the house had been blocked.

It looked like they were on their own.

Chapter Four

Katherine

MISS KATHERINE SMITH had thought marriage to a man she didn't respect the worst thing that could happen to her. A prison with a sentence of life.

Now she faced a much worse prison. A real one. Or worse. She rested her palm on the base of her throat, trying not to imagine how a hangman's noose would feel.

Someone walked past, jostling her arm, but she barely noticed. It had all happened so quickly. One moment he had been there, grabbing at her, and the next, lying dead at the bottom of the steps. She hadn't even pushed him. But Lord Perrin had been in his cups, slurring his words and unsteady. It hadn't taken much to make him fall.

Katherine's stomach twisted. She had killed a man. She hadn't intended to, but the earl was dead just the same.

A porcelain cup was lowered before her gaze. She blinked and looked up. The attorney, Mr. Evans, held the cup out to her.

He gave her a sympathetic smile. "Hot tea will be good for your nerves. And I added a splash of a little something extra. This situation has distressed us all."

She forced herself to smile back. No one could be as distressed as her, and she, the least deserving of feeling that emotion.

But Mr. Taylor had told her how pointless it would be for the accident to destroy two lives. She'd been too shocked to disagree.

"Thank you," she murmured. The cup rattled in its saucer as she lowered it to her lap.

Mr. Evans squatted at her side. He had the body of someone who worked hard labor, tall and strong, rather than a man who sat at a desk all day writing contracts, but his face was kind, his whiskey brown eyes warm.

It was those eyes that almost undid her, making the backs of her own burn.

He rested his hand on the armrest of her chair. "I promise, you and the other women will be safe. I'll make sure of it."

"Safe?" Katherine's father frowned. He stood across from her on the other side of the low table. "Of course, she'll be safe. Why wouldn't she be? No one would want to harm *her*."

The room quieted, all eyes turning toward her father. His voice did tend to carry. He shrugged. "I've said it before and I'll say it again. There's no need to lionize the dead. Perrin could be a right sot."

Katherine's chest ached. And yet her father had intended to marry her off to such a man. When he had first approached her about the idea of marriage to Perrin, she had thought her father at least respected the earl. That he could give his daughter into the care of a man he didn't like had never occurred to her.

Her sisters had been happily settled. While there might not have been ardent feelings toward their husbands when they'd married, they were now quite content with their stations. She had trusted her father to provide the same situation for herself.

Until Katherine had met Lord Perrin. Then she'd known she would never be content married to him.

But perhaps it had been easier to find suitable matches for her sisters. Her eldest sister was exceptionally beautiful. Her likeness had been used by a renowned painter as the face of the goddess Venus. Her other sister was exceptionally brilliant and kind, a combination that wasn't often found together. Katherine wasn't exceptionally anything, except perhaps exceptionally sharp-tongued.

And that was not a useful commodity in the marriage market.

And now it didn't matter. None of it mattered. Perhaps she had deserved no better than Lord Perrin.

"How can you speak so?" Miss Walker jumped to her feet. "Lord Perrin was lovely. Just lovely."

Katherine's father arched an eyebrow, dipping his chin. "He toyed with people. Made promises he never intended to keep."

Miss Walker flushed, and suddenly, Katherine could no longer stand it. All the falsehoods. The pretense. The authorities might not be able to reach them now, but eventually a magistrate would come. And she couldn't let an innocent person be accused.

She scooted to the edge of her seat, pressing a hand to her abdomen. "I—"

Someone squeezed her shoulder. Tightly. Looking up, she saw Mr. Taylor shake his head.

The confession died on her lips. It wasn't only herself she'd implicate. How could she bring trouble to Perrin's secretary when all he'd done was try to help her? Katherine dug her nails into her skirts. Though the fact that he could have taken that knife and....

She swallowed. She didn't know quite what that said about him. She knew that Mr. Taylor fancied her, but she hadn't realized his regard was strong enough to help her cover up her crime.

"It has been a trying night," Mr. Taylor said. "I suggest we all retire. Sleep will help us all think more clearly."

To rethink her confession, he meant. Katherine sighed, her shoulders drooping. If she were able to fall asleep, the oblivion would be welcome.

She looked up, and her gaze caught Mr. Evans's. He had a curious expression on his face as he looked at her, to the hand on her shoulder, and up to Mr. Taylor's face. As unobtrusively as possible, Katherine slid out from the secretary's grip and rose.

"Bed does sound like a good idea," she said, looking everywhere but at Mr. Evans.

"Are you not afraid to be alone?" the attorney asked, tilting his head.

If a murderer had been on the loose, Katherine supposed she would be. Exhaustion dragged at her limbs, making her too tired to even attempt to feign concern. "It is as my father says. Lord Perrin had an enemy. I don't believe anyone else is at risk."

Lord Havenstone took his wife's hand and tugged her to standing. "We also are retiring. And we will be taking the rear staircase up to the first floor. My wife doesn't need to see *that* again."

Lady Mary clapped her hands together. "Quite right. Everyone should use the servants' stairs. And I would suggest that Lord Perrin be removed to the ice house until a magistrate can inspect the body. Stevens, can you direct some men to make that happen?"

The butler nodded. "I'll have some lads clear out space in the ice house now."

"Good." Lady Mary patted the lace cap over her ivory hair. She had a decided air of authority, which, as the sister-in-law of the earl, she most likely deserved. "Well, then, since nothing more can be done tonight, I suggest we all go to bed."

Chapter Five

Lady Mary

I WAITED BY the doors of the sitting room, smiling and nodding as Perrin's other guests passed by on their way to their rooms. Either by fortune or by his own devices, Mr. Ryder was the last to exit.

I grabbed his arm and dragged him back into the room. "What," I said, trying to keep the irritation out of my voice, "are you doing here?"

He ran his fingers through his hair, the patches at the temples just going white. "As I said, I was invited," he replied mildly.

"You knew Perrin?" I tried to think on what occasion my proud brother-in-law would befriend the president of the London Society for Morality and Decency. Perhaps as a former attorney, Mr. Ryder had assisted Perrin in a dispute.

"The barest of acquaintances." A loud knock upstairs indicated that one of the guests had closed a bedroom door with excessive force. Ryder poked his head out into the empty hall before returning his attention to me. "The earl's invitation did indicate that you would be in attendance."

My eyebrows snapped together. "And that induced you to come?"

He rubbed his jaw. "Not that it isn't lovely to see you at any time—"

I huffed. The last time we'd seen each other, he'd been trying to get me to shut down my club. The Minerva Club was the only social club in London, probably in all of England, whose members were women. Men seemed to enjoy their time at White's, and the more unsavory clubs; I saw no reason women shouldn't have the same opportunity to shake out their skirts. Perhaps if Perrin had been the type of man to allow my knife-throwing demonstration, he wouldn't have been at the receiving end of the blade.

My face heated at my uncharitable thought. My annoyance only increased at Ryder's next words.

"—but I wondered at the invitation. Why would a member of your family invite someone to a party you were attending whose presence so obviously would perturb you? What did Perrin hope to gain by asking me to be a member of the party? It raised my curiosity."

His dulcet baritone almost had me believing that he'd been concerned. About me. The fact that the man wanted to close my club proved that a lie.

As I had no answer to his questions, except for the obvious one that my husband's brother did, in fact, wish to provoke me, I stomped past him and back to the body. Without the crowd around it, Perrin's lifeless form somehow seemed more macabre. Only his boots showed beneath the blanket, and the tented fabric above the chest made the presence of the knife even more glaring.

I looked at the carpet around Perrin's body. It was large, spanning almost the entire space of the hall and was in muted colors of tans and light greens. Frowning, I bent beside the body and flipped the blanket back.

Perrin's eyes stared at the ceiling.

"What are you doing?" Mr. Ryder lowered gently into a squat next to me, the skin between his eyes creasing.

"Does anything seem strange to you?"

His eyebrows flew skyward, and I hastily added, "Aside from the body with a knife sticking out of it?"

He disapproved of the question, I could tell. But to his credit, Mr. Ryder made a thorough perusal of the body. "What are you seeing that I am not?"

My tongue burned with the myriad responses I had to that, but I restrained myself to the present matter. "Blood. There's very little of it. That knife has a three-inch blade. I would expect it to create a pool of blood or at least drips on the surrounding area." I chewed on my bottom lip. "And on the killer."

The butler and two footmen entered with a wide, rough plank of wood.

I straightened, and Mr. Ryder stood, one of his knees making a popping noise. We watched as the footmen recovered the body, then lifted it onto the plank.

"We've made space in the ice house," the butler said. "It's starting to flood from these incessant rains, but my lord should be well above the water line."

I nodded, my gaze transfixed on the space where Perrin's body had lain. No blood there, either. I waited for Perrin's servants to leave the room before turning to Ryder. "He wasn't stabbed to death. I'd bet my club on it."

"How can you possibly know that?" Ryder placed his fists on his lower back and arched, earning another satisfying pop. The moralist was tall and trim, but his body was as susceptible to age as the rest of ours.

The thought was oddly comforting.

"We hosted a surgeon as a guest lecturer at The Minerva Club last year. He discussed several famous murders in history." My lips curved. "The ladies' queries flew off on some tangents. He was kind enough to oblige our questions. And one aspect of murder by stabbing that he discussed was how much blood it typically produced. But if one is already dead, if one's blood has already stopped pumping...."

"A knife could enter a body without much of a mess." Ryder

looked back at the clean carpet. "Why would anyone stab a dead body?"

That was indeed the question *du jour*. My brother-in-law angered many people, but putting a knife in his lifeless chest seemed excessive.

I pushed my spectacles up my nose and turned for the stairs leading down to the kitchens. "I bid you goodnight, Mr. Ryder."

"The guest rooms are all upstairs," he called out.

"I know." The stairs down to the kitchens were not in as good condition as the others, and I carefully picked my way down. The butler sat at a large, wide table with several other servants, large glasses of what I assumed liquor before them.

He quickly stood when I entered. "My lady, I—"

I flapped my hand at him. "Please, sit. I was hoping I might be able to speak with the stable master. Has he retired yet for the night?"

"I don't think anyone will be getting much sleep tonight, milady." He nodded to one of the footmen, and he scurried off, presumably to fetch my quarry.

There was an awkward silence as we waited. I didn't think Perrin spent much time in the kitchens, which was his loss. Everyone knew that midnight pudding always tasted better when shared with those who had cooked it.

"What are we going to do?" one of the maids finally asked. It was the one who had found Perrin's body. She was a hearty girl, one you could picture milking a cow and carrying the buckets with ease. Her red hair and pale skin spoke of an Irish heritage, though any brogue had long since left her voice. "Our employer is dead. Do we wait for the 'eir to take over? Look for other employment?"

The butler frowned. "Hush, child. That isn't Lady Mary's concern."

My heart sank. It felt like it was, at least until Perrin's heir could arrive. Perrin was the father of two boys, young men now, but neither would be able to attend to their duties quickly. The eldest was in Rome, on a tour of the continent, his father had said, when all of society knew he had taken orders in the papist religion. The younger was in the Navy. I didn't know when he would be released from service.

I leaned against the table, fatigue catching up with me. It had been quite the day. "I can't make that decision for anyone, but if you do decide to stay on until the next owner takes possession, I'll make sure your wages are paid."

The butler inclined his head. "Most generous, milady."

The stable master arrived, unwrapping himself from a dripping blanket he must have covered himself in to try to avoid the rain. "You wanted to see me, Lady Mary?"

"Yes. I just wanted to confirm that our last guest arrived after Lord Perrin's body was found?"

"He did." The man rubbed his bristly jaw. "We had a hell—" He cleared his throat. "A difficult time getting his carriage from the road. We'll be cleaning mud from the axles for a long time."

I nodded. I hadn't truly thought Mr. Ryder would be involved in Perrin's death, but it was nice to be able to eliminate him as a suspect altogether. "This is a delicate question, but with your master dead, murdered, the time for delicacy is over. Do any of you know any reason why someone would want to harm Lord Perrin? Has he had any threats made against him recently? Any enemies you know of?"

Everyone looked to the butler. He grimaced. "I think I can speak for all the servants when I say the master wasn't the easiest man to work for. He was as free with his tongue with his associates as he was with us." He ran his fingers through his thinning hair. "But I know of no specific threat against him."

Of course, it wouldn't be that easy. I said my goodnights and made my way up to the first floor where my guest room was. My lady's maid, Jane, was there to meet me with a small brandy and an exasperated look.

"I can't say I'll cry any tears over your brother-in-law, but another murder?" She shook her head, a lock of iron-grey hair escaping from her cap. Jane had been with me since I was but a child of ten. Although her back may have bent and her step become unsure, she had lost no strength in her tongue.

Toeing off my slippers, I dropped into the tufted chair by the window. "You act as though it is my fault another person has been killed in my vicinity." I sipped the brandy, feeling the need for a good brood coming on.

Jane dragged the dressing chair from its position and sat across from me. "Of course, it's not your fault, but you're going to put your nose into this, aren't you?"

I slouched deeper into the cushions. "We are staying under the same roof as a killer." Perhaps. Perhaps Perrin had simply fallen down the stairs? But why put the knife in his chest? "I must ask some questions, at least until the magistrate or constable arrives." I looked toward the window. The curtains were drawn, but the sound of pounding rain hadn't lessened one whit. It might be days until a message could be sent out, much less have the authorities arrive. I handed Jane my glass, and she tossed back the rest of the liquor.

"I've asked the servants whether they know any reason someone would harm Perrin and received no answer other than Perrin's disagreeable nature." My mind flashed to all the little digs he'd thrown my way in the short time I'd been at his home. My husband's brother had certainly been unlikeable. He'd had a motive with his pointed remarks toward me, one I probably now would never know. "But they aren't likely to be completely forthright with me. If you could ask around, see if you can learn more...."

Jane sighed heavily. "I suppose there isn't anything better to do, what with being trapped indoors. I'll see if I hear anything."

If boredom was the only reason to gain her assistance, I'd take it. Jane hadn't approved of my investigation into the murder at my club last year, and it didn't seem as though her view had changed even though the victim was now a relation.

Perrin had been one of the last connections I'd had to my

husband. I blinked against the burn in my eyes. I mourned that loss, but I couldn't say that I mourned the man himself.

I sighed. I wasn't the sort to dwell in malaise, but this day was trying my self-possession.

And the worst part was, most of my sorrow was just me feeling bad that I didn't feel sadder about Perrin's death.

Chapter Six

Lady Mary

THE HOUSE WAS quiet at this time of morning, only the incessant rain sounding as it plinked against the slate shingles while the sky lightened to mercury gray.

The maid from last night, the one who'd asked about looking for employment, emerged from the rear sitting room, a bundle of cloth held as far from her body as she could possibly stretch her arm. When she caught sight of me, she grimaced. "Oh, milady. I didn't think any guests would be awake yet. I've just started cleaning the sitting room." She shook the bundle. "I think this fellow partook too much. I found 'im nose-down in the spilled wine."

"The wine?" My mind raced, any cobwebs from sleep quickly evaporating. "You found an animal dead in the wine?"

There was a scrabbling of nails, an excited yip. Southey ran circles around my skirts, his rear end wriggling like mad.

The maid sniffed. "If this one 'ad done 'is job, I wouldn't 'ave to be cleaning up dead mice."

The terrier got a little too familiar poking his nose under my skirt, and I gave him a gentle tap with my toes. "Can I have it? The mouse?" I held out my hand.

She blinked. "All right," she said, drawing out the words. She passed it over and wiped her hands on her apron.

"What's your name?" Southey must have sniffed out my new possession because he started leaping for the bundle, barking to wake the house.

"Marie Murphy." She gave me a quick curtsy. "Are you sure you don't want me to get rid of it?"

"Get rid of what?"

I started at the voice behind me. Mr. Evans stepped to my side and looked down at the dog. "Hush."

Amazingly, the dog did.

"A mouse died in the sitting room." Marie nodded her head back toward the room. "Lady Mary asked to 'ave it." The maid's tone indicated what she thought of my request.

The attorney wrinkled his forehead. "A dead mouse. Why....?" His forehead cleared. "The wine. You think he was poisoned? But the knife...."

"I think nothing yet. I only know there was next to no blood from the stab wound and that Perrin died somehow." I headed into the sitting room, almost tripping over Southey. I suspected much, but I didn't need to alarm the whole household until we knew for certain. I stopped at the puddle by the sideboard. It had mostly dried, staining the wood beneath. I took Perrin's amber wine decanter and poured a fresh glass. I sniffed.

"Well?" Mr. Evans asked.

"It smells like his normal foul wine." I shrugged. "The wormwood would hide any other odor. Or taste."

Southey sniffed at the puddle, and the attorney used his boot to prod him away. The terrier turned his attentions to my gown once more, taking the hem in his mouth and tugging.

"We need another animal to test it." If someone had poisoned Perrin's wine, it had been a wise choice. I knew of no one else who would dare try it.

A tearing sound made us both look down. Southey sat back on his haunches, a triangle of fabric hanging from one tooth.

Mr. Evans and I looked at each other. He hastily scooped up

the dog and backed away. "I'll look for another mouse. Make sure no one touches that wine."

I refrained from rolling my eyes at the obvious order. I plopped down in a chair to wait. And wait. Apparently catching a mouse was a more difficult task than I had imagined. Finally, Mr. Evans returned, a small bit of brown fur in his hand. He rubbed his thumb softly over what I saw was the animal's head. "Can you pour the wine into a saucer? It might drown if we dip it into the glass."

I decided not to point out that there was a strong chance the mouse would be dying regardless and did as he asked.

Mr. Evans took the saucer and held it for the mouse to drink. It obliged, making me wonder if mice had any sense of taste.

"How long will this take?" I asked.

He shrugged. "I write contracts. I've never studied medicine."

I sat back down. "It would have been better for Perrin if he'd invited his physician to this party instead of his solicitor."

"I doubt his physician could have finalized the wedding contract, which was the reason why I was invited." Mr. Evans kept stroking the small beast, trying to provide it comfort.

I studied the attorney's face. His features were blunt, unrefined, but appealing in their way. If I had seen him on the street I would never have guessed law was his profession. "I was surprised when I heard Perrin might remarry. Miss Smith is quite young for him."

He pursed his lips. "Not if he wanted more children. I've written contracts with larger age differences."

"Was there anything unusual about this contract?"

He raised one eyebrow. "Aside from the fact it was unlikely to be signed? The earl angered the bride's father, and I don't believe Mr. Smith was amenable to a renegotiation."

I scooted forward. "What did Perrin do?"

Mr. Evans hesitated.

"Your client is dead." I waved him to the chair next to mine, tired of looking up so high. "Someone stuck a knife in his chest.

We need to discover why."

"When a magistrate comes—"

"It will be days." I shouldn't be annoyed. Mr. Evans didn't know I had some experience at solving murders. He most likely thought me a nosy, old woman, not someone who could be of use. "And we are all stuck here together. The time for discretion is past."

He sank down next to me, the mouse tucked against his chest, its nose twitching. "Perhaps you are right. Many people won't be safe until we discover the killer." He blew out a breath. "Your brother-in-law asked me to rewrite a term in the marriage contract. There was to be an exchange of land grants. Mr. Smith owns a parcel of land not too far from here. Used to be a mine, I believe, but it has some lovely coastline as well. As part of the contract, he was to trade that land for a section on the north of Perrin's estate, one that produced an income. It turns out Perrin had already sold off that part of his estate. Perrin wanted me to change the contract and substitute another parcel of land. Of course, I had to tell Mr. Smith of the changes."

"Of course." Perrin had hired an honest attorney, a decision he most likely had regretted.

Evans scratched the mouse under the chin. "Well, Mr. Smith didn't appreciate the attempt to deceive him. He said the wedding was off."

There was a clatter of dishes in the dining room next door, the low murmur of voices as breakfast was set up.

"Perrin was always striving for his next deal." I crossed my ankles and stared at the ceiling. "It doesn't surprise me he ruined one deal by making another. Or that he angered Mr. Smith." Perrin used to drive my husband mad with all the investment schemes he wanted Cavindish to invest in.

The attorney's silence had me looking his way. "Do you know of other botched deals and angry associates?"

He cleared his throat. "Well, I suspect Lord Havenstone wasn't feeling too fondly towards the earl after their meeting yesterday. Perrin had a new business association he wanted Havenstone to invest in, but after losing all of the baron's investment in their last deal, I don't think Havenstone reacted the way Perrin wanted."

"They fought?"

"Loudly." He pressed his lips together. "I was in the cloak room looking for something I'd left in my coat pocket. They were on the other side of the wall in Perrin's study. Havenstone made it clear he wouldn't be investing with Perrin again."

"Interesting." I knew Lord and Lady Havenstone socially. I'd heard at one time the baron had been forced to sell some land in the north, but their habits in London society had never changed. Had the loss of that investment been a financial burden to the baron? "Do you know how much he lost?"

Mr. Evans grimaced. "It was substantial but obviously not devastating."

"And you won't tell me the amount?"

"I will not."

Fair enough. If I gained access to Perrin's study in order to write to his sons, I most likely could find the information out myself. If the earl had kept orderly records. "Anyone else here who lost money with Perrin?" I took back my previous thought. Having Perrin's solicitor at the house was deucedly more useful than a physician. He knew all the *on dit*.

"Only one other, though I don't know how much." Evans sighed. "I was hired after the event took place and only know of it through correspondence."

"And...?" I rolled my finger in a circle. An attorney with a looser tongue would have been even better.

"Apparently Perrin lost a sum gambling to Mr. Withers. He paid it off with the note to a tin mine he owned." Evans sniffed. "But Mr. Withers didn't know the mine was already played out. He wanted recompense from Perrin, but the earl refused. I understand Mr. Withers leases the land out to a wool business now."

The wool markets were a big industry in the southwest of England. As was mining, mainly tin, copper, and silver. But with the wool industry becoming mechanized, the land for shepherding was becoming less and less profitable. The population of Modbury was smaller than the last time I'd come through it, with people moving to the cities to look for work as the factories took more and more jobs away from the countryside. Bertram had every right to be angry at Perrin.

But Perrin was his brother-in-law, as well, the husband of Bertram's sister. Whatever differences the men might have had, they would have made allowances for it, for the sake of family harmony. And I knew Bertram was quite comfortable financially. The loss of a gambling win was hardly enough to make the man murderous.

I tapped the armrest. "My brother-in-law was not well-liked, and for good reason." I still didn't know why he had been trying to provoke me. What had he known or thought he'd known? "But he didn't deserve death. Perhaps he died naturally, however, and someone stabbed him after out of misplaced anger or some misguided devilry."

"I fear not." Mr. Evans rose, his mournful face looming over mine. He held out his hand. "The mouse is dead."

Chapter Seven

Henry

T HE MOUSE WAS limp in his hand, a pathetic little creature. Henry couldn't help but feel guilt over its death.

"Well, this muddles the matter." Lady Mary stood and started pacing. "Poison could have been put in Perrin's wine at any time, and I know very little about how poisons work. Do you?" She looked over her spectacles at him in irritation.

"Not a part of my legal education." Poisoned and stabbed. Someone wanted to make sure the earl wouldn't survive. Henry had known the earl for several years, first when he'd apprenticed with a senior solicitor, and then becoming Perrin's attorney after the other man retired. He'd never particularly cared for the earl, but then, it wasn't his job to like his clients. Only to give them the best legal service he could provide.

He looked down at the mouse. Even as disagreeable as Perrin could be, Henry still found it hard to fathom someone killing him. But the proof was in his hand.

Lady Mary picked up the decanter of wormwood wine. "I'll make sure this goes under lock and key, then I'll head to Perrin's library. Perhaps he had more of an interest than we did of substances that kill and I'll find a book on poisons." She glared out the rain-streaked window. "If only this dratted weather would let up. I feel in this instance we'll need a magistrate."

Henry pursed his lips and watched her go. Which instance like this one had she felt she *hadn't* needed the proper authorities? Sighing, he went out the glass doors onto the terrace, trying to stay under the shallow overhang. The rain seemed to delight in coming at him sideways, drenching his trousers in moments. He found a large potted lily of the valley at the corner of the terrace and dug a hole in its dirt. He laid the mouse inside. The bell-shaped white flowers seemed a fitting memorial for the animal. "I'm sorry you died before your time, but your life held meaning. Or your death, at least."

He covered the carcass, then brushed dirt from his hands.

Lady Mary was right. If they were to be stuck in this house for the next few days, they needed to discover who had killed Perrin. Either that, or lock everyone in their rooms until the constable could arrive.

He didn't think the rest of the guests would stand for that.

Turning on his heel, he went back inside and headed to the earl's study. Cabinets lined a side wall, with diamond-shaped cubbies built in above and stuffed full with surveyors' maps and grant deeds. A low bookcase ran under the window on the far wall, and Perrin's wide desk sat before the double windows looking onto the front drive.

He made a quick perusal of the contents in the desk drawers. Ink and paper. Some recent correspondence. A pair of button hooks. He pulled out a file of newspaper clippings. At the top was an opinion piece in *The Times* by Mr. Enoch Ryder railing against Lady Mary's The Minerva Club. He flipped through the pages. All of the clippings had to deal with Lady Mary in one way or another. Efforts to shut the club down. Details of a gruesome murder that had happened within its walls. A fire. Another fire.

Henry let out a low whistle. He hadn't thought Perrin had invested in his sister-in-law's business, but perhaps he was wrong. Perhaps cutting out these articles was Perrin's way of keeping track of his investment. He returned everything to their drawers and turned to the cabinets.

Henry started with the top drawer, removing the stack of documents and seating himself at the desk with the papers spread out before him. He looked for any contract or communication with any present guest and put those aside in the corner of the desk. By the time his stomach started grumbling in earnest, he'd gone through eight drawers in two cabinets.

He leaned back, stretching. He hadn't eaten any breakfast, and the clock by the door told him it was nearing two in the afternoon. Well past time for a repast.

There was no one in the dining room, but crumbs were on the table and a napkin on the floor. Henry picked it up on the way to the sideboard, folding it neatly before picking up a plate. Thankfully, food remained on the dome-lid covered dishes. The kitchen staff had seemed to be trying to make up for the lack of its popular chef by providing an abundance of food. If they didn't have quality, then quantity would have to do.

He loaded his plate with cold ham, several hard-boiled eggs, bread and jam, and the end of a nut loaf that remained. The coffee and tea were cold, but Henry didn't have much of a thirst, not knowing that someone liked to put poison in the beverages.

He sat and tucked in. Didn't poison have a warning taste? Scent? The acute bitterness of the wormwood wine would most likely have covered any warning signs, he supposed. Did the killer know that no one else would touch Perrin's special wine, or did he simply not care if anyone else died?

Movement at the glass doors caught his eye. Henry stood, wondering who would be out in this weather, and caught sight of Mr. Taylor leading Miss Smith down the terrace, his hand at her elbow, a rain umbrella in his other hand. They passed from sight, walking in the direction of the sitting room next door.

Henry gritted his teeth. In other circumstances, it would be none of his business. But seeing as how nothing connected Perrin's secretary and his almost-betrothed except the dead earl, Henry decided to make their little assignation his business. He left the dining room, emerged from the house out a side door, and walked as softly as possible to the corner.

"You don't have to worry," Taylor said. He bent down, a look on his face that Henry could only assume was meant to be comforting but looked eager instead. "I've taken care of everything. There's no…." The wind whipped away the rest of his words.

Miss Smith had her back to the house, a look of distress on her face. Probably from the wet and cold.

Henry frowned. Couldn't Taylor make sure she was properly dressed before taking her out-of-doors? At least the man could give her his damned jacket.

Her words were quieter. All Henry could make out was "I think we should…" before the storm's voice drowned out hers.

Taylor stepped closer to her, making the hair raise on the back of Henry's neck. "We can go away together now. I have the money. We can—"

The doors to the sitting room opened. A small bundle of fur shot through, followed by Miss Walker's head. "Oh, hallo. Southey needed letting out. We didn't expect to find anyone else out here in this weather."

The terrier sniffed at a garden hedge before doing his business. He seemed not to care about the rain and mud. The servants would likely feel differently when he came back inside.

Miss Smith sidled past Mr. Taylor and gave Miss Walker a bright smile. "The weather is atrocious, but sometimes one just needs some fresh air. Mr. Taylor was kind enough to attempt to block the worst of it from me. It is chilly though. Time to come inside, I think."

Taylor opened his mouth, his brows drawing down. Whatever he wanted to say, he thought better of and closed his mouth again.

Henry went back to the side door, desiring to get inside before Southey discovered him and gave him away.

The secretary and the affianced. Henry hadn't noticed a relationship between them before. Taylor was more amenable to her than the other guests, but she was a pretty girl. His attendance had seemed natural.

But was there more to it than that? And if Perrin had discovered his intended in a relationship with his secretary, what hell would he have put them through?

Henry headed back to the study, his shoulders set. The question that burned most in his mind was the money Taylor professed to have come into. Henry needed to look through the ledgers thoroughly. Perrin hadn't been a romantic man. His pride would have been hurt if he'd lost his intended to his secretary, but not his heart.

But Perrin did care about money. If Taylor had been stealing from the earl, and Perrin had discovered it, Perrin would have done everything in his power to destroy the young man.

Perhaps Taylor had decided to strike first.

Chapter Eight

Katherine

KATHERINE STOPPED AT the top of the stairs, sucking in a deep breath. She could do this. It was only dinner. She would smile. Nod. And no one would know she had killed Lord Perrin.

Except for Mr. Taylor. She started down the steps. Their conversation earlier had left her feeling…unsettled. Her gaze flew to the spot at the bottom of the stairs. The spot where Perrin had lain, crumpled. Mr. Taylor had said he wouldn't be able to testify against her if they wed. He said he loved her. She couldn't help but notice that Mr. Taylor had waited to make such declarations until he saw a clear path to matrimony to her – and access to her father's money.

She stopped on the third step from the bottom, still staring at the carpet. If Mr. Taylor only pressed for her hand because he wanted to increase his wealth or status in society, he would be sorely disappointed. The money her father would endow if she married well would disappear if she married beneath her station.

"Not even a depression in the carpet remains."

Katherine started at the voice behind her. She shifted, turned, then gasped as her heel twisted off the step, spilling her backwards. She windmilled her arms, but gravity had its way. She squeezed her eyes shut, waiting for the pain.

A pair of iron arms wrapped around her instead.

Opening one eye, Katherine saw an expanse of dark brown wool inches from her face. She turned her head, and the edges of a cravat tickled her nose.

"Are you all ri—. Oh, no."

She began to respond, but they were already moving, tumbling that last step down. An 'oof' escaped his lips when he hit the ground. Her landing was better padded, his body cushioning her impact.

"Mr. Evans? Are you injured?" Katherine pressed up to kneeling, examining the attorney. He was staring at the ceiling, a muscle in his jaw twitching. But there wasn't that horrible, vacant look in his eyes like last time. There wasn't….

She looked around. They were lying roughly where Perrin's body had come to a rest. Her stomach twisted. "Oh, God." She scrambled back, her hands pushing against his chest, her knee pressing into—

An oath exploded from his mouth. Faster than she could apprehend, he rolled, tucking her body beneath his.

Katherine was left blinking at the ceiling. She tapped his shoulder. "Mr. Evans?"

"Give. Me. A. Moment." His voice was guttural, each word sounding as though it had to be forced out.

His body was warm and draped over hers in a most interesting manner. This close, she could smell the soap he had used for his ablutions. It wasn't unpleasant having this large man's body covering hers.

It also wasn't decent.

She pushed again at his shoulder. "Mr. Evans, you really must—"

"A moment," he gritted out.

She sighed, their bodies shifting. And then there was another problem to consider. One more immediate. She pounded on his shoulder. "I can't…breathe."

With a sigh of his own, Mr. Evans pushed off of her and

flipped to his back. "You have very pointy knees."

Katherine didn't know how to respond to that. She'd always thought her legs, knees included, rather shapely.

The sound of a throat clearing had Katherine jackknifing into a seated position.

Mr. Evans remained supine.

A maid, Marie, Katherine thought her name was, stood by the foot of the stairs, a stack of folded towels in her arms. "Can I 'elp you with anything? A brandy? A footman to carry you to your room?" There was more pertness than solicitude in her voice, and Katherine flushed.

"A footman will certainly well *not* carry me to my room." Something that sounded very much like a growl emanated from the attorney's chest. "I just need a moment."

Katherine climbed to her feet and ran her hands over her hair. "You've had plenty of those now." She toed his hip. "Get up." The story of how she and Mr. Evans had been rolling together on the floor would most likely make the rounds in the servants' quarters, but she didn't need another witness to her humiliation.

She turned to Marie. "We slipped. On the stairs."

"Yes. Congratulations to whoever is tasked with polishing them." Mr. Evans heaved himself to standing. His face was a bit gray, but otherwise he looked unharmed. He tugged on the cuff of his jacket. "Perhaps a carpet down their length wouldn't go amiss, however. A person could kill themselves...." He darted a look at the floor, the section where Perrin had lain, and pursed his mouth.

Katherine's stomach fluttered. "Yes, well, mayhap the next owner will see to that. We'd best get to dinner before it gets cold. I hear Cook Clem has returned to the kitchen. We don't want to miss his efforts."

Without waiting to see if Mr. Evans would follow, Katherine trotted to the dining room. Everyone else had already arrived. The looks she received were a mixture of annoyance and relief.

"Finally." Lady Mary snapped her napkin into her lap. "We

only wait on Mr. Evans now to partake in Clem's *coq au vin*. I hear it is sublime."

"You need wait no longer." Mr. Evans followed her in, his arm brushing her shoulder.

Her face heated just remembering how much of him she'd felt before. Keeping her gaze down, she found her seat. "Yes, I can't wait to sample Cook Clem's fares. I've heard so much of his skill. I wonder if he will remain here for the next Lord Perrin or look for employment elsewhere."

Lady Havenstone waited for a footman to pour her wine. "I'm certain Cook Clem will want to leave this dreary place. He will go to those who will appreciate him most."

Lady Mary narrowed her eyes. "I quite agree. A talented chef like him will want to join a fine house in the city, I would think."

Lady Havenstone nodded. She slid a small packet from her left sleeve and poured the contents into her wine. She swirled her glass, making the powder dissolve. "For my digestion, you know."

Mr. Evans took the seat next to hers, his elbow brushing her arm. Katherine squeezed her arms to her side and looked across the table to her father. "How was your day, Father?"

"Deadly dull." He frowned. "No one here offers any challenge in billiards, and Perrin's library is dreadfully lacking in anything interesting to read."

Lady Mary leaned forward and inhaled deeply as a bowl of consommé was laid before her. "The library is full of histories and treatises on philosophy and natural sciences."

Katherine's father snorted. "As I said, nothing interesting. Every library should have at least one mind-rotting novel or two." He turned to his own soup, and his complaints appeared soon forgotten, his focus only on his meal. "It's a good thing you brought some of your own books with you, Katherine."

"I'm so glad Cook Clem is feeling better." Miss Walker was seated at the foot of the table. Whether she had been placed there or decided to take that spot opposite the place of the master of the house for herself, Katherine didn't know. As Perrin's intended, well, almost intended, the space across from Perrin should have fallen to her, she thought. As Katherine hadn't been eager to marry the earl in any event, she was happy to let that transgression go uncontested.

"Indeed." Lady Havenstone scooped up another spoonful of the soup. "It seems his is the only cooking that doesn't upset my stomach. I have a delicate digestion, you know."

Katherine's father snorted, but kept his attention on his own dish.

Lady Mary leaned back from her empty bowl. "Now that we are all together, I feel I must bring up the matter of Lord Perrin's death."

Lord Havenstone blotted his lips with his napkin. "Must we now? Perhaps after dinner would be more appropriate."

There were some grumbles of agreement to that statement.

"No time like the present." Lady Mary rested her hands in her lap. "Perrin didn't die from the knife to his chest."

Katherine put down her spoon, no longer hungry. She knew. Katherine didn't know how Lady Mary knew, but Katherine's secret was out. She darted a glance at Mr. Taylor, but his face didn't show the concern she knew hers did.

Lady Mary gazed around the table. "He was poisoned."

Katherine gripped the edge of the table. "I didn't intend…. Wait. What?" She felt Mr. Evans's gaze fall on her, but she kept hers focused on Lady Mary. "What do you mean he was poisoned? How do you know?"

"I suspected he hadn't been stabbed when I noticed the distinct lack of blood from the wound. Then a maid found the mouse. It was because of the spilled wine, that atrocious wormwood concoction Perrin liked." Lady Mary sniffed. "A mouse died from drinking it. We tested it on another. Same result."

A spoon clattered against china, and everyone looked down the table at Miss Walker. She pressed her hand to her throat.

"Poisoned? That's horrible. Is our food safe?"

Several people pushed their bowls away.

Lord Havenstone cocked his head. "The wine had a very strong flavor. Most poisons wouldn't be detected in it. Smart."

Katherine stared at the base of a candlestick in the middle of the table. Poison. He'd died from poison, not falling down the stairs.

She hadn't killed him. She darted a look at Mr. Taylor. He hadn't needed to desecrate Perrin's body in an attempt to protect her.

And she didn't have to marry to protect her secret.

She clutched her hands together under the table, a fine tremor running through her body.

Mr. Taylor tapped his fingers on the table. "Surely there is no way to know for certain that he was poisoned. He could have been killed in other ways."

Katherine's stomach turned to lead. Lady Mary was giving them a reprieve, one the secretary seemed intent to ignore. There could be only one reason. Mr. Taylor wanted to trap her in marriage just as surely as her father and Lord Perrin had intended.

"I'm certain the magistrate will confirm it." Lady Mary nodded to the footman who took her bowl. "I've had the butler place the bottle of wormwood wine somewhere secure."

Lord Havenstone raised his wineglass, paused, then put it back down. "I'm trying to remember last night. How did Perrin act before we found his body? Was he sweating? Slurring his words? There would be symptoms."

"You seem to know a fair amount about poisons," Mr. Evans said. Katherine couldn't help but notice he was the only one who didn't seem surprised by Lady Mary's revelation. "Are poisons a particular hobby of yours?"

Havenstone chuckled. "Hardly, but as someone who owns a few mining operations, it behooves me to be familiar with noxious substances."

"What poisons come from mines?" Lady Mary asked.

"Arsenic, primarily. As well as being mined for itself for use in paint and agriculture, it's also a consequence of tin and copper distillation." He scratched his jaw. "But really, many ores can be toxic if ingested in large enough amounts."

Miss Walker stared at the plate of chicken a footman placed before her. She prodded the meat with her fork. "Poisons are unfortunately all around us. A good garden can have foxglove, belladonna, and hemlock for medicinal uses. Even yew trees have been used to treat certain maladies. If one isn't careful, many plants can kill you, as well."

Mr. Withers cut into his own chicken. "My goodness, we are surrounded by experts in poison." He popped the bite into his mouth, his eyes closing in pleasure. "Delicious."

Miss Walker stiffened. "Your sister and I had many long talks about the tonics and poultices we could make from our gardens. Lady Perrin was especially adept at herbalism. She made a lovely tonic for my father's gout."

Lady Mary sighed. "So our options are endless. We can leave the type of poison used for the magistrate to discover."

The scents of red wine and garlic teased Katherine's nose. She looked at her plate. "Mushrooms can be deadly, as well, can't they?" She speared one rounded hood and chewed on her bottom lip. Nothing seemed safe.

"I think Perrin would have noticed chopped up bits of mushroom in his wine." Lady Mary patted her ivory hair. "I believe the *coq au vin* is safe." And putting word to action, she put a bite in her mouth, her eyes closing. "Heavenly."

Everyone watched her, waiting to see if she collapsed.

Lady Mary arched an eyebrow. "Unless you all plan on starving, I suggest we go on thinking Perrin was the intended target and the killer has no reason to harm the rest of us. However, if you are too fearful, I am more than happy to be the sole recipient of Cook Clem's efforts. This meal was worth the wait."

After a couple of moments, the rest of the guests joined Lady Mary and Mr. Withers in partaking of the food. Though if they'd been poisoned, no one would have known until it was too late. After dinner, despite the entreaties of Miss Walker to remain in the sitting room for entertainment, everyone made their excuses and went to bed.

And hoped the servants wouldn't find them all dead in their beds the next morning.

❧ ⸻ ✦ ⸻ ☙

Chapter Nine

Lady Mary

I THOUGHT I had bested my foe. That my cunning plan would keep his attention off me and where it belonged.

I'd thought wrong.

"Go away, you infernal beast." I snapped my skirts out of reach of Southey's teeth. "Go find someone who will appreciate your company." I stepped into my bedroom.

He wriggled inside before I could close the door.

I stepped outside.

He followed.

We did a little dance, hopping back and forth over the threshold, the little nuisance faster than my attempts to shut him out. "Jane? Jane!" I slapped my thigh. Where was the woman? She was always around to give me her unwanted opinion but never when I needed her. And if I wanted a decent night's sleep, I needed to rid myself of this dog.

"This won't do." Keeping my head held high, I marched down the hall, holding my single candle aloft. I turned a corner and headed for the doors to the ballroom. That room was large, running the length of the house on the back side. Floor-to-ceiling windows ran along the far wall, large mirrors along the opposite. It was apparently being used to store furniture, ghostly white-draped tables and chairs cluttering the parquet floor.

Of course, Perrin would use his ballroom as storage. I wondered when the last time was he had done anything so merry as hold a dance within his walls. But it looked a good place to hide.

Or a good place for a dog to get lost in.

A flash of lightning illuminated the room, strange shapes dancing in the mirrors' reflections. The windows shook with the thunder, and Southey whined, pressing into my leg.

"That one was close." I blinked, my eyes seeing only gray dancing spots until the candle came back into focus. "But there's nothing to be frightened of, silly dog. It's only a storm." And I was speaking to an animal. Who was the silly one?

"Right then." I pretended to hold something in my hand. I waved my arm back and forth, getting the dog's attention, then pretended to throw the imaginary object. "Fetch."

The terrier sprinted off, nails scraping on the floor, and I made my escape, closing the door behind me. "Ha." It was a small victory, but at this moment any success was welcome. Besides, it was Southey's own fault. I had instructed a maid to give the dog a large bone, one it should have taken him several days to devour. Days where he was happily chewing and I was left in peace. But the beast had decided to forego that pleasure in order to aggravate me.

Several loud yips broke the quiet. It could only have been my overactive imagination that made them sound accusatory.

I started down the hall, the barking seeming to get louder the farther I went. I paused at the junction in the hallway. I'd chosen the wrong room to imprison the animal. His barks echoed. Pretty soon someone would come to investigate. And then there would be questions. *Who would leave a dog in the ballroom? What kind of person would abandon an animal?*

The next bark was a veritable howl. I hadn't realized terriers could make such a forlorn sound. I swallowed, the back of my throat going thick.

"Fiend seize it." I stalked back and flung open the door. Southey barreled out, dancing about my feet. "I was going to tell a servant where you were." Eventually. "Now let's go find Jane."

We turned down the hall, blessed silence once more reigning. At the junction, I started to turn left when movement slowed my feet. A shadow detached from the wall, flickered, disappeared.

I held my breath, not moving. The stairs up to the servants' quarters were in that direction, farther down that hallway. It could be a maid, going to her bed. And if Perrin Manor had a mouse problem, it could also have bats. There were any number of explanations for movement in a darkened hall. But if it was a servant, why were they walking in the dark without a lamp or candle? And why had they stopped moving when I had?

A lick of ice trailed down my spine, and I was suddenly glad Southey was by my side. I glanced down. Except he wasn't. He was halfway down the hall back to the guest rooms, a jaunty spring in his step, not caring in the least that he was leaving me to… to… well, something untoward. "Oh, for goodness sake."

"A problem?"

I yelped and spun, glaring at the man who had crept up quietly behind me. "Mr. Ryder, you should wear bells when you walk about. You gave me quite a start."

He smiled, holding up an amber-shaded oil lamp. I ignored the fact that he had quite a nice smile. For someone who had made it one of his missions in life to close down my club, it should have looked more devilish.

"I heard…." He went to one knee when Southey came trotting back. "Oh, there you are. I thought you might be in trouble, little one." He rubbed behind the terrier's ears, earning an approving yip.

Holding my candle aloft, I stepped toward where I'd seen the shadow. With Mr. Ryder and Southey with me, it didn't seem as frightening.

As well it shouldn't. There was nothing there. Blowing out a breath, I turned toward my intended destination. "I didn't realize you were such a dog lover, Mr. Ryder. Southey needs a new master. Perhaps you can keep him in your room for the duration of our stay."

Ryder rose and followed behind. "It would be a strange creature who doesn't like dogs. They are faithful and true, unlike many humans."

I pinched my mouth shut as I descended the stairs to the ground floor.

"What are you doing here at this time of night?" Ryder took the stairs by my side. "It might not be safe to go about alone."

I refrained from pointing out that he, also, was 'going about alone,' as he put it. "I heard the dog barking, as well." It wasn't a lie. "And now I'm looking for Jane." The rooms on the ground floor were all dark so I went to the stairs down to the kitchens.

"With Perrin dead, Southey might be a good companion for you." Ryder turned the wick up in his lamp, the white hair at his temples shimmering gold in the warm light. "He's small, but will rouse the household if you were in trouble."

I snorted. "I can do my own rousing." A light in the room next to the kitchen drew me there. Voices raised; someone shouted in triumph. When I stepped through the doorway, I had to stop from rolling my eyes.

The table where the servants ate was crowded, but it wasn't food that was on the table but coin. Jane slowly shuffled a deck of cards, her bent fingers expertly mixing the cards for the next deal. A tidy sum of blunt was before my lady's maid, but nowhere near as large as that in front of young Marie.

Perrin's maid was shaking her head. "I've said you shouldn't play casino, Bert. Everyone can read 'ow good your cards are from your face. You should stick to 'azard."

Ryder loudly cleared his throat. All eyes swung toward us. "I apologize for interrupting your sport," he said, not sounding sorry at all, "but I was hoping Cook Clem was not yet abed. I find myself still hungry."

Some tidbit of tonight's meal did sound good. It had been days since this kitchen had put out anything decent, and this night's supper only whetted my appetite for more excellent food. And a conversation with the chef wouldn't go amiss. Pretty soon the carrion birds would be circling, and I wanted to get to him first.

Marie hooked her elbow over the back of her chair. "Oh, Clem went up to bed 'ours ago. Feeling better, 'e is, but still a bit unsteady, if you take my meaning."

"I understand." Ryder's shoulders dropped. He hooked his thumb in the pocket of his waistcoat. "Perhaps it is time for everyone to be abed. It's a more wholesome alternative than some entertainments." He looked meaningfully at the table.

I sighed. "Do you go about looking for people amusing themselves in order to ruin their sport? They're only having a bit of fun."

He raised his chin and looked down at me. "It has been shown that gambling induces dishonesty, as well as takes money from those who might need it most. I hope The Minerva Club hasn't added this vice to its many others."

Inhaling sharply, I planted my hands on my hips.

Jane stood as fast as her arthritic bones would allow. "I have been trotting too hard. Perhaps it is time to call it a night."

The other servants rose, murmuring their good-nights and departing. With a nod of his head, Mr. Ryder also excused himself. Soon, it was only Jane, Marie, and I.

And Southey.

"Why did you bring that man down?" Jane asked, digging her knuckles into her back.

"I was trying to rid myself of this animal." I pointed at Southey, who panted happily up at me. "I was looking for you to assist when I ran into Mr. Ryder."

Jane frowned, the grooves on her forehead deepening to veritable chasms. "I don't know why that dog upsets you so. Any tear he makes to your gowns you know I can repair."

I huffed out a laugh. "You? *You've* repaired the damage?"

Jane shifted her weight. "Well, I know who to send them off

to for repair. It's the same thing."

I restrained myself from rolling my eyes.

Jane sniffed. "Well, it's too bad you brought that Ryder down here. I was winning."

Marie scraped her pile of coin into her apron and twisted the fabric into a knot. "No, you weren't. You again didn't 'ave any spades in your 'and, and I was about to reach twenty-one."

I examined the girl. I'd known she was quick, but perhaps underestimated just how clever. "How about a spot of tea before we turn in?" I settled myself at the table, shaking Southey off of my foot. "I have a few questions that I hope you can answer, Marie."

"I'll get the water going," Jane said.

I looked at the enormous pot and shot Marie an imploring look.

She nodded. "You sit and think about why you tried to build to that nine when Bert 'ad already shown 'is." She lugged the pot to the fire and kindled it. "What do you want to know?" she asked me.

I pushed out a chair for Jane. "Did you or anyone else see someone around Lord Perrin's wine yesterday?"

"Not that I noticed." Marie climbed over one of the benches and sat. "I can ask the others, but I think they would've said something after we found out 'e was poisoned."

"What about arguments?" I drew my feet farther underneath me. Instead of his bone that I could see sitting near his bed near the fire, Southey seemed to find my boot leather more palatable. "Did any of the servants hear Perrin fighting with one of the guests?"

Marie hesitated. "Well, there was a banger of a fight between the master and Mr. Smith. I don't think 'e was going to let Miss Smith marry my lord any longer."

I nodded. That accorded with what Mr. Evans had said about the marriage contract dispute. "Anything else?" I pushed.

Marie stood and went to a tin on the counter. She pulled it

open, sniffed, then chose another. "There is always a bit of yelling. The master did 'ave a temper. But nothing specially bad."

I toed Southey over to where Jane sat, hoping he'd transfer his attention. "And?"

Marie's shoulders dropped. "It's not what we 'eard. It's what we've seen. Lord Perrin told us to look through the guests' belongings, looking for anything interesting. The lord always asked us, whenever any guests stayed over."

"Perrin asked you to spy?" My heartbeat raced. I don't know why I was surprised. That sounded like just the thing my brother-in-law would do. It was still shocking. "How ghastly."

"Just go through pockets and drawers while we cleaned. Their luggage if they didn't unpack. Keep our ears open, that sort of thing." Marie took the pot off the fire and poured it into a teapot. She added tea leaves from one of the tins and brought it to the table, reseating herself after placing cups in front of us.

Jane leaned forward. "Did you find anything interesting?"

"Jane!" This was people's privacy we were talking about. It was an abominable question.

But one that needed answering. "Yes, but, uh, did you?"

Marie shrugged. "I 'eard Lord and Lady 'avenstone speaking poor of the earl, but that's not so surprising." Her forehead wrinkled. "The baron does 'ave a case of tonics in 'is room. 'e seems to like to take a tipple from some of them with the morning tea, and Lady 'avenstone, well, she's got a remedy for everything. But they're not the only ones who didn't trust Perrin Manor to have the medicine they need. Mr. Bertram Withers also brought some powdered chamomile and calomel. 'e asks for a cup of hot water every night to put them in. Must 'ave a weak stomach."

Neither of those powders would kill someone in mere hours. But what of the Havenstones' tonics? There were many ailments that might induce the couple to travel with their personal apothecary shop. Might one be a poison, however? "Next time you're in Lord Havenstone's room, can you look to see if the tonics are labeled? Write down what all he's brought? You can write, can't you?"

The girl huffed. "Yes, ma'am."

Jane poured them all tea. "I thought spying on guests was wrong." She pushed my cup toward me, her lips pinched.

"It is." I took a sip of tea, wincing at the bitterness. I placed the cup down. "It's abominable behavior. But would you mind terribly to keep on doing so while we investigate?" I leaned forward, resting my forearms on the table. "Someone here killed Lord Perrin. We must discover who."

Marie grinned over the rim of her cup. "Trying to catch a killer. That'll be all the crack."

"Yes, except for the fact a man is dead," I said dryly. My chest went tight. Marie was smart and had experience poking through what didn't belong to her. She would be all right.

I pushed back my chair and stood. "One more thing." I bent and plucked up Southey. I put him into Marie's unsuspecting arms. "Hold onto this beast until I can get to my room, please. I fear to think what he would do to my slippers if he had all night to chew."

Chapter Ten

Lady Mary

I STRODE INTO the dining room, a small skip to my step that morning. I wasn't the only one cheered by the break in the storm, or the thought of what Clem might have made for breakfast. Miss Smith stood by one of the windows, her face uplifted to a solitary ray of sunlight shining through a break in the clouds, a soft smile on her lips.

"Good morning, all." I nodded to the guests as I made my way to the sideboard.

"Good morning." Miss Smith closed her eyes. "Glorious day, isn't it?"

Glorious seemed several complimentary adjectives too far, but the house no longer felt like a shroud, and that was something.

"When do you think we shall be able to send for the constable?" Lady Havenstone asked.

"Not for another day or two, I wouldn't think." Mr. Evans refilled his coffee from a silver urn. "The rain hasn't fully stopped, and it will take time for the mud to dry enough to become passable."

Lord Havenstone stole a sausage from his wife's plate. "Well, we will be returning home the first moment we can. If the constable wants to talk to us, he can hire a carriage and come find us."

"Will he let us leave?" Miss Walker pushed her half-eaten plate away. "I would like to get back to my father. My aunt is staying with him, but she's nearly as old as he."

"We shall have to wait to see what the constable advises." Mr. Evans said this with some authority; as he had been Perrin's attorney, no one disagreed. At least not aloud.

I moved to an empty seat, my plate loaded, when Southey came barreling through the door, headed straight for me. Sighing, I plucked a slice of bacon from my plate and went to the casement doors that led to the terrace. I opened one, tossed the bacon through, then closed the door in triumph as the dog chased it. I returned to my seat.

"It is still quite cold outside," Miss Smith pointed out.

"He has fur. He'll be fine." Especially with one of my slices of bacon to warm his belly. I looked to the sideboard but decided it wasn't worth the trip to replace it.

"If you keep feeding the dog, Lady Mary, he is certain to follow your footsteps even more fervently." Mr. Ryder looked over the offerings at the sideboard, sniffing appreciatively.

I frowned. "That is hardly possible." But I made a note. No more treats.

Miss Smith wrapped her shawl more tightly about her. "More coffee, Father?"

He held up his cup. "Thank you, my dear." He watched as she replenished it. "I'm sorry for your sake you won't be a countess, Katherine, but as for my part, I never concerned myself about titles. It seems the loftier a gentleman is, the more likely he is to be a scoundrel. No, we'll find a nice industrialist for you instead."

"Because they are always so honest?" Miss Smith arched her eyebrow as she placed the steaming cup in front of her father.

"A man who's had to work for his wealth is far less likely to squander it in gambling and risky investments," Mr. Smith retorted.

I pursed my lips. There was some truth in that, perhaps.

Mr. Ryder sat next to me, holding his own cup of coffee. "Vice isn't limited to any strata of society. Every member of society falls victim to it. Especially gambling."

My body heated. The man just couldn't help himself. "No breakfast? I do hope you aren't feeling ill, Mr. Ryder."

"I am in the best of health," he said mildly, though he could hardly have missed my sarcasm. "I don't eat breakfast."

Of course, he didn't. Having too full a stomach was probably some sin in his mind.

"What about love?" Mr. Taylor flushed when all eyes turned his way. "I'm just saying, if a title isn't important, surely the thing that is important is that your daughter is loved by the man who marries her." He turned his limpid gaze on Miss Smith.

Mr. Smith burst out laughing. He dabbed his eyes with his napkin. "Love. That's a good one, boy. You must have amused Perrin with that wit."

Miss Smith frowned at her father, the idea of love clearly not as amusing to her.

I looked between her and Perrin's secretary. I couldn't see it. I had no problem with marriages between those of different social standings and wealth levels. My nephew, the duke, had married a woman that had almost had him ostracized from society permanently and they were the happiest of couples. But a marriage between people of different temperaments and intelligence was another matter. I'm sure Mr. Taylor was a competent secretary, but he didn't seem suited to the little I knew of Miss Smith.

Bertram rose and went to the window. He tapped his fingers on his thigh as he looked out. "I do hope that dog doesn't destroy my sister's garden. She spent many a happy hour in it."

"If the storm didn't destroy it, I think it is safe from a small dog." I pinched my mouth. Everyone was so concerned, either about the dog's health or the garden's. But what of the health of my boots and my gown's trim? No one seemed to consider that.

"Remember the Christmas we all spent here, you and Cavindish, me and my wife and sister?" Bertram turned, his gaze looking as though it were seeing something far away. He tapped his hand against his thigh. "What a grand time we had."

Bertram had forgotten to include Lord Perrin in that assembly, but I understood why. The holiday would have been all the more merry if Perrin had stayed more to his rooms. "It was a lovely time," I agreed. And it had been. We'd come together at a time when my marriage was still young and hopeful. Even when we'd lost a bit of that hope, Cavindish and I had still enjoyed our life together, but once we'd tasted that first bitterness of sorrow, even the good times were slightly tainted.

I cleared the lump from my throat. "I remember your wife leading us in the carols. She was quite an accomplished musician."

"I can play the pianoforte." Miss Walker leaned forward. "After dinner tonight, I can entertain us."

Only Mr. Ryder made a sign of encouragement for that idea.

Bertram cocked his head. "I wouldn't think those would be fond memories for you, Lady Mary."

"Why is that?"

He lifted one shoulder. "Perrin mentioned you weren't happy in your marriage."

I sucked in a breath, my jaw locking. I didn't know what angered me more: that Perrin would say such a thing or that Bertram would repeat it here in front of others. Bertram had forgotten his manners.

My spine went straight. "I can assure you that wasn't the case. Cavindish and I were very happy."

"As you say." Bertram ran his hand up the back of his head. "I should go. I have a letter to write." He put his cup down on the sideboard and left the room.

His exodus started the others leaving. Mr. Ryder rose. "Can I interest you in a game of speculation?" he asked me.

"I thought you didn't approve of card games." I was still

annoyed at Bertram and might have let that irritation flow unjustly onto Mr. Ryder.

His chocolate eyes twinkled. "I've never said that, though it is amusing how you try to twist my words to keep me your bogeyman. Perhaps another time."

Hmph. And because I didn't know to which room Ryder had retreated, only knowing he was no longer in this one, I refilled my cup of tea, added an extra lump of sugar, and reseated myself. Only I and Mr. Evans remained.

Mr. Evans moved chairs to sit across from me. "I hope you don't mind my joining you for another cup of tea."

I inclined my head.

Evans took a sip then gently placed his cup before him. "I also hope you won't mind the impudence, but was there an issue in your marriage?"

"I do mind the impudence." I glared at the attorney. "Very much."

He sighed. "I don't mean to pry, and if Perrin hadn't been killed I wouldn't dream of it, but as you yourself have pointed out, we need to investigate anyone who might have a reason to want the earl dead."

"And you think I have one?" My eyebrows shot up.

He tapped his index finger on the table. "I hope not. Perrin asked me a couple months ago about England's libel laws. He wanted to write a letter to *The Times,* hoping it would be published for all and sundry to see. He said someone had wronged his family and wanted that person to pay."

I drew back. "Me?"

"He didn't say. But he also said he had to consider his actions carefully as he didn't want disgrace to fall on his family by the association, which led me to believe it was someone close to his family. And Perrin never had anything nice to say about you."

I swallowed. What exactly had Perrin known about my marriage to his brother? There was no way he could know the truth. Cavindish would never have spoken of it, not even to his brother, and I had never unburdened myself to anyone, not even to Jane.

But Perrin had been needling me since I'd arrived, seeming to hold some specific animus against me.

No. I pushed my spectacles up my nose. He couldn't have known. "I don't know whom Perrin was speaking of, but I can assure you he had nothing to write to a paper about me. I wasn't overly fond of my brother-in-law, but I had no reason to kill him."

Evans studied me and slowly nodded. "Of course, my lady. I had to ask."

As I was poking my nose into everyone else's business, I had a hard time faulting him for turning the tables on me. That didn't mean I liked it.

I stood. "Good day, Mr. Evans." I swept from the room, my mind going back again and again to one question.

What had Perrin thought he'd known about me and Cavindish?

Chapter Eleven

Henry

S HE WAS QUITE charming when she was trying to be stealthy. Henry paused when she did, ducking behind the corner when she looked behind her. When he poked his head around the wall, Miss Smith had disappeared out the same side door he'd used the day before.

He gave a passing thought to letting her be. It really was most ungentlemanly to follow a lady. He was tired of looking through Perrin's office, however, and suspicious activity should be investigated. So, after waiting thirty seconds, he followed her out-of-doors.

The chirping of robins was the only sound he heard. The birds were probably just as happy the storm was breaking as Perrin's guests. The path to the left was a pit of mud, unblemished by any recent footprints. The right led to the rear terrace. Henry went right.

A quick glance around the corner showed Miss Smith in the same spot he'd found her in yesterday, and with the same companion. She and Mr. Taylor hovered near the potted lily of the valley at the far corner of the terrace, their heads bent close together, their voices too low to hear.

Henry's muscles tensed. Nothing the secretary had to say

could be so interesting. And how foolish of Miss Smith to meet with him. After what had happened to Perrin, no woman should gallivant about, meeting with strange men in dark corners.

Unless Miss Smith knew Perrin's secretary better than she let on.

Henry had never cared for Mr. Taylor. Perrin's secretary had been overly obsequious to his employer and then turned around and spoken poorly of him to others. Perhaps Taylor was talented at turning that cloyingly sweet tongue on a woman. Although Henry found his scrawny neck and thin shoulders less than physically impressive, mayhap his slenderness evoked a tender feeling in some women.

There was another, darker, reason Miss Smith might want a moment in private with the secretary.

Had they hatched the plot to murder Lord Perrin together? Had Miss Smith been so against the idea of marrying the earl that she'd resorted to murder?

He examined the woman, but no signs of villainy were apparent in her features. Her brown eyes were wide-set and lovely. Her full lips were a bit tight at the moment, but irritation was a common reaction to Mr. Taylor. And with the sun's rays finally breaking through the clouds, Henry could see golden streaks illuminated in her honey-brown hair.

Henry shifted his weight. She really was quite lovely. She reminded him of a painting he'd seen once at a Gainsborough exposition. The portrait of a Mrs. Sheridan, he believed. With her soft eyes and pretty mouth, Perrin would have been a lucky….

Miss Smith turned her back on Taylor, and he grabbed her arm, quick as a snake. A wince crossed her face.

Before he knew it, Henry's feet were moving. "Unhand the lady."

Taylor looked up, his face blanching at whatever he saw on Henry's face. "We are only having a conversation. A private one."

"One which has now concluded." Henry stopped next to Miss Smith, calculating how many of the secretary's fingers he could break when he pried them off her arm.

Unfortunately, the point became moot. Taylor dropped his hold on her and stepped back. "You might think you're in charge here, Evans, but once the magistrate arrives, things will change." He gave Miss Smith a hard look. "In more ways than one." And turning on his heel, he stomped off.

Henry looked down at the top of Miss Smith's head. She seemed determined to examine a bug that crawled along the stone floor. "Lovely company you keep, Miss Smith. Is Mr. Taylor a beau of yours?"

She clasped her hands behind her back, her lips whitening.

"Mr. Taylor was correct in one respect," he continued. "The magistrate will be arriving soon." The butler thinks it will be safe to send someone on the morrow if the rain keeps at bay. "I will have to relay my opinions to him, and right now, you and Mr. Taylor are acting most suspiciously."

She nudged the beetle with the toe of her boot.

Henry loosed a breath. "Fine. If you wish to keep your own counsel, that is your right, but you should speak to your father about hiring a good barrister skilled in criminal law."

He made it halfway across the terrace before he heard her move.

"Wait." She muttered softly before stamping up to him. "I will tell you what you want to know. Perhaps we can find someplace without eavesdroppers, however."

Ignoring the insult, he nodded and led her around the building to the side door. Both sitting rooms were occupied but the library was free. They went inside and he shut the door behind them.

Sunlight struggled through the far windows, casting dim shadows on the floor-to-ceiling bookshelves. A couple of chairs and a settee formed a loose circle around a low table, and a large, wingback chair faced the now cold fireplace.

"Shall we sit?" He went to one of the chairs, waited until she seated herself on the settee across, before lowering himself down.

"Now. Tell me, why all the clandestine meetings with Mr. Taylor?"

She jumped to her feet and went to a bookcase. "There is nothing romantic between Mr. Taylor and myself, except he has said he loves me and wishes to marry."

"Nothing romantic indeed." Henry debated whether to stand. He had just settled himself, and the chair was deucedly comfortable, but proprieties demanded he not be seated while a lady stood. He pushed up.

"Well, nothing romantic on my part." She ran her finger along dusty spines. "I am grateful to him. Mr. Taylor tried to help me out of a dire situation."

"What dire situation?"

She chewed on her bottom lip.

Henry strode up to her, getting closer than was proper. He didn't like to use his size to intimidate, especially a woman, but he was tired of her dodges. A man had been murdered. He placed his finger under her chin and lifted her face to his. "What situation?"

Something whispered to his right, and he jerked his head. He saw nothing but the seats they had left and the back of the large wingback. Perhaps the mice had invaded this room, as well. He should tell a maid to let Southey loose in here.

Miss Smith sighed, her breath gusting over his hand. "I thought I had killed him, you see. Lord Perrin. And in order to divert suspicion from me, Mr. Taylor stabbed Perrin's corpse. He brought attention to the knife in the sitting room, then stabbed the body while there were witnesses to me remaining in the room. A perfect alibi."

Henry blinked. Not much surprised him, but he had a hard time wrapping his mind around her words. "You thought you'd killed Perrin. But you didn't?"

"No." She jerked away and started pacing. "He grabbed me at the top of the stairs, you see. I thought he was in his cups and trying to take improper liberties. I pushed him away, and he fell down the stairs. And never got up." She pressed her hand to her throat. "He was probably struggling for help from the poison when he grabbed at me. Poor man."

Henry rocked back on his heels. Pushed down stairs. Stabbed. And poisoned. He rubbed his forehead. Perrin had truly had some horrible last moments. "It sounds like it was an accident, or you were defending yourself. Why not just call for help?"

"I intended to, but Mr. Taylor found me next to Perrin's body. When I explained, he thought I could be in trouble. He said he'd take care of it and to return to the sitting room and not tell anyone."

"And you agreed." A sour taste filled his mouth.

She grabbed his arm. "You don't understand. Perrin had been pulling at my dress, my body, and then he was dead, and I felt numb. I didn't ask Mr. Taylor to do it. I wanted to speak up, many times, but if I did, then I would get him in trouble, as well."

A soft snort sounded. Frowning, Henry went to the door and flung it open. No one. If he was the type of man to believe in ghosts, he would think Perrin's spirit was haunting them. He closed the door again and returned to Miss Smith. "So Mr. Taylor desecrated a body out of the kindness of his heart, and now he wishes you to marry him as repayment for that favor. Do I have that right?"

She frowned. "It isn't like that. He said that if we were married, neither of us could testify against the other. And he might care for me a little. He had shown interest when he thought I was Perrin's intended and quite out of his reach. There's a chance I might have an affectionate husband." She eyed him up and down. "I don't suppose any of your contracts ever contain a clause about that. That a husband, after buying his wife, must at least show her some tenderness."

Henry ignored the scorn in her voice. He wasn't an expert on criminal law, but he didn't think Taylor's reasoning was strictly true. A husband and wife couldn't be compelled to testify against each other for acts or speech that occurred during the marriage, not before. But he wasn't here to give Miss Smith legal advice. "If he is so affectionate, why did he grab you?"

She rubbed her arms. "He was upset. I told him that since Perrin was killed by poison, we no longer needed to marry. I wasn't responsible for his death. Mr. Taylor said that I could still be in trouble for pushing Perrin, and that it would be reckless not to marry. He may be right."

Henry shook his head. She couldn't be that naïve.

Apparently, he wasn't the only one to think so.

"He's only upset because dreams of his life of ease are disappearing." Lady Mary's head popped up over the back of the wingback chair. "Really, girl, you might not have the finest mind in London, but use what brains the Lord did give you. That man is using you." She sniffed. "And mucking up my investigation in the process."

Chapter Twelve

Katherine

KATHERINE PRESSED HER hand to her racing heart. "You've been sitting there the whole time?" She cleared her throat, not liking the squeak in her voice. In a lower tone, she said, "You should have announced yourself when we entered."

Lady Mary rose and pushed her spectacles up her nose. "And if you want a private conversation, you should check behind every chair and curtain. Amateurs."

Katherine's eyebrows shot up. "So it is my fault that I've been spied upon? Twice now?"

"Three times really." Mr. Evans crossed his arms over his wide chest. "I listened the first time you and Mr. Taylor snuck out on the terrace for conversation."

Katherine's cheeks heated. She threw her hands in the air. "And I'd thought Lord Perrin the most ill-mannered person here." She flounced to a settee and dropped onto it, crossing her own arms.

Lady Mary tossed a book onto the seat of the wingback and leaned against the armrest. "I was trying to determine which poison might have killed Perrin, but this book has not been helpful. Do either of you remember what symptoms he displayed the night he died? I remember he was sweating a bit, but I had thought that was due to proximity to the fire."

"He was irritable," Mr. Evans said.

Lady Mary dipped her chin. "He was always irritable."

Mr. Evans scratched his chin. "He rubbed his chest frequently. His chest might have been hurting."

"Good." Lady Mary looked at Katherine expectantly. "You?"

"Me?"

Lady Mary tapped the toe of her boot. "Did you notice anything that might point to which type of poison killed him?"

Katherine pursed her lips. Had she? "Well, he staggered up to me and grabbed for me. I thought he had a lewd intent, but he could have been dizzy? Or his legs may have no longer held him."

"So, weakness in the body, as well." Lady Mary shook her head. "That might not narrow the list down much. Did you learn anything new in Perrin's study?" she asked Mr. Evans.

"No, but there is still much to go through." He rubbed his jaw. "It could take me weeks to read every document."

Lady Mary nodded. "As it stands, we know three people here who have financial reasons to want Perrin dead. Four if you include that Mr. Taylor," she said, nodding her head at Katherine.

Katherine chewed on the inside of her cheek. "Mr. Taylor had no financial motive."

"With all due respect to your charms, I don't see Taylor killing simply for your company." Lady Mary gazed at the ceiling. "No, he would want your money and the status marrying an heiress would bring him."

Katherine inhaled sharply, trying to control her tongue. She would not get into a battle of words with the aunt of a duke. Smiling as sweetly as possible, she said, "Be that as it may, Mr. Taylor had no way of knowing I would give Lord Perrin the gentlest of nudges just as he was dying from the poison and that Perrin would fall down the stairs, leading me to believe I had killed him. And without the threat of exposure, Mr. Taylor must have known he had no chance to convince me to marry him."

Mr. Evans nodded. "It does sound more like the secretary was an opportunist after the fact."

"Perhaps. Some people, however, are most deluded in their own worth and prospects. He might have thought he could woo Miss Smith here to wed him instead of an earl."

Laughter burst from Katherine's lips. She covered her mouth and feigned a fit of coughing to cover just how ridiculous *that* idea was.

"All right, all right." Lady Mary grimaced. "But the man plunged a knife into a corpse. Better than sticking a living person, I'll grant, but still not an action a decent person would take. I don't trust him."

A small smile crossed Mr. Evans's face, his eyes lighting with humor, and something in Katherine's belly fluttered. He truly was a handsome man, if one ignored his sneaking about and listening in on private conversations. "You don't have to trust him," Mr. Evans said. "That still doesn't make him a killer."

Lady Mary sniffed. "Well, he remains on my suspect list with the others. He might not have known Katherine would push—"

"Nudge!" Katherine couldn't have others exaggerating.

"—Perrin down the stairs, but he could have poisoned him just the same. The opportunity to extort Miss Smith could have just been the cream on top of the pudding."

"The others?" Katherine sat up straight, remembering Lady Mary's earlier words. "You mentioned three people with financial motives? Who?" Dread spiraled through her gut.

Mr. Evans ran his hand through his dark hair. It needed a trim, but the unrefined look somehow added to his appeal. "Perhaps we shouldn't discuss—"

"Well, Lord Havenstone, of course." Lady Mary rubbed the bridge of her nose. "He invested in one of Perrin's schemes and lost everything. That kind of humiliation doesn't sit right with most men."

"Then why come to Perrin's house party if he disliked him so?" Katherine leaned forward, grasping the armrest of the settee. "And why would Perrin invite him?"

"Both excellent questions." Lady Mary looked about and sighed. "I do wish I had my walking stick, but I usually only use it when I go out of doors."

Mr. Evans hurried to her side. "Are you feeling unsteady, my lady?"

Lady Mary scowled. "No. It is simply more satisfying making points when I have the stick to jab into the floor for emphasis." She turned to Katherine. "As to your first question, the only reason I can see why Havenstone accepted the invitation is for revenge. Which puts him near the top of my list."

There was talk of that list again. Did everyone have a list of people they suspected of killing Perrin? Should Katherine have one? "And the other two?"

"Mr. Bertram Withers." Mr. Evans gave Lady Mary one last concerned look before stepping away. "Perrin lost a good sum of money to him gambling and paid it off with a worthless mine."

Lady Mary cocked her head. "Bertram and Perrin were related. There have been family events since that incident they've both attended with no acrimony. I'll admit Bertram wasn't overly fond of the earl, but not being sad someone has passed is a far cry from killing him."

"Very few murderers have what most people would consider good reasons for killing." Mr. Evans cocked his shoulder against a bookcase.

Katherine popped up. "Why are we even discussing this? Uncovering who killed Perrin is a job for the authorities." She started for the door.

"Don't you want to know who the third person is?" Lady Mary called.

Katherine stopped, her shoulder blades drawing close. "No." Because she already knew. Just as she knew he couldn't have done it.

"Your father has one of the strongest motives of all," Lady Mary said. "He came to this house party expecting to finalize your marriage contract and instead learned that Perrin was trying to trick him into trading for another parcel of land than the one agreed upon."

"The deception would have angered my father, like it would anyone, but it isn't a financial blow." She bit down on the inside of her cheek. There were periods when her father became 'cash poor' as he was wont to call it, having tied up his money in purchases of land or businesses. There were times when their finances had become tight waiting for his investments to produce. But while cash might become limited, her father was still wealthy. He could sell one of his assets if he ever needed to.

She turned to face them. "Besides, my father wouldn't know the first thing about poisoning someone. If he were to kill, it would be in a different manner."

"That's not a defense I would recommend using before the magistrate." Mr. Evans arched an eyebrow.

"My father doesn't need me to defend him. Besides, both of you are ignoring the prime suspect and motive. Unrequited love. Miss Walker wanted nothing more than to become Lady Perrin. It was obvious in the way she treated Perrin Manor as her own, the way she spoke to the earl, and the low way she treated me when I arrived."

Lady Mary pursed her lips. "That seems like more a motive to kill you than Perrin."

Mr. Evans nodded in agreement.

"She has been his neighbor her whole life. Watched, heart-broken, as he married Mr. Withers's sister, and thought she finally had a chance upon her death." Katherine warmed to her idea. She could see it in her head, the bitter, spiteful woman Miss Walker had become after waiting so long. "She thought she might finally have her chance, but Perrin goes and chooses someone else. Again, she's spurned, and she's finally had enough."

"A dramatic story," Mr. Evans said dryly, "but you've absolutely no evidence."

"And you do?" Katherine stepped up to him, needing to tilt

her head back to look him in the face. He was most annoyingly tall.

He examined her, tilting his head. His eyes were the color of a fine whiskey, and they seemed to see more into her mind than she wanted. She shifted on her feet. With his brawny size and blunt features, Mr. Evans appeared more a laborer than a professional. She would have to remember there was a sharp mind in that attractive head.

Lady Mary interrupted their little battle of stares. "Right now, all we have are suspicions. What we need is proof, and I suggest we look for it."

Katherine snapped her head around to look at Lady Mary. "What? You want us to look for a killer? Are you mad?"

"I've been called that before." Lady Mary pushed her spectacles up higher on her nose. "But I tend to get results and that's what matters. There is a killer in this house, and the magistrate is still days away."

"Yes, the magistrate is just days away." Katherine shook her head. "There is no reason we cannot wait for his arrival."

"I don't like waiting." Lady Mary sniffed.

"It might not be safe to wait," Mr. Evans agreed.

They *were* mad, the both of them. Katherine took a step back.

Lady Mary made an exasperated sound. "I'm not asking you to climb through windows or interrogate anyone. Just keep your eyes and ears open. If you say your father is innocent, this would only be of help to him."

Katherine narrowed her eyes. Well, that was low, but it wasn't wrong. Her father would be under suspicion. Lud, she might still be, as the unwilling bride.

She nodded. "I won't investigate, but I will look and listen. If I learn of anything important, I'll let you know." And she knew right where she would start. Mr. Evans and Lady Mary might not think much of her theory, but Katherine knew better than most that a heart shouldn't be trifled with. Knew what it was like to dream of a future only to have it ripped out from under you.

Her father might be at the top of Lady Mary's list, but Miss Walker was at the top of hers.

Chapter Thirteen

Lady Mary

I T MIGHT HAVE been stocked merely for appearances' sake, but the library in Perrin Manor held an exemplary collection. And with steady sunlight now streaming through the windows on the first truly clear day since I'd arrived, I desired nothing more than to find a good book and take my seat in the wingback by the fireplace with a plate of Cook Clem's pastries by my side.

Unfortunately, I didn't have time for leisure. Also, a maid had said the last of the previous day's sweets had already been claimed. I sniffed.

To further my pique, I found my chair already occupied when I entered the library.

"Good day, Lady Mary." Mr. Ryder rose and inclined his head. A plate dusted with crumbs rested on the side table next to him. "Lovely morn."

I eyed the plate with suspicion. "Yes." Turning my back, I wandered to the bookcase that held botanical reference books. I hadn't found anything about plants that could be used as poisons yesterday, but I'd only skimmed through half the shelf devoted to botany.

"I didn't realize you were interested in gardening." Ryder spoke from right behind me. He reached over my shoulder and removed a book on garden design. "Do you have much of a garden at your home in London?"

"It's adequate." There was space for me to sit in the sun in good weather and plenty of colorful plants to cheer my eye. I left the care and tending of it up to my staff. I pulled out a book, flipped through the pages, and replaced it. What I needed was a book with illustrations of flowers so I could see if poisons lurked in Perrin's own gardens.

"I saw you took *An Enquiry Concerning the Principles of Morals* up to your room last night." His arm brushed against my shoulder as he reached for another volume.

I frowned and stepped to the side. "What of it? Does it surprise you, a woman reading something other than a novel?"

Ryder tapped the book he held against his thigh. "My only surprise is that you would enjoy it. I've always found Hume's writing dry and his conclusions uninteresting."

I muffled a snort of laughter. I hadn't expected that. I gave him a considering look. My assumptions about the president of the London Society for Morality and Decency led me to believe he would have approved of any book with 'morals' in the title. But then, Hume found morality largely to be based on passions, not reason, and that theory I could easily believe Mr. Ryder to find abhorrent. I couldn't imagine the man ever succumbing to passion.

Seeing a book entitled *British Botanist*, my hopes rose. I pulled it out and, yes, there were illustrations. Quite detailed and lovely ones, in fact.

"Did you find anything in your late night reading to help you understand why someone would kill your brother-in-law?" Ryder tucked a thumb into the pocket of his waistcoat, the movement showcasing his admirably flat abdomen.

I sighed. I shouldn't forget how shrewd the man was. Of course, he would know I would continue to look into Perrin's death. "Do I detect disapproval in your tone?"

He looked at me, his milk chocolate eyes serious. "You

shouldn't spend your time investigating murders. Leave it to the authorities."

I tapped the toe of my boot against the floor. "And what, pray tell, should I be doing with my time instead?"

His forehead furrowed. "My advice was intended as a warning about placing yourself in harm's way, not a criticism of your hobbies. But now you mention it, there are more appropriate activities a woman of your station could pursue. Needlework?"

Needlework? I ground my back teeth. Of course, he would wish to relegate me to the most boring activity ever devised. "I have bad eyes."

He rubbed his jaw. "Pianoforte or harp?"

"I lack an ear for music."

"Charitable works?"

"I'm already on the boards of London Ladies of Mercy and The Charity for the Houseless Poor." How much more charitable did a person have to be? "My French is atrocious, I detest journaling, and I couldn't paint anything recognizable if you held a pistol to my head. As you can see, not all women have the capacity, or inclination, to excel in the feminine arts you seem so desperate to relegate us to."

"But you are skilled in argumentation, one of the most feminine arts of all," he said dryly. He shook his head and wandered to one of the windows. The bits of silver in his golden-brown hair caught the sun. "You remind me of my wife."

I blinked. "You're married?"

Ryder chuckled. "You don't have to sound so surprised a woman would consent to marry me." His face sobered. "I was. My wife died only two years after we wed. She fell down the stairs in our home after imbibing one too many glasses of wine."

"Oh." I didn't know why I'd never considered that Ryder would have had a wife. He looked well enough now; he was probably quite handsome in his youth. He was well-spoken and intelligent, and if—

"Just one moment." I planted a hand on my hip. "Are you

implying I overindulge? I have a glass of wine with dinner, and a glass or two of something stronger only if the situation demands it." My brandy was more medicinal than anything else.

He held up his hand. "I wasn't implying that you drink too much, and that wasn't my wife's habit, either. The comparison was purely of the stubbornness of the two of you. You know what the sensible course of action is, but you refuse to follow it."

That only partially unruffled my feathers. "It would be quite a dull life if one only did what was sensible."

He twisted his lips. "Perhaps. Well," he said, arching an eyebrow, "what have you learned?"

I narrowed my eyes. His turn seemed too good to be true. "Not much. There are four guests here with known motives to want Perrin dead." Five if you include Miss Smith's harebrained theory.

"I hope I am not included in your tally."

"No." I tucked the botany book under my arm. "You arrived too late to be the perpetrator. The stable master confirmed it."

His lips twitched. "How fortunate for me." He sat back on the windowsill. "Of course, you did notice how attentive Perrin's secretary was to Miss Smith. And the clandestine meetings the two of them have had since Perrin's death."

"Of course." I rolled onto the balls of my feet. "I've spoken with Miss Smith and she is no longer a suspect in my eyes."

"But Mr. Taylor hasn't been similarly cleared?"

I inclined my head. "He has not."

"A pity." Mr. Ryder smoothed a hand down his cravat. "No one here seemed to be overly fond of Lord Perrin, except perhaps for Miss Walker. She seems quite distraught at his death."

"Too distraught?" I asked. I joined Ryder at the window. The man might be infuriating, but he did seem to have a strong ability to read people's motivations. I was curious if he thought Miss Walker might be overplaying her hand.

"Too distraught over the man, perhaps." He cocked his head. "But over the loss of a dream, of wealth, status, no, her mourning might be in proportion to all that."

Yes, a lost dream was one of the hardest things to mourn. I stared out the window. A large pond glittered in the sunshine, making me believe spring had finally arrived. The ice house stood nearby, a small domed structure dug into the earth that had been Perrin's resting place these past three days. I should be thinking about how soon he could be laid to rest in a proper grave. Instead, I wondered what he might have known about my and his brother's lost dream.

"Have you noticed Lady Havenstone's eyes?"

I blinked, the change in topic jarring. "No. What about them?"

"Her pupils have been unusually large on several occasions. Some women attempt that for cosmetic purposes, but I have seen her rubbing her lower back frequently. I believe she suffers from some ache."

"And?" My brow cleared. "Oh. And a treatment for pain relief is belladonna. Drinking the juice from the berries also dilates the pupils, and in large enough amounts, kills. Lord and Lady Havenstone may have access to a poison that could have killed Perrin." I'd ask Marie to confirm that one of the vials in Havenstone's potion case was belladonna.

I gave Ryder an approving look. "For all your complaining about leaving these matters to the proper authorities, you seem to have a natural talent at investigating yourself. Anything else you've noticed?"

"Only that Mr. Withers enjoys gambling more than is healthful." He pressed his lips into a white slash. "He tried to make his townhouse a stake in a game of hazard he and Havenstone played last night. Fortunately, Havenstone was not so reckless."

My breath hitched. I knew Bertram liked his games, but I hadn't realized he liked his stakes so high. Perhaps when Perrin had swindled him out of his gaming winnings, it had been a bigger blow to Bertram than I'd thought. Perhaps he had needed those winnings to cover great losses he may have sustained elsewhere.

There was no way to ask Bertram the question without both putting him on notice he was a suspect and having him tell me it was none of my business to my face.

But there was someone of my acquaintance who might have answers. He also might tell me to mind my own business, though in a much more civilized manner. Then again, he might not. I'd send a letter to him as soon as the post was able to reach London.

Mr. Ryder held out his book. "If you want to understand why someone would kill, there is no better instructor than Thomas Aquinas."

I reached for it, but he held on for a moment, the book connecting the two of us. I swallowed. "Thank you. More light bedtime reading, I'm certain."

Ryder grinned, his eyes crinkling at the edges. "You are a most challenging woman, Lady Mary. I do hope you will remember that while sensibility might lead to a bit of tedium, its opposite can have much more hazardous effects. Do be careful."

As I could see he was in earnest, I bit back a flippant response. "I will." Or I would try, at least. I always did try to be careful; matters just went askew at times. I pulled the book from his grasp.

Ryder lifted his face and sniffed. "Is that....?" He pulled his watch from his pocket. "Two o'clock. I believe luncheon has been set out. Shall we see what Cook Clem has prepared today?" He crooked his elbow.

I took his arm. Having someone to keep pace with seemed the only way to restrain myself from racing into the dining room and greedily piling my plate unbecomingly high. "Let's."

Chapter Fourteen

Lady Mary

I FINALLY FOUND my quarry in the front sitting room. Marie was kneeling on the floor, a bucket of muddy water by her side, a wet rag in her hand. The late afternoon sunlight glinted off her auburn hair. "Hardly anyone uses this sitting room," I said. "I wouldn't think it would need much cleaning."

The maid looked up, a scowl on her face. "It wouldn't, except *someone* keeps putting Southey outside and when 'e comes back in, 'e trails this muck everywhere."

"The outside air is healthful to dogs." I cleared my throat.

Marie narrowed her eyes and scrubbed at a brown streak on the peach-colored rug.

I winced. I hadn't meant to give the maids more work, but the dog did need to go out to do his business. And a bit of mud was of no comparison to the damage that beast was making of my skirts and boots.

Skirts and boots.

"Marie, before Perrin was killed, do you remember needing to clean mud off anyone's clothes or shoes?" If someone picked a poisonous leaf from the garden here, he or she might have tromped through some mud to get to it.

She tossed the rag in the bucket and rose, stretching her back.

"I didn't notice, but I can ask the girl who does the laundry. But that wasn't something Lord Perrin instructed us to look for. A bit of dirt isn't scandalous enough to threaten someone with exposure, if you take my meaning."

Someone gasped.

Marie and I turned toward the door.

Miss Smith stood there, three books bundled in her arms, a shocked expression on her face. "Do you mean to say that Lord Perrin had the servants looking for reasons to…to…extort his guests?"

I dropped my chin. "Come now, we already knew Perrin was a scoundrel. No need to act surprised."

She walked into the room and dumped her books on a side table. "Did you look through my things?"

Marie shifted her weight. She raised one shoulder. "You 'ave lovely pantalets. I especially like the ones with the blue lace trim."

Miss Smith's cheeks went pink. "Thank heavens I didn't marry that man."

Marie twisted her mouth. "Is Mr. Taylor going to be any better?"

"I'm not marrying Mr. Taylor, either." Miss Smith frowned.

"Oh." Marie scratched her head. "Does 'e know that?"

I bit back a laugh. This maid had some cheek, I'd give her that. I was surprised Perrin would suffer such forthright talk to her betters. Perhaps he hadn't. Perhaps the girl was clever enough to know around whom she could loose her tongue.

Miss Smith stiffened. "There is nothing between Mr. Taylor and myself."

"Begging your pardon, miss, but all of us who serve this 'ouse know of Mr. Taylor's fondness for you. 'e didn't want you marrying the master. Made that clear, 'e did. And we thought 'e intended on marrying you, after Perrin's death and all. 'e thinks you are, at least."

The color on Miss Smith's face deepened. She balled her hands into fists.

I watched the maid. "Did Mr. Taylor want Miss Smith enough to kill for her?"

"Oh, really," the woman in question muttered.

"People 'ave done more foolish things for worse reasons," Marie said, sounding wise beyond her years. "You're better off, begging my pardon for saying so. Lord Perrin wouldn't be a proper 'usband."

"Why do you say that?" I asked.

"The master was supposed to get engaged during this party. To 'er." Marie bobbed her head at Miss Smith, a strand of hair coming loose from under her cap. "And still Lord Perrin invited Mrs. Draper 'ere. Luckily, she declined, which put the master in a right foul mood, it did."

Miss Smith's forehead creased. "Who is Mrs. Draper?"

This time it was Marie who went pink. "Well, she's a woman Lord Perrin used to…well, they used to…." She huffed out a breath. "Let me put it this way. We all thought 'er name was quite fitting, seeing as she used to drape 'er arms about the master, drape 'er skirts over 'is lap, drape 'er ti—"

"Yes," I broke in. I appreciated when a person spoke their mind regardless of their perceived social status, but perhaps the girl could learn a bit more discretion. "We take your meaning, Marie."

"And Perrin invited that woman to this party?" Miss Smith planted her hands on her hips. "A party to which he'd also invited me, his presumed affianced?"

Marie winced. "Yes." The word came out sounding more like a question.

"What a lovely man." Miss Smith's eyes narrowed to slits. "It's no wonder the house is filled with the sounds of mourning. Orphan and widow alike will fall to their knees in grief on hearing of his passing."

I ignored the girl's overly-dramatic sarcasm. "Are you certain about Perrin's indiscretions?" Though it was hard to hide something like that from the servants.

The maid rubbed her lower back. "The last party at Perrin Manor, the master was quite open about it. Touching 'er shoulders. Giving 'er meaningful looks. And right in front of poor Miss Walker. That was one of the few times I actually felt bad for the woman." Marie made a face. "Though mayhap she deserved it."

"Why do you say that?" I asked.

Marie wrinkled her nose. "She's not as nice as she puts on. She can be cruel, she can. Said some right nasty things to Mrs. Draper, and when that lady fell off of the master's 'orse, Miss Walker laughed. Didn't think anyone was around to 'ear it, but I did."

Miss Smith gave me a look full of triumph. "She has a streak of viciousness in her, it would appear."

I flapped my hand at her. "Was Mrs. Draper badly injured?"

"Some nasty scrapes and bruises, but nothing more serious."

Miss Smith leaned against the back of a settee. "How did Mrs. Draper fall from the horse? Did someone startle it?"

Did Miss Walker startle it, she meant. Miss Smith was determined to make Miss Walker the villain. But was she wrong?

"No, miss. The girth snapped, throwing 'er off while she was galloping." Marie picked up her bucket.

The maid seemed eager to get back to work, but I was loath to let her go. She was turning out to be quite the valuable font of information. "Were you able to check the case in Lord Havenstone's room?" I ignored the look Miss Smith shot me. I wasn't going to feel guilty that I'd asked the maid to keep spying on the guests.

"Oh, I forgot." She put the bucket back down and slid a folded bit of paper from the cuff of her sleeve. She handed it to me. "A list of the labels for each potion. None of the vials were empty."

"Why is that significant?" Miss Smith asked.

I scanned the paper as Marie answered. I didn't recognize many of the potion names, but one did catch my eye. *Belladonna.*

So it was confirmed. Havenstone did have access to a potential poison.

"I just thought if I were to poison someone, I'd dump the whole lot in the wine. Make sure to get the job done."

And the belladonna vial hadn't been empty. Havenstone could have brought a second vial. Or perhaps a lethal dose was smaller than I'd expect. "Thank you, Marie." I tucked the paper up my own sleeve. "You've been most helpful."

She dipped a curtsy, picking up the bucket in the same motion. Most economical, I thought. "Yes, ma'am. Well, more pawprints to clean. I'm off." And with that parting shot, she left.

"I told you Miss Walker was a good suspect." Miss Smith walked around the settee and dropped onto it, pulling one of her books off the side table and onto her lap.

I sniffed. "What are you reading?"

"These are home apothecary books. I'm looking for any garden remedies that could be poisonous in excess and what the symptoms of the poisoning would be. If we can match Lord Perrin's symptoms with one of the poisons, it might narrow down the suspect list."

I was impressed. "I thought you weren't going to investigate, only keep your eyes and ears open?"

Miss Smith raised a shoulder. "Reading is only using my eyes. Besides, Miss Walker has mentioned she has gardens of her own. I'll wager that the poison used was one she grows at home."

I sat next to her. "Don't close your mind to other possibilities. Now, give me a book. I'll help with your research." And see if any of Havenstone's potions were listed in these books.

But Havenstone didn't seem as promising a suspect as he once had. Could Miss Walker have tampered with the saddle's girth? And if she had tried to kill once before, how much easier would the second attempt have been?

Chapter Fifteen

Henry

THE RED BALL meandered toward the corner pocket, hovering at the edge of the drop before dipping inside. Henry put his cue stick down and nodded to Lord Havenstone. "Thank you for the game."

Havenstone blew out a breath. "Nice for you, perhaps. I need a less talented player to go against. Withers?"

Mr. Withers appeared to take no offense and picked up the cue.

Henry turned to the other men in the room. It was after dinner, and all of the men had gathered in the billiards room, drinks of their choice clasped in their hands. Henry hoped the alcohol would loosen tongues.

He went to the sideboard and picked up the decanter of whiskey. "A refill, Mr. Smith?"

"Damn right." The man of business held up his glass and took the generous pour with a smile.

Henry settled in the chair next to him. "I wanted to express my apologies once more for the confusion over the marriage contract. If I had known earlier that Lord Perrin intended to change the terms, I would have notified you before you'd come and perhaps saved you the journey."

Mr. Smith flapped his hand. "It wasn't your error to apologize for. Perrin's perfidy is on his own head."

"I know you were anticipating the use of the mine." Henry gave him a sympathetic smile. One thing he'd learned in his years practicing law was the ability to question people while making them feel comfortable. "I do hope you won't be too adversely affected by Perrin's change of mind."

Mr. Taylor leaned across a low table, breaking into their conversation. "Mr. Smith didn't need to marry his daughter off to the earl. He is well enough off on his own. He doesn't have a motive, if that is what you're implying."

Henry kept his features even. He might have a talent for keeping clients untroubled, but apparently that didn't extend to nosy secretaries. And a secretary who had a motive to make sure Mr. Smith remained unconfined and available to become his future father-in-law.

Mr. Smith gave a deep belly laugh. "Is that what these questions are about? Don't worry about me. My daughter and I are clear with the law. I have no concerns on that point."

"So your interests haven't been hurt by not trading for Perrin's land?" Henry asked.

The smile fell from Mr. Smith's face. He shifted in his seat. "Everything has worked out for the best."

Mr. Taylor scooted forward. "I'm sure Mr. Smith is successful enough where he has no need to marry his daughter to someone worthless for profit. From the short time I've been acquainted with him, I can tell he only wants his daughter to be happy, and that would include in her marriage."

Henry leaned back and cocked one leg over the other. "You seem awfully interested in the future of Miss Smith."

Mr. Taylor tugged on his lapel. "Miss Smith reminds me of my sister, so I will admit to some tender feelings on my part." He leaned back. "And what wouldn't a brother do for a sister? There isn't much."

A loud sigh came from the billiards table. "Withers, we haven't got all night." Havenstone tapped his cue on the floor. "Take your shot."

Withers did, striking the white ball so hard that when it connected with its red counterpart, the billiards ball hopped over the rim of the table and rolled in Henry's direction.

Havenstone muttered an oath and tossed his cue stick down on the table. He followed the ball, frowning when he came to the settee it had rolled under.

He dropped to his knees and reached under the settee. "This billiards game is becoming tedious. Anything of interest happening here?"

"Just talking about the earl," Henry said. "I believe someone will be able to fetch a magistrate tomorrow. The mud should have hardened enough by then."

Havenstone grunted. "Good riddance. Although the food has drastically improved, I will be ready to depart from this house as soon as possible." He pulled back, holding the ball in triumph. "Ha!"

"Damn right," Mr. Smith muttered. "I can't wait to remove my daughter from this place."

"You seem to have a knowledge of mining, Lord Havenstone." Henry rested his glass of whiskey on his knee.

"I would hope so." The baron shot Withers an apologetic look and plopped down on an empty seat. "I've owned and operated over twenty mines in my life, seven currently."

Henry arched an appreciative brow. "I was hoping you might explain the process of extracting arsenic."

Mr. Taylor huffed. "Do you suspect everyone of Perrin's murder?"

Havenstone frowned. "Are you insinuating my knowledge of arsenic makes me a suspect? I wouldn't appreciate that if it were the case."

Henry gritted his teeth and managed not to glare at the secretary. "Not at all. Perrin owns some mines of his own, some quite close. Anyone could have procured the arsenic. Your knowledge of a potential poison could help to catch the killer, however."

Havenstone pursed his lips. "Well, there isn't much to it. As I said before, arsenic is a by-product of processing tin and copper, although it can be mined directly, as well. When you take the raw metal ore and roast it at high temperatures, the arsenic burns out, turning into a vapor. When the vapor cools in the flue or chamber attached to the furnace, it condenses into a white powder that can be harvested. There was a period where I had my workers collect the arsenic and I sold it to a paint producer, but that became unprofitable."

Henry cocked his head. "Do you know if arsenic powder has a strong taste? Would it have been noticeable in Perrin's wine?"

"I never tried to taste it," Havenstone said dryly.

Henry inclined his head. Another person with knowledge and access to poison. He hadn't realized just how many ways to kill had existed.

"Well, my glass is empty." Mr. Smith placed his empty tumbler on a table. "Shall we join the ladies?"

Everyone agreed, and they filed out and went to the rear sitting room. The room was quiet, only a couple hushed conversations between the ladies.

Miss Walker was slouched in a wingchair when they entered. She popped up straight at the sight of them. "Oh, good. Fresh blood. The women here are very dull and don't want to play any games. Now that you've arrived, does anyone want to play Consequences? Charades?"

Lady Mary sighed. "What is it with you and charades? Why are you so eager to make silly pantomimes?"

Miss Walker drew her shoulders back. "It is an amusing activity for house parties. For the right sort of people at least."

Henry's gaze was drawn to Miss Smith, and he repressed his smile at her eye roll. She held an empty glass, and her lace fichu had come a bit untucked, exposing a hint of creamy skin above her bosom.

Henry shifted, and dragged his gaze back to her face. He

wondered about the lady. She had sounded convincing, but a doubt still lingered in the back of his mind. He was hard-pressed to envision her smuggling a vial of poison into the house and pouring it into Perrin's wine, but her secret conversations with the secretary still struck him as suspicious.

As if to further his misgivings, Taylor made a straight line to Miss Smith. He stood behind her chair and leaned over to greet her. Giving the man, Henry suspected, a clear view straight down her bodice.

Henry narrowed his eyes.

"Katherine," her father called as he settled in his own chair. "How about some music? Show me that my money on that piano tutor was well spent."

"Yes, Father." Katherine rose and moved to the pianoforte in the corner of the room.

Taylor followed after her, cocking his hip against the instrument as she began to play.

"If Miss Walker is so eager for entertainment, how about a game of whist?" Lady Havenstone suggested. "I know my husband is always ready for a game."

Miss Walker stood and moved to the gaming table at one end of the room. "Sounds lovely. Mr. Smith, will you make our fourth?"

Smith chuckled. "Not hardly. I've never been much for the games of gentlefolk."

Miss Walker covered her disappointment well. "Mr. Withers? Surely you won't refuse a lady's request."

He pulled a deck of cards from his pocket and shuffled the cards with one hand. One card escaped his control and drifted to the floor. Withers plucked it up, a red stain darkening his face. "I'll do so if we can play without small talk." He went to the table and fluffed out the tails of his jacket before sitting.

Miss Smith hit a discordant key, drawing some gazes. She was focused on the sheet music, but her shoulders were curled inward. Mr. Taylor hovered close, ready to turn the page of the song.

Lady Mary caught Henry's eye. She tilted her head toward the pianoforte while pulling her foot from underneath Southey's sleeping form.

Henry remained where he stood. He'd done his part for the investigation for the night. On the morrow, they could relay all that they knew to the magistrate and be done with it. No one else seemed to be in danger.

Frowning, Lady Mary again nudged her head in Mr. Taylor's and Miss Smith's direction.

Henry grumbled. There was no way to discreetly circle behind them in order to listen in on their conversation, if there was any. He didn't see the point.

But, as he had little else to do, he made his way to the pair.

With a sharp glance at Henry, Miss Smith muttered to Mr. Taylor, "I've told you, I do not wish to marry. I have told my father and others about what happened, and I will tell the magistrate the same. As Perrin was poisoned, I have done nothing to cause me trouble. I thank you, but no."

Taylor flipped another page over, his movement jerky. "You are making a mistake."

"Perhaps, but it is mine to make." Her forehead wrinkled as she played a section of the song that had a particularly quick tempo.

Taylor's knuckles went white. "What are you doing loitering about, Evans? Can't you see I'm assisting Miss Smith?"

"It looks more like you are annoying the lady," he said mildly. "She has given you her answer. Stop pressing the question."

"You know nothing of what we were speaking." Taylor straightened, his height still a good three inches shorter than Henry's own. "You need to mind your own business."

Henry smiled, but there was no kindness in it. "On the contrary, I know exactly what you were speaking of. And I know what you did." He didn't know which was worse, desecrating a body or attempting to pressure Miss Smith into marriage. Both actions were contemptible. And they made it easier to believe the man might also have been the one to kill Lord Perrin.

Taylor's face went ruddy. "You told him?"

"Keep your voice down." Miss Smith spared him a quick glare before turning back to the music. "And yes, Mr. Evans is one of the people to whom I confessed my actions. And yours."

Taylor tightened his fist further, and Henry hurried to his side. As discreetly as possible, he pushed his way between the secretary and Miss Smith. Taylor looked ready to lash out, and Henry wouldn't put it past the man to strike a woman.

"Calm yourself," Henry said. "You made the decision to do what you did. If there are consequences for it, you will have to face them."

Taylor ignored Henry. He gripped the edge of the pianoforte and bent over to speak around Henry's middle. "I would have taken care of you. I would have shared my good fortune. You have shown yourself not to be worthy of my attentions, however. You will regret not accepting my proposal."

Miss Smith finished the song with a flourish, then neatly folded her hands. "I think not. I think marrying you would have been worse than marrying Lord Perrin. Perhaps even worse than prison. I'd thought there was a possibility you'd acted out of kindness, but now I see that isn't a characteristic you possess."

Henry casually knocked Taylor's hand from the instrument, causing the man to stumble forward a step. "I will turn the pages for Miss Smith. Your services are no longer needed."

Taylor's face darkened to brick red. "I'm better off," he said before stomping out of the room.

Henry's shoulders lowered an inch. "I can't believe you seriously contemplated marrying that man."

Miss Smith's nostrils flared. "I didn't feel I had many choices. I still don't. My father will find another man of means and contract my services to him." She nodded to the sheet music.

Henry closed his gaping mouth and turned the page. Surely she didn't mean *services* in that way. A lady would hardly allude to that. He cleared his throat. "Your father won't take your preferences into account when he makes his decision?"

She gave him a look from the corner of her eye. "The fact that it is his decision to make is the problem."

Henry couldn't deny that a woman of Miss Smith's station often wasn't able to choose her own husband. Miss Smith lived in comfort and never had to worry about her next meal, but she had fewer freedoms than women from his own class. Most women he knew would gladly trade their poverty for their independence, however.

"I'm certain your father would only have you marry a man who he thinks will take care of you."

Miss Smith's fingers slowed to a finish. "Are you?" she said quietly. "Are you certain? I wish I could be."

The sorrow in her voice tugged at something deep inside of him. The problem was he wasn't certain. People traded other people all the time, often times those to whom they were closest.

She stood from the piano bench, the faint scent of flowers wafting from her body. Her big, brown eyes held an almost accusatory glare in them when she lifted her head to his gaze.

He hesitated a moment, his body having the inexplicable urge to lean closer to hers, to lower his own head to meet hers.

Which was all kinds of foolish. He stepped back, giving her space. But he couldn't stop from holding up his hand, nor the quick surge of pleasure that raced through him when she gave him hers and he helped her step out from the bench.

Perrin would have been a fortunate man had he married Miss Smith.

He let her go and watched as she joined her father for a drink.

And perhaps it was Miss Smith's good fortune that Perrin was dead.

Chapter Sixteen

Katherine

THERE IT WAS again. The squeak. Katherine hadn't closed her window's drapes, and the moonlight cast blue shadows in her bedroom. She sat up in bed and scanned the room, but saw nothing to account for the sounds.

Shivering, she pulled the covers closer about her. Her fire had been but embers when she'd readied for bed and now the grate was cold.

The sensible thing to do would be to lay back down, pull the covers over her head, and search for the so-far elusive sleep. And, for the most part, she was a most sensible person.

A sound like a wail torn by the wind made her flesh pebble. But she wouldn't be able to sleep if these noises persisted, and as her sisters and father could attest, when she lacked a good night's sleep, she became decidedly unreasonable. A grumpy badger, she had been called, and that was the kind epithet. A crazed shrew was the term her eldest sister preferred.

All Katherine knew was that if there was a ghost haunting the hallways of this house, it was incredibly rude to be wailing when people needed sleep. And if it were other guests keeping her awake, she wanted to give them a piece of her mind.

She tossed her covers aside and slid out of bed. Reaching for her wrapper, she slid it on, knotting it tightly, as she made her way to the door. Pressing her ear to the wood, she held her breath. There were definitely voices, and was that laughter?

"Oh, for heaven's sake." She flung open her door and stuck her head out. "Anyone there?" she called softly. She didn't want to be the annoyance that kept anyone else awake. *She* had manners.

Silence settled around her. Windows at the ends of the hall gave some illumination at the edges, but pitch dark loomed in the space near her. Katherine waited a minute, listening and knowing everyone else was having sweet dreams but her, before giving up. She started to close the door.

Something wailed again, the sound full of pain but muffled as though coming from far away. She jerked the door back open, clenching her teeth. If it was that dog again, she was going to give whoever was supposed to be caring for it a tongue-lashing they wouldn't soon forget. She stomped down the hall in the direction of the sound, pausing when she turned the corner.

She narrowed her eyes. Something moved at the far end. Or was that just a cloud crossing in front of the moon, making the shadows dance? "Hallo?" she called again, even softer this time. Her feet were carrying her slowly forward even as her mind was clearing. A disturbed night's sleep wasn't the worst thing in the world, not when one was safe in one's own bed.

Something hissed, and Katherine's heart started to race. She stopped. This had been a poor idea. She'd let her irritation lead her to a stupid decision. She took a step back. There was a thump at the end of the hall. She spun, her elbow banging into a handle. As this door was closer than her own, she turned it, and darted inside the room.

She leaned back against the door, her chest heaving. She was probably being foolish. It was probably just the dog.

But she'd wait a few minutes before venturing back into that hallway.

She straightened. She'd taken refuge in the ballroom, one that looked as though it hadn't been used for some time. White sheets draped several pieces of furniture, and a potted plant had withered to just about nothing.

The parquet floor was cold against her bare feet. A draft caressed her cheek.

And a hand reached out from behind and grabbed her shoulder.

"Gah!" Katherine spun again, feeling much too much like a child's top. She pressed a hand to her chest. "You. What are you doing sneaking about?"

Lady Mary's spectacles glinted in the moonlight. "Me? I was following you. What are you doing?"

Katherine's heart began to settle. She dropped her head back on her shoulders. "You were the one at the end of the hall. I thought…" Well, it didn't matter what she'd thought. Any foolishness about the supernatural that might have flitted through her mind she would keep to herself. She raised her head and glared at the older woman. "You've kept me from a restful night's sleep."

"You aren't the only one wishing she was abed." Lady Mary sniffed. "So, you were following me and I was following you. How disappointing."

Katherine tilted her head. "Wait. I couldn't have been hearing you out in the hallway while you were in your room hearing me out in the hallway. Something made a noise that lured one of us out of our rooms first. There has to be someone else out there."

Lady Mary tugged on her white sleep cap. "I thought I saw someone creeping up the staircase from the front hall. What would anyone be doing creeping about here in the dark? If it was a servant, he or she would carry a lamp or candle."

"Perhaps, though neither of us was clever enough to seek out an open flame to light a candle of our own before creeping about."

"*I* didn't want the person I was following to see me." Lady Mary lifted her chin. "And I wasn't creeping."

Katherine tip-toed to the door. "Fine, you are the superior sneaker." Her voice was cross, and she knew she'd have to apologize to the woman after she'd had some sleep. She opened the door an inch and peered out.

Nothing moved. Feeling a bit braver now that someone else was with her, she asked, "Are we going to keep looking for the source of the noise or return to our rooms?"

Lady Mary blew out a breath. "I'm tired. Let's make a quick circuit around this floor and, if we see nothing, retire."

Katherine agreed. Shoulder to shoulder, they made their way around the first floor. The hallways formed a convenient square. The dark corner at the first turn, the one Katherine had thought she'd seen something moving in, proved empty. As did the second turn. They made their way towards the third, passing the main staircase leading down to the ground floor.

Katherine paused. This was where she'd stood when Perrin had grabbed for her. When she'd pushed him away. She didn't think the sight of him bouncing down the stairs, his head rattling against each step, would ever leave her memory.

Lady Mary tilted her head. "Do you hear something?"

"No." Katherine shook herself. "No, nothing." She sighed. "There's no one about. Let's—"

Glass shattered, the sound rising like an explosion from the ground floor. The air shifted, a chilling draft swirling their nightdresses. Something else shattered, and Katherine grabbed Lady Mary's arm. "Do we go see what that is?"

"If I'd brought my pistol, maybe." Lady Mary looked about. "And there is nothing handy around here that can be used as a weapon."

A door opened around the corner of the hall. Footsteps hurried their way. Mr. Ryder trotted up to them as more doors opened. "What happened?" he asked.

"We were just about to go investigate." Lady Mary gave him a genteel smile. "However, if you would like to do that for us…."

Mr. Evans joined them, tying the knot of his banyan. "Stay

here," he told them, nodding to Mr. Ryder. The two of them trotted down the stairs as Lady Mary and Katherine were joined by the other guests.

Katherine blew out a breath. It looked like no one was going to get a good night's sleep.

Chapter Seventeen

Lady Mary

WHILE I'D HAD my reservations about investigating a darkened ground floor, I wasn't about to be told to stay put. Gripping the banister, I hurried down the stairs, following Mr. Ryder and Mr. Evans. Ryder picked up the oil lamp that was kept burning by the front door on a low wick and started for the front sitting room.

"The disturbance came from that direction." I pointed at Perrin's study. At least that's where the sound had seemed to emanate.

Evans picked up a large candlestick. Plucking out the candle, he tossed it aside then prowled towards the room, holding the heavy silver stick aloft like a weapon. Ryder was only a step behind.

"What has happened?" The butler blinked sleepily at me as he and several other servants gathered around, most of them holding candles of their own.

"Rocks," Ryder called from the study. He came to stand at the doorway. "Someone threw a rock at each of the windows in here. It's a mess."

We all surged forward, wanting to have our own looks at the destruction.

Miss Smith inched over the threshold, toeing a large piece of glass aside. "Who would do this?"

Evans scowled at her and clomped forward. He had taken the time to shove his feet in boots before rushing out of his room. Reaching her, he bent, wrapped one arm beneath her rear, and stood, holding her most inelegantly. He carried her from the room and set her down near the large round table in the middle of the hall. "There is much glass and you have bare feet." He stomped back to the room, examining everyone's feet as he passed.

"It would be best if everyone left the room," Ryder said. "There's nothing to see besides."

I ignored that suggestion. After all, I had put on my slippers before I'd left my room, and I was still thinking about Miss Smith's question. Who would have done this, and why? I surveyed the gathered crowd. All the guests had come down and joined the servants in the main hall. Everyone seemed to be accounted for.

I pressed my lips tight. I should have counted heads at the top of the stairs to see if anyone were missing then. There had been plenty of opportunity since we'd all descended for the malefactor to have rejoined the assembly after having his sport with rocks. It was poorly done.

But I couldn't go back in time, so there was no use nursing that annoyance. If I couldn't determine who, I would have to ponder on the why. It seemed so petty, smashing up windows. Childish. If it was the killer who had done it, surely he would have already achieved the ultimate satisfaction in destroying the master of the house. Attacking the house itself would be a poor satisfaction in comparison.

A gust of wind blew a stack of papers from the desk, and Evans muttered an oath. I bent to retrieve them as Ryder herded the last of the onlookers from the room and Evans searched out the butler.

"Are there wood and nails available to board these windows?"

he asked.

The butler nodded. "By the stables. Johnny can fetch it." He pointed at a young footman.

Evans clapped the boy on the shoulder. "Let's go," he said, and followed the footman out.

Mr. Ryder stood in the threshold. He looked between me and the rest of the party in the hall. "Well, there isn't much we can do here. We may as well go back to bed."

I stared at the windows. One of the rocks had made all of the glass fall out of its pane, except for some small jagged points around the frame. The other window had remained intact, however, only missing a rock-sized hole near the center.

Rocks through windows were petty, yes. It could be attributed to boys having their idea of fun, or a drunken lark. But something about this act chilled my bones. It could also be an expression of pure hatred, and if killing Perrin hadn't been sufficient for the murderer to excise his animus, then what else might be in store?

"Lady Mary." Mr. Ryder came to the desk and took the papers from my hand. He put them in a neat pile and placed a paperweight on top. "There's nothing to be done here. May I escort you to your room?"

A maid came in with a broom, and I realized that not only was there nothing I could do, but that I would be in the way, a circumstance I particularly detested. "Of course." My grim musings could be had elsewhere.

I took his arm and let him lead me out. Most everyone else had already returned to their rooms, and we followed Lord and Lady Havenstone up the staircase.

"Try to get some sleep," Ryder told me at the door of my room.

I inclined my head and endeavored to do just that.

Sadly, I failed. When I joined the others for breakfast in the dining room the next morn, it looked as though I wasn't the only one who had tossed and turned all night. There were dark shadows under many ladies' eyes, and Mr. Taylor looked as though he hadn't had the vigor to comb his hair properly that morning. Bertram looked even worse, his eyes red and his skin sallow. His hand trembled faintly as he brought a bit of toast to his mouth.

I poured myself a cup of tea, adding an extra lump of sugar, and took my seat.

"How did you sleep, Lady Mary?" Miss Smith spread marmalade on a slice of toast across from her.

I decided not to respond to that question, only gave her a look.

One which she must have misinterpreted. "I had a splendid night's sleep after all of that unpleasantness," she continued.

Yes, she was one of the only people who did look well this morn. Her hair was glossy, her eyes bright, her attitude unforgivably cheerful. And I wasn't the only one who noticed. I caught Mr. Evans giving the young woman a furtive glance or two.

Mr. Taylor, on the other hand, was scowling at Miss Smith.

"I hear the constable was finally sent for." Lady Havenstone turned to her husband. "Hopefully we can away on the morrow. There is something in the air in this house that is unwholesome. I can feel it in my lungs."

Lord Havenstone patted her hand. "We'll take some walks about the grounds today. It will fix you right up."

If the roads were clear enough to send for the constable, then I should be able to send my letter today, as well. I would have to remember to give it to the butler.

"Lord, yes." Mr. Smith rose and filled his plate from the sideboard once more. "Pack your trunk this evening, Katherine. I want to leave first thing."

"If we are given permission." I tapped my thumb against the rim of my cup. Time was running short. I had been hoping for the arrival of an authority figure since Perrin was killed, but now I saw the difficulties in investigating the murder when all of the suspects had dispersed to their own homes. Even a trained magistrate would find it trying, having to travel to get answers to his questions. Many of us were in London, Miss Walker local, but the Havenstones lived somewhere in the north. And who knew where Mr. Taylor would travel to for new employment?

I stood. "Where are the rocks that were thrown through the windows?" I addressed Mr. Evans, hoping he would know.

He paused, his fork holding a bit of pork inches from his mouth. He lowered his hand. "By the front steps. Why?"

"I would like to see them." Ignoring the curious looks, I made for the front hall.

"Why do you want to see the rocks?" Evans followed me out the front door and down the short flight of steps to the graveled drive.

I turned and spotted two stones that appeared out of place nestled along the side of the stone staircase. I pointed at them and the attorney nodded. "I want to see how heavy they are. Could a woman have thrown them through the windows?"

I strode to them. One was about the size of two of my fists held together, the other a bit larger. I bent and lifted the larger one. My back protested when I straightened. "Well, I can hold it, but tossing it at a window might prove difficult." I would have to be standing quite close to the window. One of the rocks had traveled to the far shelves, though I supposed it could have rolled most of the way.

Evans cleared his throat. "They are a bit unwieldy, I grant, but perhaps it wouldn't be too difficult for a younger woman...."

He trailed off at my glare.

"Did you notice anyone late to join the gathering in the hall last night?" I asked. "And aside from Mr. Ryder, did you notice who came out of their bedrooms after the noise?"

"No and no." He ran his hand up the back of his head. The sun fell full on his face, and he squinted. "I'm afraid I wasn't thinking about trying to identify the rock thrower until it was too late."

As the same thing had happened to me, I couldn't judge the

man. I also couldn't hide my disappointment. "I fear this is hopeless. We will have learned nothing of import by the time the constable arrives to take over."

"No one else has been harmed." Evans took the rock from my hands and replaced it on the ground. "That is what we were trying to prevent. When the constable arrives, I will be happy to place this burden into his hands."

I frowned. It was a sensible opinion, but one I didn't share. I didn't like leaving things unresolved, and if I left for London now, it would eat at me.

Not having any other ideas, however, I decided to turn my attention to something I could accomplish. I bid my *adieus* to Mr. Evans and circled around the house to enter the kitchens by the servant's entrance. Discretion in this matter was advisable.

The expression on the scullery maid's face when I came inside was comical. She jumped to her feet, but I waved her back down. "I need nothing but a word with the…"

Mr. Ryder stood by the oven, his hand on Cook Clem's shoulder, for all appearances in a deep discussion.

"…cook," I ended. Inhaling sharply, I stomped over to the pair.

Ryder dropped his hand and gave me a pleasant smile. "Lady Mary. I would like to say I'm surprised to see you down here, but—"

"Don't smile and simper at me, Mr. Ryder." I planted my hands on my hips. "All that nonsense about accepting Perrin's invitation because you were concerned about me was a load of hogwash. You came because you want to steal Cook Clem away from Perrin Manor." I hadn't thought Ryder had means enough to hire a highly sought-after chef, but Cook Clem's meals were succulent enough to suffer other privations to obtain.

Ryder had the decency to flush. "Both things can be true. I was concerned, and curious, about such a brother-in-law. But the head of my social club heard I had been invited to Perrin's home. He asked that I try to tempt Cook Clem away from his current employment and work for us. London must be a more interesting locale to live in than the countryside of southeast England," he said to Clem. "And now with the earl gone, you might not have employment here for long, in any case."

"Yes, London is more suited to a young, virile man like Cook Clem." I turned my most engaging smile on the cook. "But you wouldn't want to work for some stuffy club. No, a private home is a much better situation. If you come to work for me, I can guarantee you will be admired by the cream of London society, including my nephew, the Duke of Montague."

I rarely entertained, but Clem didn't need to know that. I felt a bit shameless dropping Montague's name into the conversation, but a chef as talented as Clem would want to be admired by the highest in society. "I can guarantee your wages will be higher with me, as well."

"Now just a moment." Ryder drew himself up straight. His baritone voice deepened even further. "My club can—"

Clem flapped both hands at them. "No fighting, no fighting. My cooking is supposed to bring joy, not disharmony."

"But...."

He held up a plump finger, stopping my entreaty. "I have many kind offers that I will have to consider."

I narrowed my gaze. Who else had been offering for him?

"Now," he continued, "I need someone to taste the new cakes I have been experimenting with." He ushered us to the wide plank table the servants ate at and sat us down. He returned with two teacup-sized dainties and placed one before each of us. "You must tell me your thoughts. I am uncertain if the citrus and caraway flavors meld together as they should."

I picked up a fork, glaring at Ryder.

His lips twitched as he picked up his own fork.

We both dug in at the same time. My eyes closed at the first taste. Exquisite. "Is that lemon?"

Clem tucked his thumbs in his apron and smiled. "Nothing so pedestrian. It is a hint, just a hint, mind you, of grapefruit."

The flavors shouldn't have worked together. I couldn't imagine anyone else trying to pair the herb with the exotic fruit. But it was delicious, and I wanted Clem working for me more than ever.

Clem made excuses and left us as we finished our treats. "Who else do you think approached him?" I asked Ryder. "I'll bet it was those Havenstones. She is always saying how Clem's is the only cooking that doesn't upset her digestion."

Ryder licked a crumb from his fork and sighed. "I don't know, but I will be at my club every afternoon if we obtain his services."

"You won't." I finished my own last bite.

Ryder raised his eyebrows. "Is that a challenge?"

"We could make it a bet, but I know how you feel about those." I stood and gave one last look at the counter where more of the cakes cooled. I did hope Clem had made enough so I could enjoy this dessert again tonight. With a nod of my head, I left the kitchen and headed for the stairs.

I might not be able to discover who killed Perrin, and that defeat would sting.

But if Cook Clem was in my kitchen, I felt sure I would be able to overcome any disappointment.

Chapter Eighteen

Lady Mary

THE CONSTABLE DIDN'T come to the house that day. Apparently he had been knee-deep in digging out a well that had collapsed in the rains. But he arrived at Perrin Manor bright and early the next morning, looking as though he hadn't slept since the storm had begun.

He rubbed his eyes as Marie brought him a cup of tea. "All right. So the Earl of Perrin was found at the bottom of a staircase with a knife sticking out of his chest. A woman here"—he flipped to a page in his notebook—"a Miss Smith, admitted to being in an altercation with the lord where he either fell down the flight of stairs or was pushed. Yet you believe Perrin's cause of death was poisoning."

I waited for him to take a restorative sip of the hot brew. "Constable Adams, I realize this is a confused situation, but the combined facts that there was very little blood around the knife wound and that two mice died from drinking Perrin's special wine is strong evidence of my theory."

"And you eliminated falling down a flight of stairs as the cause of death because…?"

I folded my hands and rested them on my knees. "Perrin was already in distress when he approached Miss Smith. Again, there was no blood from a head wound from hitting the stairs. No broken neck. No, the rational conclusion is that the poison that was causing him to grab at Miss Smith was what also killed him."

He placed his cup down and pinched the bridge of his nose. We were in the front sitting room, the constable having agreed to speak with me first as a close relation of the deceased. Adams was a young man in his mid-twenties who had country manners and intelligent eyes. His boots were streaked with mud, both fresh and dried, and Marie pinched her lips together when she saw the state of her floor. She gave a quick curtsey and departed, probably to ready her bucket.

He rubbed his smooth jaw. "The former constable of Modbury, Constable Greeley, only left his position last month, and I had only been apprenticed to him for a year before that. Normally I would only assist the magistrate in such a serious matter."

"But the magistrate for this county is dead." I could see his dilemma.

He shot me a look. "I'll be sending word to the magistrate the county over, asking for assistance. Until then, I'd like to interview everyone here and see the body. I'll have our local leech examine Perrin, but he's most likely as out of his depth here as I am."

"You're young. There is no shame in acknowledging your lack of experience in certain areas." I nodded, approving. "It's a wise man who knows his limitations."

"I'm so pleased that you approve," he said, his last words distorted by a jaw-breaking yawn. "Will you send people in one at a time?"

I stood, ignoring his sarcasm. I suppose I might have sounded a tad patronizing, but speaking from experience was one of the benefits of age. I paused at the door. "Most of the guests are quite eager to return home. Might I suggest that you advise them to remain until the magistrate can arrive? Questioning suspects would be difficult once they have dispersed about the country."

"Had experience with that, have you?"

As his question was not anticipating a serious response, I merely gave him a small smile and left to do as he'd asked. Hopefully my fellow guests wouldn't be too put out with me for advising that they remain.

The interviews seemed to go on forever. I'd had four cups of tea in the rear sitting room and one trip to the necessary as the guests and servants went to the constable one by one and gave their statements. I finished *Summa Theologica*, much to the amusement of Mr. Ryder when he saw it in my hands. I pondered which of Aquinas's four temptations, wealth, pleasure, power, or honor, would most likely seduce me into murder. I tallied up the remaining renovations that remained to be completed on The Minerva Club after a fire had damaged it last year. I was starting to count the fleur-de-lis on the paper that lined the wall when the constable joined us.

"Oh, thank heavens." I sat up straight. "Have you finished with everyone?"

"For the most part." He tucked his notebook into his jacket pocket. "I'd like to see the body now."

Mr. Evans and I both rose. "Of course," I said. I assumed the role of macabre host, showing the constable the dead body, before the attorney could. Holding out my hand, I indicated the main hall. "We can go out the front door."

It was when I was digging out my walking stick from the cloakroom by the front door that I realized everyone was coming with us.

I couldn't blame them. We had been trapped indoors for days, then forced to remain at a host-less house party. The tedium would make an excursion to the ice house seem exciting.

We tromped across the front drive and towards the hut by the pond. The ice house was circular, about ten feet in diameter and dug partially into the ground. Three worn steps led down to the wood door.

Constable Adams told us all to wait outside as he ducked his head and stepped inside. He had been sensible enough to bring an oil lamp with him, and a faint glow came from the open doorway.

We waited in hushed anticipation, as though we expected the constable to shout 'Aha!' But when he came out, he only shook his head sadly. "Thank you all for your continued patience. I'll send for the magistrate immediately. He should be here either tomorrow or the next day. Remember, remain at Perrin Manor until then."

There were some angry mutters, a few glares.

I lifted my chin. Really, what did they expect? The group started drifting back to the house.

"Miss Smith?" the constable said. "A moment."

He didn't ask me to remain, as well, but I felt it prudent.

Mr. Evans also stayed. "What is this about?" He took a step closer to Miss Smith.

"I only wanted to ask if Miss Smith was certain she didn't strike Lord Perrin around the face." Constable Adams crossed his arms over his chest. "If he was attacking you, it would be understandable that you would strike him."

Miss Smith's forehead wrinkled. "No, I don't think so. I remember he grabbed my arm, then his hand went to my..." Her face flushed. "I pushed at his chest, just to try to get him off of me."

"So you didn't strike him?"

"She has answered that question." Mr. Evans put himself between her and the constable, drawing his shoulders back. He seemed to grow taller, and for the first time I could imagine that he would be a force at the negotiating table. "If you are treating Miss Smith as a suspect, I would recommend that she not speak to you without first consulting with a barrister."

Constable Adams held up his hand. "I'm merely trying to get all the facts straight."

I pushed my spectacles up my nose. His questions seemed specific. Had the constable seen something on the body that I'd missed? I hadn't noticed any signs of a struggle when I'd looked at

Perrin, but perhaps they had taken time to appear.

"I've gathered all the information I can for today." The constable looked at me. "Lady Mary, before we leave, can you give me the direction for Lord Perrin's sons? I'm certain the magistrate will want to contact them."

I looked at the constable's expectant face then at the ice house. I wanted to have another look at the body, but I didn't think Constable Adams would allow it. My eyebrows drew down. "One moment," I said to him before walking to Miss Smith and Mr. Evans.

I lowered my voice. "Check for any marks on Perrin's head and face. It sounds like we missed something."

Miss Smith's mouth dropped open. "You want us to what?"

Evans looked at Miss Smith. He nodded. "I'll take care of it.

"We can't—"

"Lady Mary?" Constable Evans interrupted Miss Smith's objection.

I nodded to Evans, confident he'd do as I asked. He might not want to admit it, but he wanted to solve Perrin's murder as much as I did. "Coming, Constable." I jabbed my walking stick into the earth as I made my way to the house.

Bruises or marks might not tell us much more about Perrin's murder, but then again, they might. No detail should be overlooked.

Wealth. Pleasure. Power. Honor – or as was more accurately described, the pursuit of recognition. These were the four worldly pursuits Aquinas identified as the typical substitutes man made for God. If one desired them too greatly, they became false gods, and man might do anything to worship them, including murder.

Perrin had desired them all. He'd cheated or deceived the wrong person in order to achieve them. Someone who had wanted that false god even more than Perrin had.

And it had gotten him killed.

Chapter Nineteen

Henry

"Y OU'RE NOT TRULY going to look at Perrin's body?" Miss Smith clutched her elbows. "Lady Mary must have been jesting."

Henry arched an eyebrow. "I don't think even Lady Mary would joke about that." Besides, he was curious what the constable had seen that he hadn't on that night. "Stay here."

He descended the steps and pulled open the door. He had to stoop inside the hut, wondering why the builders hadn't added a couple more inches to the ceiling. But this structure wasn't built to linger inside. Blocks of ice were stacked within, and along the far wall, the blocks were stacked to form a bed of sorts. Perrin lay atop, a blanket covering his form.

The light from the open door wavered. "Do you see any-thing?" Miss Smith asked.

"I might if you didn't block the light." He should have thought to bring his own lamp.

"Oh." She hurried down the steps and to his side. "Sorry."

"I didn't mean for you to join me down here." He pressed his lips flat.

Miss Smith circled to his other side, her gaze fixed on the blanket-covered form. She stood closer than was proper, her skirts brushing his legs, her bosom grazing his arm.

The lady was trepidatious, of course. Her body instinctively sought out a live body as comfort against the one who was dead. He understood it, and he would be lying if he said his own body didn't appreciate her nearness.

But this was a nasty business. "Go back to the house. I need to lift the blanket."

She shook her head. "I want to see. I don't remember striking him, but my memories of the event are a bit muddled. I want to know what I did."

Henry grasped her shoulders and turned her to face him. He put his finger under her chin, turning her head from Perrin's body and raising it to his. "Whether you struck him or not, you didn't kill him. Poison did. There's no need for you to see him."

She swallowed. "I know. And when I was outside, there was nothing I wanted to see less, but now that I'm here, I don't think I can leave without seeing him. I know it doesn't make sense, but if you're going to look at Perrin's face for bruises, I feel that I should, too."

He examined her. Miss Smith may look like a typical society miss, one whose biggest concern was the latest fashion, but she had a spine made of steel. He'd been impressed with her composure after learning what had occurred between her and Perrin before he died, and he was even more impressed now.

Her father might plant him a facer if he learned that Henry had allowed his daughter to examine Perrin's body, but from the determined glint in her eyes, he knew it was the right thing to do. And it wasn't as though she hadn't already seen the body.

Henry shuffled forward, a crick starting to form in his neck. Miss Smith matched him step for step, keeping close. He reached for the top of the blanket. "Are you ready?"

She nodded, her gaze again fixed to Perrin's form.

He pulled back the blanket, his shoulders lowering an inch. The face wasn't as bad as he'd feared. The skin was grey in this low light, and there was a purple bruise along one cheek that

Henry didn't remember seeing before, but the ice had done its job. There was no decay as yet, and only the faintest cloying scent reached his nose.

"That seems a large bruise." Miss Smith held out her right hand. "Wouldn't I also have a mark if I'd struck him that hard?"

If she'd struck him that hard, she'd most likely have a broken bone. He tried to picture the woman beside him winding up to sock an overly-familiar Perrin, and his lips twitched.

"You didn't cause that bruise." Henry lowered the blanket to Perrin's hips, wondering if the earl had anything of import in his pockets and why he hadn't thought to check them before. "Perrin most likely obtained the bruise falling down the stairs." He quickly stifled his disgust and swept his fingers in the body's jacket pockets, then moved to the waistcoat.

Nothing. "I'm certain Lady Mary will be disappointed, but there's nothing to learn here. Perhaps a doctor or coroner can discover something new, but we can't. We should leave."

A tremor shook Miss Smith's body, and she ran her hands up and down her arms. "Are you certain? I don't want to have to come back."

"*You* won't." He shook his head. "Let's—"

The door slammed shut, blanketing them in darkness.

"Mr. Evans?" Miss Smith's voice was high and thin.

He stumbled forward, biting back a curse when his knee struck the edge of an ice block. Feeling his way along the roof, he reached the door and pushed.

It didn't move. "Hallo? Did someone shut the door? I and Miss Smith are inside. Hallo?"

There was no answer. Henry pushed harder against the door. The wood creaked, but remained in place. There was no handle on the inside of the door, no lock. No reason why the blasted thing shouldn't open.

"Oh, God." Panic laced Miss Smith's voice. "We're trapped."

He backed up a step, braced his hands on the ceiling, and planted his boot on the door. He kicked it again. A third time, each strike making a satisfying creaking noise but accomplishing nothing.

Miss Smith's voice sounded even fainter. "We're trapped. With a dead body. In the dark."

The bigger concern was being trapped in the cold, but he refrained from pointing that out. "It will be all right." His eyes were beginning to adjust. It wasn't full dark in the ice house, a bare amount of light filtering through the cracks in the hut's plaster. Miss Smith was a lighter shadow among the dark, and he groped his way to her, knocking his head on the ceiling once in the process.

He grabbed her arm, at least he hoped it was her arm, and squeezed. "Something must have fallen and blocked the door. Someone will be out here soon and move it." He slipped off his jacket and tucked it around her shoulders. "Stick your arms inside. This should keep you warm."

Fabric rustled as she did as he said. "What about you?"

"I'm fine." He was colder than Medusa's stare but he wouldn't admit to it. He inched around the perimeter of the hut, looking for any weakness in the structure. It didn't take long. The ice house wasn't large, but it was seemingly of solid construction. Too solid. He slapped his hand against the wall, wincing at the sting. Since Miss Smith couldn't see him, at least not well, he stuck his hands under his armpits to warm them.

"Any minute now someone will notice our absence," he said. Grimacing, he picked up an ice block and went to the door. The skin on his hands started to burn from the cold. Using the block as a battering ram, he attacked the door once more. "Someone." Bam. "Will." Bam. "Come." Bam. "For us." Bam, bam.

The ice slipped from his hands and landed on his toe.

Biting back an oath, Henry rested his forehead against the door. *Blast.* He didn't even bother looking for the block when he returned to rejoin Miss Smith.

"Is it becoming difficult to breathe?" she gasped out.

"No." Without thought, he gathered her to his chest and

rubbed her back. "There's plenty of air. Take slow breaths."

She shook against him, and he held her until the tremors stopped, until her breath slowed to match his.

He rested his cheek on the top of her head. "Someone will find us, don't worry."

"I don't like small spaces," she admitted.

"Understandable." He inhaled deeply, the scent of whatever soap she used on her hair filling his nose.

"Or the dark, though this seems to be a new fear for me."

"Since there are only the two of us here, there is nothing to fear from the dark." He tucked her closer. He wanted to share his body heat with her. His confidence. If she happened to feel like a soft, tempting little armful against him, well, that was only an unlooked for bounty.

"The two of us and…."

That wasn't a pleasant direction for her mind to go. "Your father mentioned that you and he had recently returned from a trip to Paris. Tell me about that." He had mentioned it to Perrin, in their argument when he'd confronted the earl about the changes to the marriage contract. Apparently he'd been meeting with a business associate there who would fund the mining operation expansion Smith had planned for the land Perrin was supposed to give him.

"We lodged near Notre Dame Cathedral." A shudder wracked her body. "It was lovely, but the people were disagreeable. I don't know if it was anti-English sentiment, the fact that my father is wealthy, or just the nature of the French. I feel no need to return." She dug her hand into his cravat, her fingers pressing against his throat.

He flinched. "Good Lord, your hands are colder than mine." He put just enough space between them to be able to hold her hands between his. He lifted them to his mouth and blew. "What of your sisters? Did they accompany you?"

"No." She rested her head against his shoulder. "Their husbands wouldn't let them. They each do have a young child to care for," she conceded, sighing. "I used to hope my father would find me a good man to marry me off to. Now a part of me hopes he'll think he has enough money and allow me to remain unwed."

He chafed her hands between his. "Not all men are like Lord Perrin. And surely you wish to have children of your own one day."

She was silent for a moment. "I hope that I can choose the man who would be father to my children. I know better than anyone with whom I'd be compatible."

That was a grand idea in theory, but Henry knew plenty of people in unhappy marriages that they had chosen to enter into themselves. And he knew plenty in arranged marriages who seemed quite delighted in their spouse.

He would be lying, however, if he said he wanted Mr. Smith to contract his daughter to another man. She did deserve to have a say in the matter. And he didn't want to see her with another man who was unsuitable.

A small part of him didn't want to see her with another man at all.

In the dark, he felt it was safe to press a small kiss to her fingertips.

Miss Smith snugged her body against his. Her voice grew husky. "My lips are quite cold, as well."

In the dark, he felt it safe enough to drop his head and press his lips to hers. It was only responsible to keep all her bits warm.

Her breath heated his mouth. Her lips sought his just as eagerly. And when she opened her mouth and let his tongue slide inside, he had to assume that her body heated just as much as his.

He stopped thinking about the impropriety. They were trapped. Cold. She needed comfort. Heat.

He dug his fingers into her hair, angling her head to the perfect position.

After all, it was the responsible thing to do.

————— ⚬≈⚬≈⚬ —————

Chapter Twenty

Katherine

S HE COULD NO longer feel her toes. It might have been from the cold. It might have been that Mr. Evans's kiss had drawn all her attention to only the parts of her that pressed against him.

She felt her belly, tight against his hip, and the flutters that each stroke of his tongue created there. She felt her hands, held tightly in one of his own. And her lips.... Well, she definitely felt those.

She had been kissed by a couple of her beaus before, but it had never been like this. She never wanted it to end.

"Hallo?"

"Let me look, milady." Footsteps padded on the earthen floor. Then a throat cleared. Loudly.

Mr. Evans stiffened. His lips pulled away. Katherine's body chilled, reminding her that she was still in an ice house. Alone with a dead body and Mr. Evans.

And the footman who was staring at them. The light from the open door displayed his knowing smile all too well.

She jumped from the attorney's arms and shook out her skirts. "Thank you for attempting to keep me warm while we were trapped, Mr. Evans. It was most kind." And without looking him in the eye, she fled, to the light, to warmth, and away from whatever that unsettling feeling was that only Mr. Evans seemed to elicit.

He followed her. As she blinked in the sunlight, he bent to whisper in her ear, "Attempting?"

She ignored that and turned to Lady Mary. "Thank goodness you came back." She stomped her feet, trying to bring back some feeling. "The door was stuck."

Lady Mary pushed her spectacles up her nose and frowned. "It wasn't stuck. It was blocked."

"What do you mean?" Mr. Evans asked, trotting back down the steps to examine the door.

The footman toed a thick plank. "I was heading to the stables when I saw Lady Mary trying to move this. It was wedged between the top step and the door. It is quite heavy, milady. You shouldn't have tried to move it yourself."

Lady Mary waved his comment away. "Did you hear anyone out here? Who might have done this?"

Katherine flushed. She hadn't been hearing much of anything. Although they hadn't been… doing what they'd been doing when the door had been blocked. They weren't distracted then. She shook her head.

"Nothing," Evans agreed. His face was grim. "So this was intentional. Why? What would killing me or Miss Smith accomplish?"

"Kill?" Katherine pressed her hand to her throat. "Surely no one wanted that."

Mr. Evans planted his hands on his lean hips. "The human body can't take such cold temperatures for long. If we hadn't been found, we would have died."

"But that would have taken several hours." Lady Mary bent to peer into the ice house. "If I hadn't come out here, someone else would have, looking for you. I don't think this was a serious attempt. It feels more like mischief-making."

"Mischief implies childlike fun." Katherine shoved her hands inside the jacket's pockets. "There was nothing innocent about this at all."

"Fine. Evil mischief then." Lady Mary rested her hand on the ice house's door. "There isn't very much space in there, is there?"

Katherine swallowed. "If I may, no one needs to inform my father of what occurred. I am unharmed, and no one need worry him."

"Or tell him you were alone in an enclosed space with Mr. Evans." Lady Mary gave her a shrewd look.

Katherine could feel said man tensing next to her. "Quite so. My father doesn't need another reason to marry me off, leastways for supposed impropriety." She didn't want Mr. Evans to feel that she would use the situation to try to trap him in marriage.

Her stomach twisted. Or to think that he could trap her. There were more than a few men who would delight in forcing her into marriage, laying their hands on her father's money. She didn't *think* Mr. Evans was of that mold, but a hint of doubt gnawed at her still.

"Marriage as the solution for an unmarried man and woman being caught alone together is silly, regardless of whether or not impropriety occurred." Lady Mary cocked her head. "Although it has been known to lead to a happy marriage or two."

Katherine stared at her boots. She slipped out of Mr. Evans's jacket, holding it out to him. She could pretend all she wanted that nothing untoward had happened when she and the attorney were trapped, but there were three other people who knew the truth.

A muscle ticced in Mr. Evans's jaw. He tugged his jacket free from her hand and shrugged it on. "I would hate to be the source of a lifetime regret on Miss Smith's part. I think we can all agree not to mention this incident." He gave the footman a hard look.

The young man quickly nodded.

"Well?" Lady Mary jerked her head toward the ice house. "Did you find anything?"

Mr. Evans crossed his arms. "There is a bruise on Perrin's face that raised sometime after his death, but I don't think it tells us anything other than that his head hit the steps as he fell down them. I don't believe he was involved in any physical altercation prior to his being poisoned, shoved down the stairs, and stabbed."

Katherine narrowed her eyes. She hadn't *shoved* him down the stairs, and Mr. Evans knew it. It wasn't her fault that her concern over appearances had insulted his male pride.

Lady Mary ducked her head to go inside.

"There's no need for you to look at Perrin's body," Mr. Evans said. His brows lowered. "I accurately described his appearance."

"I'm sure you did." Lady Mary lifted one shoulder. "That does not mean I don't want to see for myself. Please stay out here and make sure no one comes along to lock *me* in there." And she disappeared down into the ice house.

"What is it with you women needing to see everything for yourself?" Mr. Evans glared at her, as though Lady Mary's action was in any way her fault.

"Perhaps it is because we women have learned from experience that not everything a man says can be trusted." Katherine pinched her lips together.

Lady Mary emerged from the hut. She rubbed her arms and loosed a long breath. "You were right. I see nothing that changes any of our theories."

Mr. Evans shot the footman a glance. "Thank you for your assistance. We don't want to delay you any longer."

The young man didn't seem all that eager to return to his duties, but with a dutiful nod, he cut across the field toward the stables.

When he was no longer in earshot, Mr. Evans said, "I don't think it wise to let too many people know that we have theories about the murder. It might lead to more attacks against us like this one."

Lady Mary blew out a breath. "Do you think the other guests haven't taken notice of the questions we've asked?"

Evans opened his mouth to respond, but Lady Mary held up her hand. "However," she said, "I will be more discreet in future."

"Good." Evans looked to the house. "Has the constable left?"

"Not yet." Lady Mary flicked at a bit of dust on her sleeve. "He's decided to search the house for a possible source of the poison."

Katherine's chest tightened. She had nothing to hide, but still, the idea of a stranger looking through her belongings didn't sit right. "He had this idea all on his own?"

Lady Mary whacked at a loose stone with the end of her walking stick. "It might have been suggested to him. I believe his choice was made, however, when Marie mentioned that she'd heard a noise in the attics above her room two nights past in the middle of the night."

"She didn't go to see what made the noise?" Katherine asked.

"That would hardly be sensible." Evans extended his arm toward the house, and they began to trudge their way back. "What woman would be foolish enough to go investigate a strange noise in the middle of the night?"

Katherine and Lady Mary exchanged a look. What woman indeed?

Katherine's shoulders drooped. The fear from being trapped, followed closely on its heels with the exhilaration of being in Mr. Evans's arms, had left her feeling curiously drained. The backs of her eyes burned. She wanted nothing more than to be home, in her own rooms, safe.

She looked to the house, hoping Constable Adams would find something to uncover who had killed Perrin. Something to end this.

Movement in one of the windows caught her eye. A face pressed against the glass inside the ballroom.

She stopped, her breath catching. It was human, she was sure, but it looked wrong, distorted, as though the individual features had been sewn together incorrectly.

"Is something wrong?" Mr. Evans's voice still held a bite of irritation, but there was a note of something else there, as well.

Katherine looked at him. The edges of his whiskey-colored

eyes were crinkled in concern. When she'd first met the man, she'd thought him pleasant but plain looking. Now that she knew how strong that jaw felt in her palm, how comforting his arms felt wrapped around her, she couldn't deny his appeal. She raised her hand and pointed at the window.

But when they all looked to where she pointed, the face was gone.

Chapter Twenty-One

Lady Mary

THE CONSTABLE JOINED them in the rear sitting room, a brown glass vial in his hand. He'd asked everyone, guest and servant alike, to gather in one room while he searched.

"I found this tucked behind some boxes in the attic." He held it up. The vial was empty except for some dusty residue inside. "I'll give this to the magistrate to have analyzed, but I'll ask all of you first. Is there any legitimate reason such a bottle would be stored up there?"

The butler shook his head. "Any tonics or medicines are kept in the pantry off the kitchen. We don't clean up in the attics often, however. There's no telling how long it could have been up there."

"There's no dust on the outside of the glass." I cocked my head, wondering if the constable would allow me to have a closer look at the substance inside. Was that small residue ground up mineral, leaf, or seed? "If it had been there long, we'd see the evidence of it."

"But why put it up in the attics?" Havenstone asked.

"The killer must have assumed our rooms would be searched at some point." I should have asked the butler to search the rooms immediately after Perrin's death. It would have angered the guests, but perhaps we would know who the killer was if I had. "Or that a maid might come upon it while cleaning. The attics are as good a place as any to dispose of the evidence."

"He truly was poisoned then. By one of us." Mr. Smith shook his head. "I didn't fully believe it until now." He stood, his jacket pulling taut around his soft middle. "I want to take my daughter out of here. The magistrate can contact us at home."

There was a general murmur of agreement.

Constable Adams tucked the vial into his pocket. "There is no reason any of you should be a target. Lord Perrin was obviously the intended victim. I am going to ask that you all remain until the magistrate comes to question you himself. It's only a day or two more."

"The constable is right," I added, loath to have my suspects disperse in a most unmanageable manner. "Besides, it might look suspicious for any of us to appear too eager to leave. Like we had something we wanted to hide." It was the lowest form of emotional manipulation, but I was hard-pressed to feel guilty over it. Perrin had been my husband's brother. While I hadn't liked him much, I couldn't just let his killing go unanswered.

Marie nervously tucked a strand of her red hair behind her ear. She darted a glance at the baron. "That looks like one of the little bottles in Lord Havenstone's case."

The room grew silent.

"How do you know that?" Havenstone exploded. "Did you search through my belongings?"

Marie had the grace to flush.

"It wasn't her fault." I leaned forward in my chair. "Lord Perrin told her to look through his guests' rooms. She was only following the orders of her master."

"He did what?" Lady Havenstone's jaw dropped open. "That is abominable."

Miss Walker frowned. "He must have had good cause."

"No, he was simply a miscreant." Bertram inhaled sharply. "I told my sister not to marry the man. I told our father his title wasn't worth it, but they didn't listen."

The constable held up his hand. "This discussion is fruitless. What I would like to know is if anyone saw someone in the attics who shouldn't have been there. Marie said she heard noises two nights past."

"That was the night the windows in Perrin's study were broken." Miss Smith rested her hand at the base of her throat. "The night Lady Mary and I heard noises in the hallway and went to investigate. I saw something by the stairs up to the servants' quarters, but I thought my eyes were merely playing tricks on me."

Lord Havenstone hmphed. "You most likely just saw a servant retiring for the night."

Possibly. It did seem odd that the killer would wait so long to dispose of the vial, but someone disturbed enough in mind to murder might not be thinking clearly. I thought about the shadow that I'd seen days earlier. Had it been the killer creeping up to the attics to hide the vial?

I was surprised when my Jane stepped forward. "It wasn't the middle of the night like Marie said, but I saw Mr. Taylor going up to the attics that evening." She shrugged at my look. "My rheumatism was flaring up. You know I like to walk to ease the pain."

Mr. Taylor pushed off the wall he was leaning against. "I had every right to be up in the attics. It's where the paper supply is kept."

"As your employer is now dead, what did you need the paper for?" Mr. Evans gave the secretary a smile worthy of a shark.

"I have inquiries to make, don't I?" Mr. Taylor's face went red. "A new position to find. I won't be the one who is implicated in his death."

His excuse made sense. A secretary who suddenly found himself without a position would send out inquiries. However, if his boasting to Miss Smith about having enough money to marry her bore any truth, then he might not be looking for another position. On the other hand, if his claim to future blunt was his assumption that Mr. Smith would provide for the married couple, and Miss Smith turned him down, perhaps he had gone back to seeking honest employment.

I rubbed my temple. "I don't suppose you have any evidence of these inquiries? The addressed letters? Any responses?"

"I've already sent out the letters, and it's too early for any responses, but the butler can tell you I gave him letters for the post."

We all looked to the butler, and he nodded. "They went with Lady Mary's letter and two of Mr. Smith's."

Mr. Taylor sneered. "I can understand why you would want to divert attention to someone else. With what Perrin knew about you, you have the most reason of anyone to wish him dead."

My stomach turned a lazy spiral. "What are you talking about?"

"The earl wanted to ruin you," Taylor said. "He knew the truth about your marriage to his brother. Knew you weren't the doting wife you pretended to be."

I slowly straightened in my seat. "There was no pretense. I loved my husband." And there was no way Perrin knew about my and Cavindish's issues. Cavindish would never have spoken of them to anyone.

Mr. Evans stalked forward, looming over the shorter man. "You'd best be careful what you say next, Mr. Taylor. We have laws against slander in this country. Your insinuations against a respected member of society would not go without a response."

"It isn't my words but Lord Perrin's," Taylor said. "I'm merely repeating what he told me, on many occasions. He asked my opinion on how best to format his letters to the newspapers."

"And did Perrin explicitly state just what he was accusing Lady Mary of?" Constable Adams asked.

"Well, no." Taylor frowned. "He gave hints and insinuations, but it wasn't difficult to surmise his meaning. Let's just say Lady

Mary is no lady."

I barely heard the shocked gasps in the room over the blood pounding through my ears.

Next to me, Mr. Ryder gripped the armrests of his chair, his fingers going white.

Jane hobbled forward. "That's all that I want to hear from the likes of you." She poked Taylor's thin chest. "You don't know what you're talking about. My mistress—"

"Jane." I held up my hand, pasting on a smile I was nowhere near feeling. "There is no need to defend my honor, mainly because I have done nothing to injure it. My husband and I had no secrets between the two of us, and we loved each other very much." Love hadn't been the problem. But love hadn't been enough to solve our problems.

Mr. Smith dipped his head in my direction. "Those of us who know you would never doubt that, my lady. No one of value will heed any such rumors."

I appreciated the sentiment, especially considering my acquaintance with the gentleman extended less than a week. I didn't know if I would be so fortunate in my support back in London, however. I was already thought eccentric. I ran a club for women that was disgraceful in many eyes.

I made a point not to look in Mr. Ryder's direction. I could only guess his thoughts on the matter.

No, I was under no illusions that if Perrin's accusations became public knowledge, my reputation would take a severe hit. Aside from the effect it might have on my club's membership, I wasn't sure I cared.

I did care if anyone thought worse of my husband, however.

I pushed to standing. "As exciting as this conversation is," I said dryly, "I have correspondence of my own to attend. I assume my presence is no longer needed this afternoon?" I asked the constable.

"Uh..." He rubbed the back of his neck. "No, milady, but please make yourself available for the magistrate when he arrives."

I nodded, my smile tight. Mr. Taylor's little outburst might very well have placed me near the top of the suspect list. And if the investigation centered around me, it would ignore the true culprit.

I left the room, chin high, with as much dignity as I could muster. I heard Jane following behind, but I didn't turn my head.

"My lady." Jane wheezed behind me. "Don't take what that young scoundrel said to heart. He knows nothing."

"I realize that." Even if Taylor believed Perrin's ravings, he would know little of the truth. I pushed into my bedroom. "You should have told me you saw Taylor sneaking about. You know I'm investigating Perrin's murder."

Jane shut the door behind her. "Oh, is that what we're going to talk about? Nice diversion."

"No diversion." I went to the window and peered out. The surface of the pond glinted in the sun, blinding. "That is the only topic worth speaking of."

Jane went to my bed and sat on the edge. "Fine. I hesitated to tell you because I know you are investigating. I'm not sure it's good for you."

"Investigating?"

Jane pointed a crooked finger at me. "The last time you stuck your nose where it didn't belong, your club was almost burned down and you were almost killed."

I arched an eyebrow. "That is a gross exaggeration." Though the repair bills to The Minerva Club might argue to the contrary.

Jane sniffed. "You run a ladies' club. You're the aunt of a duke, a member of high society. I don't think becoming a lady detective is an asset to either of those endeavors."

The edges of my lips curled. I quite liked the sound of 'lady detective.' But my humor was short-lived. "Someone in this house killed Perrin. The authorities might very well think I had a hand in it. You must see that I have to look into the matter myself."

Jane shook her head sadly. "No. If it were any normal person, I wouldn't see that." She sighed. "But since it is you, I will have to accept it."

I went to the small desk in the room and busied my hands straightening the few pieces of paper resting on top. Jane should know my character by now. We had seen each other through both great joy and sorrow. Still, there were some things I had thought remained private.

"How did you know?" I asked softly.

She pushed off the bed and came to stand behind me. She rested one hand on my shoulder. "About the decision you and Cavindish made?"

I nodded.

"It's near impossible to keep a secret from one's lady's maid, and absolutely impossible when that lady's maid is me." She squeezed my shoulder. "I knew how much you and the master wanted children. What you decided…it was hard, but it was the logical thing to do."

I crossed my arm over my chest and grasped her hand. The back of my throat burned, and it was a moment before I could speak. "Hiring you was the best decision I ever made."

"In point of fact, you didn't hire me. Your father did, and then your husband continued my employment."

I huffed out a laugh and pushed her hand away. The other advantage of having Jane as my maid was she always knew when to lighten the moment. "And I could have terminated your employment at any point. I still can."

She snorted and went to lay out a dress for dinner.

I returned to organizing the already organized desk. Jane was right. It had been the logical action to take.

But I didn't know any longer if it had been the right one.

Chapter Twenty-Two

Lady Mary

WELL, WE HAD finally done it. We had given in to Miss Walker's imprecations for an after-dinner entertainment, and now we all paid the price.

I huddled in my chair, hoping the large wings on it would make me invisible to the woman. I had refused to play Blindman's Bluff, much to her irritation, and I feared I wouldn't be able to escape her next suggestion, either.

Miss Walker clapped her hands together. "Charades it is," she exclaimed, even though no one had agreed to that idea. "Who will go first?"

Mr. Smith stared into his brandy, avoiding all eye contact.

Mr. Evans engaged Miss Smith in light conversation in the corner of the room.

Mr. Taylor scowled at the pair of them, his expression so fierce I doubted even Miss Walker would have the nerve to interrupt his thoughts.

"Lady Mary." Miss Walker waved at me to stand. "We'll let you go first."

Like it was some great honor. With a scowl almost as fierce as Mr. Taylor's, I rose. The thought briefly crossed my mind to mimic something outrageous that would keep me from being invited back to this game, but I suppressed the urge. If I was to continue investigating, I needed these people to talk to me.

I shot Mr. Ryder a look. He was sitting in another corner of the room, a book in his hand, but I knew he watched. And maybe some small part of me didn't want to do anything that would truly disgust him. He thought me nefarious enough.

I made the motion for a book.

Though perhaps I could shock all of them, just a little.

The motions my hands were making soon drew the attention of the room. Lady Havenstone gasped at a particular gesture, but her husband muttered, "Come now, she can't mean that."

"*The Banished Man*," Miss Walker guessed, her eyebrows drawn together. "*The Romance of the Forest?*"

I shook my head and repeated my pantomime.

There were a couple of other awkward guesses, no one wanting to put into words what my gestures brought to mind.

Bertram leaned forward in his chair, resting his elbows on his knees. "*An Apology for the Conduct of Mrs. T.C. Phillips.*"

I paused my pantomime and looked to him, eyebrows raised.

"Lady Mary indicated the title only has two words," Lady Havenstone sharply reminded him, and included Miss Walker in her disdainful look.

And neither of those two words were in any way close to the title Bertram had just guessed. I gave a small shrug. Oh, well. Charades wasn't a game for everyone.

"What's to keep her from saying no to all our guesses, even if we're right?" Bertram narrowed his eyes. "There's no way to check if she's lying."

I dropped my hands. "It's a game, Bertram. Why would I lie?"

The butler glided into the room. "Excuse me, milady. With the roads so bad, the post has only just arrived. I have a few letters." He gave one to Mr. Ryder and one to Lord Havenstone. My heart dropped when I saw there was no letter for me.

No matter. I was certain Mr. Cooke would reply when he was able, even if it was only to tell me that the clientele of his businesses were confidential.

"Do continue, Lady Mary." Miss Walker brushed a light brown curl from her cheek.

"Please don't," Mr. Smith objected. "Just tell us what book you were trying to ape."

I clasped my hands primly in front of my abdomen. "*The Wanderer*. Otherwise known as *Female Difficulties*."

"Written by Fanny Burney." Mr. Ryder's eyes glinted suspiciously but his face otherwise remained impassive.

"Well, that explains some of those gestures," Mr. Smith muttered.

Lord Havenstone abruptly stood. He waved the letter he'd been reading in front of his wife's face. "Even from the grave he tests me. We will leave this house as soon as possible." Face red, he stormed out.

Lady Havenstone smiled tightly and rose. "I apologize. He received bad news from my father." And she followed after her husband.

"Can anyone guess who is testing him from the grave?" Mr. Taylor sneered. "I tell you, there is no one here who liked the man, it wasn't just me. But whoever killed him will pay."

"You have more faith in our judicial system than I." Mr. Smith raised his glass in salute. "Here's to your words becoming reality."

I had to agree with Mr. Smith. One could hope for justice, but the reality often fell far short. And considering how many people Perrin had angered, justice could be hard to come by.

Murder was always wrong, but I couldn't help feeling that in some circumstances, it might just be understandable.

Chapter Twenty-Three

Henry

THE SMELL OF gunpowder was an oddly reassuring scent. Henry nudged Southey out of the way with his boot before planting his feet and taking aim. When the hunting dogs flushed out a flock of pheasant, he and the other men took their shots.

Southey whined.

"And that's why you'll never be a hunting dog," Henry told him. "If the noise bothers you so much, go back inside."

"I don't think it understands you." Mr. Smith handed his double-barreled flintlock fowler to a footman to reload. Katherine's father was surprisingly adept at shooting for a man who had been born and raised in the city, as he liked to say. The two noblemen whom he'd married his elder daughters off to must take him hunting whenever he visited.

"You'd be surprised how much he understands." They were waiting for the magistrate to arrive, and going outside to make a lot of noise had seemed a good idea to relieve the tension in the house. Clouds were beginning to gather, and Henry hoped any rain would hold off until the roads had fully dried from the previous storm.

Southey gave an excited yip and trotted over to the group of ladies who had come out to watch. Lady Mary tried to shoo him off with her foot, but the terrier turned it into a game, attacking her boot when he was able to get in close.

Miss Smith wore a lavender gown today, one that stretched nicely across her bosom.

His gaze flicked back to her face, hoping to see some acknowledgement of his presence, but she kept her gaze on her father. He'd thought they'd talked through any awkwardness the night before. True, she had redirected any attempts on his part to address that kiss, but the conversation had flowed.

Lady Mary yanked her skirts from Southey's teeth. "I would like to try my hand with a firearm." She glared down at the dog.

Henry shared a look with the other men, giving a brief shake of his head.

"These guns have quite a kick, Lady Mary." Mr. Smith put his to his shoulder and shot at a lone bird circling in the sky, missing. His shoulder did jerk backward most emphatically. "I'm afraid it would knock you on your—"

"Knock you over," Mr. Ryder injected smoothly. "Have you ladies come to admire our aim?"

"If anyone's aim is worth admiring." Lady Mary picked her way over to the cart the footmen were loading their kill on. "You've been out here for an hour and this is all you've bagged?"

Mr. Smith pinned Withers with a look. "Some of us have skill more admirable than others, to be sure." His gaze softened when he looked at his daughter. "Have you come to call us for lunch?"

"Sadly, no." Lady Mary rested her hip against the cart. "The constable is back and with some bad news, apparently. He'll join us shortly after a snack from the kitchen."

"So he gets to eat but not us," Mr. Smith grumbled.

"I am excited to see what Cook Clem will do with these birds." Lady Mary nudged one speckled brown wing. "If you gentlemen can provide enough for all of us."

"We aim to please," Mr. Ryder said dryly. "Send the dogs out farther," he told the footman. When another group of birds were ousted from a hedgerow, he smoothly raised the fowling piece to his shoulder and pulled the trigger. A bird fell from the sky.

Henry was man enough to admit that Ryder had provided the lion's share of the birds already in the cart. For another city dweller, he was a surprisingly good shot.

Lady Mary looked impressed, as well.

Henry strolled to where Mr. Taylor stood at the end of the hunting line. He had handed his gun to a footman to load, seeming unsure how to do it himself. He'd yet to hit a pheasant. "First time shooting?" Henry asked.

"It wasn't an activity Lord Perrin encouraged for his secretary." Taylor grabbed the gun from the footman and turned, the muzzle of the weapon arcing toward the group of women.

Henry grabbed the barrel and jerked it up. "Only point at what you are willing to kill."

Taylor narrowed his gaze, and Henry rethought his warning. He didn't know just what Taylor might be willing to kill. "Keep your gun aimed down field," he gritted out.

"Fine." Taylor swung in the opposite direction and took a shot, stumbling backwards. Nothing fell from the sky. Henry didn't even know what he could have been aiming at.

He jerked his head at the footman, silently asking him to move away. When he had, Henry said, "I wanted to speak with you."

Taylor stiffened. "Regarding?"

"Where did you go yesterday after the constable went to the ice house to look at Perrin?" There might be others at Perrin Manor who had the maliciousness to shut him and Miss Smith into the ice house, but the secretary was the only one he knew about for certain.

A dark shadow crossed the secretary's face. "Go? None of us can go anywhere."

"So you remained in the sitting room with the others?"

Taylor lifted one bony shoulder. "I don't remember. Some of us went to our rooms. I might have dropped into the library for a book. I wasn't trying to remember my movements."

"Or you could have been writing inquiries on the paper you took from the attic." A knot formed in Henry's stomach. The more he learned of this man, the more it angered him that Taylor had thought for one instant that he could have Miss Smith.

The knot moved up to his chest. Though apparently no one would be good enough to marry Miss Smith.

"Maybe I was." Taylor rested the butt of his gun on the ground and leaned on it. Henry didn't feel the need to warn him that his chest was now over the double barrels.

"Good afternoon, everyone." Constable Adams waved as he hiked up to their position. "I have some unfortunate news to relay."

"What now?" Havenstone muttered.

"The magistrate of Dorset is unable to travel here for several days." The constable took off his hat and turned it in his hands. "As such, I must request that you remain here for a bit longer than you wanted."

"Oh, come now," someone muttered while another said, "This is insufferable."

Mr. Smith stepped forward. "If this magistrate doesn't have the courtesy to make his way here in a timely manner, I don't see why we should feel any need to stay on his account."

"We all intended to stay the week when Perrin was alive. As there has been a murder here, I think we can find it in ourselves to remain an extra day or two," Lady Mary said pointedly.

"A murder is all the more reason the blighter should make haste and come to us." Mr. Smith laid his weapon on the cart and rested his boot on the wheel. "And a murder of a fellow magistrate."

Constable Adams raised a hand. "Due to the severe storms we had, a mine collapsed in the magistrate's jurisdiction. Eighteen men are trapped, and he is leading the rescue efforts. While he is digging through mud looking for bodies, we ask that you remain at a fine house, having shooting parties and feasting. I hardly think it is too much to ask."

Mr. Smith rubbed the back of his neck. "It isn't all sunshine and roses here," he muttered, but no one else raised an objection.

Lady Mary looked like the only person happy to receive that news. Henry would have to write his office, inform his partner of his delay and rearrange some of his appointments. He didn't look forward to the crush of work that would face him upon his return.

But the delay would give him more time to go through Perrin's papers. He still had only read about a third of the earl's documents, not that he expected anything he found to help discover Perrin's killer. He'd uncovered motives for most of the guests here. They already had reasons to want him dead. More reasons couldn't make him deader. But he was trained to be thorough, and one never knew what fact would be key to winning a case.

Miss Smith raised her face to the sun. A line etched her forehead, and his fingers itched to rub her worries away. The extra time would give him the opportunity to learn more about Miss Smith, as well. He didn't understand why she appealed to him. He'd met many a debutante who were just as soon forgotten. Perhaps it was only close proximity that made Miss Smith intriguing to him. Perhaps when he went back to Exeter he wouldn't give her another thought.

And perhaps that was but wishful thinking.

The movement was subtle. Henry almost missed it. Taylor had tucked the butt of his fowling piece up under his arm. When he turned, the muzzle turned with him, aiming straight at the grouping of women.

Henry grabbed the gun just as it fired. His palm and fingers burned as the barrel heated. He jerked his head toward Miss Smith, his pulse racing.

She and the rest of the women were unharmed. The ground a few feet in front of them had taken the brunt of the blast. Miss Smith pressed a hand to her abdomen and released a long exhale, her gaze locking with his.

She was all right. His shoulders lowered an inch. But it had been close. His heart pounded for a new reason. Anger.

He yanked the gun from the secretary's limp hands. "You almost shot someone, you absolute ninny."

A footman hurried over and took the gun, taking it to the cart.

"You bloody arse," Mr. Smith roared. "You almost shot my daughter."

Had that been his intent? Henry gritted his teeth as he glared down at Taylor. The ice house could have been nothing more than a prank, but almost shooting someone....

"I didn't mean to," Taylor stammered. "I was just holding it and it went off."

Guns didn't just go off. Henry took a step closer to Taylor. Whether through malice or ineptitude, Taylor had caused the piece to fire. He grabbed the back collar of Taylor's jacket, lifting the man to his toes. "We are going to have a talk about gun safety."

Taylor squeaked, his eyes going wide. "I said it was an accident. Wait... Stop!" The smaller man tried digging his heels into the earth, but Henry had several pounds of muscle and righteous anger on his side. He dragged the man toward the house, away from witnesses.

Taylor swung his fists wildly, but Henry's next shake was enough to rattle the man's teeth and stop his struggle.

"Aren't you going to stop him?" Miss Walker asked. To whom, Henry didn't care. His focus was all on teaching Taylor a lesson he wouldn't soon forget.

It was the constable who answered, his voice growing faint as Henry ate up the distance to the house. "I don't think so. Some actions, and some men, deserve a good thrashing."

That was a sentiment with which Henry could wholeheartedly agree.

Chapter Twenty-Four

Katherine

A LIGHT DRIZZLE had forced everyone back inside. A newspaper that had finally reached them said the massive storm had traveled to England all the way from the West Indies. Katherine pulled a shawl over her shoulders. The returning damp had brought a chill.

Or perhaps that had been her close call with death. Mr. Taylor had almost shot her and the other women. She couldn't believe it had been intentional. Even he wouldn't be so foolish as to think he could get away with shooting a person in front of witnesses, but there was no comfort in the idea that if she'd died, it would have been by accident.

Miss Walker had drawn the Havenstones and Mr. Withers into a game of riddles. On the best of days Katherine didn't excel at that game, and today was not the best of days.

She had almost been killed, and relief and exhilaration now flooded her veins from the knowledge that even though she had been close to death, she yet lived. Watching Mr. Evans drag Mr. Taylor away by the scruff of his neck had only added to her disquiet. She wasn't proud of it, but seeing Mr. Evans manhandle the person who had been harassing her had been just the teensiest bit thrilling.

Mr. Evans was a man who could quote Wordsworth, yet looked as though he would dominate anyone else in a physical fight. A man who challenged her to the point of irritation, yet gave her his jacket when she was cold.

She sighed. Her attraction to him was now so apparent she could no longer deny it. She had developed feelings for Mr. Evans, and he was a man of trade. Her father would never allow any relationship to develop. Katherine would always have Mr. Evans to compare against whomever her father chose to be her husband. And she had the feeling that whoever that poor man was, he would never measure up.

She held the novel she'd borrowed from Perrin's library up to her face, peering over the top of it to the settee across the rear sitting room. Her father and Mr. Evans were engaged in conversation, appearing the best of friends. She knew her father approved of the manner Mr. Evans had dealt with Mr. Taylor, but that approval would never extend to allowing the attorney as a suitor. Her father had nothing to gain from such a match.

She turned an unread page. Mr. Taylor hadn't joined them for luncheon, or in the sitting room, but she had caught a glimpse of a very puffy lip as she'd entered the house. Taylor had disappeared up a stairwell and hadn't been seen since.

"Mr. Withers, that riddle makes no sense," Lord Havenstone objected.

Mr. Withers reddened. "And I say it does."

Miss Walker and Lady Havenstone attempted to bring peace, but the anger of the men didn't subside until their drinks had been refreshed with very generous pours and the promise of no more riddles that day.

A loud guffaw brought her gaze back to her father, and the hand he clapped on Mr. Evans's shoulder. Her heart twisted. She hadn't been acquainted with Mr. Evans long enough to know if he would be a man she'd want to spend her life with, but the fact that she wouldn't get to choose, that she would never be allowed to know, made her ache.

There were so many women who would love to be in her position. She never worried when her next meal was coming, never had to worry about being alone or unprotected. She had every luxury a woman could want. So many would trade their ability to choose their own husband for the chance to be as safe and pampered as she. She was an ungrateful wretch to complain. To want more.

Katherine swallowed, the back of her throat aching. And yet, she did. She couldn't help herself. And because she felt guilty, about wanting more, about being the slightest bit relieved that Perrin was dead so she didn't have to marry him, when Lord Havenstone whispered something to his wife, looked furtively about, and left the room, Katherine rose to follow.

If Lady Mary had been there, she would have had a partner in mischief, she had no doubt. But Lady Mary was taking tea in her room. Mr. Evans was chuckling at something her father said. So it was up to her to see if Havenstone was up to no good.

She'd expected him to perhaps go to Perrin's study or to the earl's private chambers. Had Lady Mary searched those yet? Katherine chewed on her bottom lip as she crept after the baron. But instead of either of those destinations, Havenstone instead turned for the stairs leading down to the kitchens.

She had to wait until the baron had gone down the entire flight and turned out of sight before she felt safe enough to follow. She inhaled a sharp breath when one of the steps creaked, but there was enough noise coming from below that detection seemed improbable. When she reached the bottom, she inched her head around the corner but saw nothing but an empty hallway.

Katherine didn't know why her heart jumped about like a rabbit fleeing a fox. While it would be unusual for a guest to visit the servants' areas, it wasn't forbidden. She could easily say she wanted an apple but hadn't felt the need to bother a servant to fetch it. But the knowledge of an easy excuse didn't calm her nerves.

She peeked into the kitchen but all she saw was the secondary cook and two maids cleaning the dishes from lunch. She hurried past the doorway. The next room was a large store room. A side of lamb hung from a hook on an exposed beam, and sacks of flour and sugar lined a shelf. A door that led outside blew inward an inch, a few drops of rain splattering on the stone floor.

Had Havenstone left by that door, or gone up the other staircase at the far end of the hall? And why come down here at all?

She entered the store room. It connected to the kitchen through a door-shaped hole in the wall. Making sure the servants in the kitchen weren't looking her way, Katherine crossed to the outer door and pulled it open.

The path was gravel, so there were no fresh footprints to indicate if the baron had left by this exit or not. She frowned as the front of her dress dampened from the rain. If Havenstone had left this way, he would reenter the house wet, but she could hardly prowl about every entrance waiting for his return to test the dryness of his clothes.

She closed the door. The change in air pressure caused the other remaining door on the side of the room to snap closed.

In for a penny, in for a pound, as her grandmother used to say. She hurried across the floor and pulled the door open. The watery light streaming in from the store room's windows gave a dim illumination to the pantry. More food stuffs were stocked along two walls. The third wall held more interesting items.

Katherine ran her fingers along several small envelopes. Dover's Powder was written on one of them. Calomel on another. She grimaced. She remembered having to take that purgative. There were several glass bottles also, with labels from laudanum to tincture of rhubarb. Lord Perrin's collection of home remedies was extensive.

Had Lord Havenstone come downstairs for this? She'd learned just how many medicines could be deadly if given in too large a dose. And if Havenstone had come here, did that mean someone else was in danger?

She placed a tin of sulfur powder back on the shelf and exited, closing the door tightly behind her. She met one maid on her way back upstairs, but simply nodded and smiled and kept on her way. She went back to the sitting room, hoping to find that Lady Mary had joined them. Katherine didn't know what to think of Havenstone sneaking about. It might mean nothing other than he suffered from indigestion and didn't have a remedy in his personal travel case of medicines.

But it might mean something. She felt sure Lady Mary would know which category to put his actions under. But the older woman still hadn't left her room. Mr. Withers had joined her father and Mr. Evans in conversation, each man boasting of one time or another when a disagreement of theirs had turned to fisticuffs and he had emerged the victor.

Katherine rubbed her arm. She didn't want to admire Mr. Evans for simply thrashing a man who had almost hurt her, but she couldn't deny it did funny things to her belly. Besides, Mr. Taylor had deserved it.

Before Miss Walker could make eye contact and invite her to join in another game, Katherine crossed to the casement doors that led to the terrace and gazed out.

This rain didn't seem to be coming down hard enough to close the roads, and she hoped for all their sakes that the magistrate wouldn't be further delayed. The constable had gone home after relaying his message, and the house felt vulnerable without someone of authority watching over it.

Southey trotted over to her. He wagged his tail, his whole rear end swaying with the movement, as she bent to pat him. He nudged at the door with his nose and whined.

She opened the door to let him out. Instead of running to the garden to do his business as was his wont, the terrier raced to the corner of the terrace, pawing at something that lay behind a large potted plant.

Katherine's eyebrows drew together.

"Close the door," a woman called.

Katherine drew her shawl more tightly about her shoulders but ignored the order. She took a step outside, staying under the small covered section. She tilted her head. It didn't make sense. Why would a boot be laying there like that?

She took another step, her mind refusing to acknowledge what her eyes saw. Because that boot was attached to a leg, and the farther she walked, the more of the body she saw.

She came abreast of the potted lily of the valley, blinking rapidly.

Southey yipped and pranced about, looking for all the world like he'd just won a game of hide-and-go-seek and wanted a reward. She bent and picked him up, absent-mindedly scratching behind his ear, her eyes never leaving the body.

She'd told Lady Mary and Mr. Evans that he hadn't killed Perrin, and now she had proof that she was right. Because Mr. Taylor lay at her feet with a large knife sticking from his chest, his eyes open and vacant.

Mr. Taylor might have deserved many things, but he hadn't deserved this.

Chapter Twenty-Five

Lady Mary

THIS TIME, THERE was blood. A lot of it. There was no question in my mind that Mr. Taylor had died from the knife in his chest.

I angled my head and inched forward. It looked to be one of the dinner knives. Not that we'd needed such a sharp blade since Cook Clem had begun preparing our meals for us. The roast lamb we'd eaten last night had practically fallen from the bone.

A footman stood near the body, holding an oil lamp in one hand. Dusk was coming on, but from the way he wrapped his palm around the glass cover, I figured he wanted the lamp more for warmth than light. He cleared his throat as I neared.

I pressed my lips flat. I wasn't planning on touching the body, although now that I thought of it, I wouldn't mind checking the man's pockets. But I could hardly complain about the footman's vigilance. After all, I had been the one to tell him to stand guard.

"Lady Mary." Mr. Ryder stepped out onto the terrace, a slight frown creasing his face. The last of the sun's light turned the white hair at his temples a soft honey. "The constable has arrived."

Constable Adams followed him out, wearing an even larger frown. "Has returned, is more like. I was just sitting down to a spot of tea when I got the message. Now I don't know if I'll even get back home for supper."

"There's plenty to eat here." I stepped back as the constable knelt beside Mr. Taylor's form. "You will be fed."

Ryder extended his hand back toward the sitting room. "Perhaps we should leave the constable to his work." The man couldn't keep the judgment from his voice. Ever the moralizer.

I ignored him and leaned on my walking stick to watch Constable Adams. I'd decided to keep a cane with me even indoors. With a killer among us, one never knew when it might come in handy. "That's one of the dinner knives," I informed the constable. "Miss Smith found his body about half past three. No one saw Mr. Taylor alive since he went up to his rooms around noon."

Constable Adams raised an eyebrow.

"I might have asked around a bit while waiting for you," I said. "There was precious little else to talk about."

Ryder snorted behind me.

"So a roughly three and a half hour window for him to be killed in." Adams rubbed his jaw. "You don't suspect poison was involved in this one, do you?"

"I do not." I pointed at a bunching of fabric in Taylor's jacket. "Can you check his pockets, see if he carries anything?"

Constable Adams did just that, slipping his fingers into the jacket's pockets before unbuttoning it to expose the waistcoat. He pulled a broken bit of a lead pencil and two quid from those pockets.

"Was it all that you hoped for?" Ryder asked.

I glared back at him before pointing again at the body. "What of his hands? Do you see any scrapes or bruises to indicate he fought his attacker?"

Adams lifted one hand, then the other, each pale and pristine. "The only marks on him are the bruises on his face, which I presume Mr. Evans inflicted." The constable's shoulders rounded. "His killer might also have left some, but I don't see how we'll ever pick out which bruises came from where. I should have stopped Mr. Evans when he hauled this man off. Now it's only muddied the waters."

"You couldn't have known." I patted the young man's shoulder. "I'll have a maid ready a room for you in case you want to stay the night." By the time he questioned everyone in the house again, it could well be early morning.

Mr. Ryder followed me back into the sitting room. "Why do you take it upon yourself to investigate?" he asked in a low voice. "Constable Adams seems… competent."

I chafed my hands together. A large fire had been built, and the heat of it warmed the room, removing some of the chill that clung to my gown. "He is young and inexperienced. And we are staying in the house with someone who has killed two people." At least, I hoped it was one person who had killed two people and not two separate murderers. "I believe it behooves us all to discover who has done this as quickly as possible."

Mr. Ryder sighed. "There are others—"

"Men, you mean."

He dipped his chin and studied me. The feeling wasn't quite pleasant. Taking a step closer so no one would overhear, he said, "It isn't wrong, the impulse society has to protect the fairer sex from unpleasantness. From harm."

"No." It wasn't wrong. I enjoyed a chivalrous act as much as any woman. "But sometimes men's idea of protection is to keep women coddled, unaware of the hazards life presents, which only puts us more in danger. And some women aren't as delicate as you seem to think."

He looked like he had more to say on the subject. As I didn't want to hear it, I inclined my head and went over to where Mr. Evans and Miss Smith stood huddled together. The attorney had planted himself firmly between Miss Smith and everyone else in the room, essentially becoming a barrier between her and the other guests. One of whom had killed again.

Miss Smith, at least, appeared to appreciate the attorney's protective impulse.

I exhaled through my nose. I already knew I was a bit different from most women. I'd accepted it. "We should talk," I said to them.

Mr. Evans looked at the rest of the room. No one appeared to be watching them, but he still lowered his voice. "Now?"

"No, after the next person is murdered." Perhaps he didn't deserve the edge in my voice, but I was too frustrated to hide it.

Miss Smith laid her hand at the base of her throat. "You think there will be another?"

Mr. Evans frowned at me, and I relented. "Most likely not, but I still think we need to discuss what we know. Let's go to the library."

We filed out. The empty grate almost made me regret my decision to leave the sitting room. I tugged my shawl higher on my shoulders. "Now. Each of you tell me what you did and saw from noon today until you found the body, Miss Smith."

Mr. Evans went to the fireplace. He added some coal from the bucket and picked the flint up from the mantel. "I went to Perrin's office to read through more of his files. Then I went to lunch. After, I joined the group in the sitting room."

Miss Smith wandered to the window. In the gathering dark, there wasn't much to see outside, yet she still stared. "Much the same. I went to my room before luncheon, then the sitting room after. I saw Mr. Taylor briefly when I first came back from the shooting field. I thought he was headed to his room, as well."

Mr. Evans kindled the fire, and I took a chair near the warmth. I pressed the tip of my walking stick into the thick rug. "It's Katherine, yes? May I call you Katherine?"

At the woman's nod, I continued. "What took you outside to find Mr. Taylor's body?"

"The dog." Katherine rubbed her arms. "He needed to go out, and he found Mr. Taylor."

The dog. I checked my ankles, surprised he wasn't nipping at them now. Someone must have trapped him down in the kitchens.

"And neither of you noticed anything strange?" I asked. "Did Mr. Taylor say anything to you after you and he…talked, Henry?"

He arched an eyebrow at my use of his given name but didn't correct me. "Nothing except he was going to make me pay. And that shooting his gun in Miss Smith's direction was an accident." He rested his forearm on the mantel, examining his fingers. "I don't know that I believed him."

"He obviously didn't kill Perrin." Katherine paced across the room. At their continued silence, she paused. "Right?"

I hesitated. "I believe you are correct. I think there is only one killer but that Mr. Taylor could well have been up to mischief of his own. But why kill him? As Perrin's secretary, could he have known something, the same something that got Perrin killed?"

Henry grimaced. "As his attorney and someone reading through all the earl's paperwork, I suppose I must be on guard now, too."

Katherine twisted her hands together. "I followed Lord Havenstone," she blurted out. "When he left the sitting room this afternoon, I followed him."

Henry narrowed his eyes. "Why?"

I nodded approvingly. "What did you learn?"

She went to the fire and held her palms out to the flame. "I thought he might go to Perrin's rooms to search for something, but he went downstairs instead of up."

My chest tightened. Why hadn't I thought of searching Perrin's rooms? It should have been one of the first acts I'd taken.

"I saw him turn the corner into the hallway to the kitchen, but when I got down the stairs, he'd disappeared." Katherine lifted her shoulders. "The assistant cook and a few maids were in the kitchen, but the storage rooms were empty. He might have gone out the door from the store room, or he could have gone up the stairs at the other end of the hall. I'd thought he might have gone down to get something from the medicine pantry, that he might have been looking for another poison. But perhaps he went to get a knife?"

I tapped my chin. "What time was this?"

"Perhaps twenty minutes before I found Mr. Taylor's body."

That didn't leave much time for Havenstone to find Mr. Taylor and kill him. I thought it more likely someone had taken a knife from the dinner table on a previous night. Which would mean Mr. Taylor's murder had been premeditated. "Why was Taylor out on the terrace? It wasn't for a garden stroll."

"That section of terrace seemed to be a favorite of Taylor's when he wanted a private conversation." Henry looked down at Katherine, his nostrils flaring.

She held up her hands. "He wasn't meeting me."

"I didn't say that he was."

I sagged back into the chair. "It all depends on timing. When was Taylor killed? If it was after lunch, was there anyone missing from the sitting room who could have done it?" My mouth twisted. "Besides me." I hoped the constable didn't think a woman of my...mature age could have the strength to stab a virile young man. I might have, if I took the secretary by surprise, but I still hoped no one else would believe it. Being a suspect in a murder investigation was most bothersome.

Henry ran his hand up the back of his head. "I think everyone was in the sitting room after lunch until Lord Havenstone and Miss Smith left, but someone else could have slipped out, I suppose. I can only say with certainty that Mr. Smith never left the room."

"Of course my father didn't do this." Katherine crossed her arms.

"I think Taylor was killed before lunch." I shot Katherine an apologetic look. "Sorry, my dear, but that keeps your father as a suspect. There are many people unaccounted for from when we all left the shooting field until we all showed for our midday meal. It makes more sense he was killed then."

"And his body was outside, mere feet away, the whole time we conversed and laughed in the sitting room?" Katherine paled. "That is a horrible thought."

Horrible or not, I suspected it was the truth. But it wasn't the idea that a body had lain so nearby as the guests had relaxed by a warm fire that bothered me most.

It was the idea that the killer had relaxed by that fire with a smile on his or her face, knowing Taylor's body grew cold just outside.

$$\rule{3cm}{0.4pt}\ \text{❧}\ \rule{3cm}{0.4pt}$$

Chapter Twenty-Six

Lady Mary

I WAITED UNTIL the constable left the next morning before sneaking into Perrin's chambers. Although I knew Adams was eager to receive assistance on this case, I didn't think that included mine.

"Will you hurry up?" Jane whisper-shouted at me. She stood near the cracked door, one faded blue eye peering out into the hallway. She shook her head, her iron-grey curls jiggling beneath her cap. "The things we do," she muttered.

"We've only just entered." I refrained from pointing out that I hadn't asked her to accompany me on this venture. She had decided all on her own that 'someone needed to watch out for me.'

I went directly to the small desk near the window. I pulled the curtain to the side to give me more light. I probably should have ordered the servants to hang black crepe in the windows, but Perrin had quite a lot of windows and there were no neighbors close enough to see the effort.

Some books lay scattered on the surface of the desk but no letters or even writing implements of any kind. Perrin must have written all his correspondence in his study. A pocket watch with a broken chain was coiled on the small table next to his bed.

I ran my hand over the coverlet. The bed hadn't been slept in for a week, but it still seemed to hold the memory of its master. Had Perrin any premonitions when he'd left it last Saturday that he'd never again dent its feather mattress? Would I know when it was to be my last day? Succumbing to a long illness didn't appeal as a manner of death, but there was something comforting about the idea of being aware the end was near. I didn't know if I hoped death would take me by surprise, or if I would have time to plan for it, to accept it.

It mattered little what I would hope for. Life, and death, didn't often give us a choice.

There was nothing but a mildly bawdy novel in the drawer of his bedside table. There was nothing anywhere in the room besides the odds and ends of ordinary life.

I leaned on my walking stick and surveyed the room, my chest hollow. This had been my brother-in-law's inner sanctum, a representation of his internal life. Shouldn't there be something more? Something that showed his desires and dreams, his personality?

"Someone's coming." Jane shut the door, with much too much force for stealth.

I prepared to beguile my way out of the situation.

The door swung inward, knocking into Jane's shoulder. Marie poked her head inside. "What are you two doing in 'ere?"

"I was looking for clothes to bury Perrin in." I was rather proud of that lie and the speed with which I'd devised it.

The effect of it was rather ruined by Jane's snort.

"Riiight." Marie slipped inside and shut the door behind her. Quietly.

I glared at Jane. "If you must know, I'm looking for anything that might indicate who killed Perrin. A threatening note would have been nice."

"I don't think Lord Perrin got anything like that." Marie rubbed her nose. "We would've 'eard about it."

Yes, the servants most likely would have. "Marie, do you

know if any of the knives were missing before yesterday?" Before one had been plunged into Taylor's chest.

"The constable asked us all that, too." She grinned. "That man is an eyeful, 'e is."

"The knives?" I tried to bring her back to the matter at hand.

Jane hobbled to the desk and sank onto the chair. "She's right, though. He is handsome."

"And that is irrelevant." Goodness, Jane had her chance for decades to ogle good-looking young men. She didn't need to start in the middle of my investigation.

Marie shifted. "We didn't keep count. Usually we do, after every meal, but with the master being dead and everyone being trapped 'ere, well, we've let a bit slide."

"Plus, we started using the cutlery as markers in our games," Jane added. "Who knows what might have gone missing then."

"You gambled with Perrin's silverware?" I arched an eyebrow.

"No need to take that tone." Jane patted her lace cap. "The silverware just represented what we owed. A knife was a shilling, a fork, sixpence. We were running a bit short on coin."

"So the murderer could have obtained the weapon at any time." Not helpful. "Marie, have you already cleaned Lord and Lady Havenstone's room today?"

"Yes."

I huffed out a breath. "Well, can you clean it again? He became quite upset when reading a letter he'd received the other day. Made a disparaging comment I presume was directed at Perrin. I want to know what was in that letter."

"You want me to snoop." The girl planted her hands on her hips.

"It isn't as though you don't have practice at it." And I was becoming more concerned by the hour that the killer might not stop with two deaths.

"Yes, but I felt bad about it, each time," Marie said. "Specially now that the guests found out we were doing it."

"It's important," I said quietly.

Marie dropped her arms. "All right, but if I get caught, I'm telling them you sent me."

"Then don't get caught." I jabbed my walking stick into the floor for emphasis.

"Come on then." Jane held out a hand, and I pulled her to standing. "I'll keep watch for you, girl."

I tried to think of an objection that wouldn't hurt Jane's feelings but came up empty.

When they reached the door, Marie turned back. "Oh, speaking of post, a letter 'as arrived for you. I put it in your room."

I hurried after them, turning left toward my room when they turned right. There weren't many people who knew I was here. It could be a letter from the club, letting me know of a problem that had arisen. Or it could be a response from the one person I'd written to while I'd been at Perrin Manor.

I only hoped he had some answers.

I'd never seen his hand before, but the address to me was just as it was in person. Bold. Hard. With a bit of a flair on the beginning and ending letters. I sat at the desk in my room and opened the missive.

Lady M—

I cannot begin to express the curiosity your letter has inspired in me. Firstly, that you wrote to me at all, and secondly, as to its contents. I was a bit disappointed that your inquiries were all pertaining to the patrons of my businesses, with not even a query regarding my health. Alas, you are forgiven. I am gratified to know, however, that I am the only man of business of ill repute with whom you are acquainted.

As to the particulars of your letter, and the three men you asked about, I can only say the following.

I do not know Mr. Smith. There are no known associations between us.

Mr. Bertram Withers is known to me. To my knowledge, he hasn't patronized any of my hells, but he is known as some-

one who likes to gamble. His games only occur in private residences, however, and he seems to only gamble within his means.

As to the third man you requested information of, Lord Havenstone, I have debated long about whether to provide you with the intelligence you requested. He is a patron of mine, and I don't readily give up information on my clientele. Not only that, but by the tone of your letter I deduced you have involved yourself in another dangerous scheme, and that isn't something I want to encourage.

However, with or without my information, I know you will persist in whatever course you have undertaken. You are stubborn in that way. And I hope that by being fully informed, you will better be able to protect yourself. To that end, I am well acquainted with Havenstone. He has come to one of my hells on a few occasions, usually when he is deep into his cups. Whether that is the cause, or because he lacks all natural skill at the games, Havenstone always leaves my establishment the poorer.

I have heard that he only tries to win at the tables when he is in dire need of funds. The first I knew of him was when he lost a sum of money to me two years past. I learned that he had already suffered a financial loss, had hoped to recoup it at my hell, but eventually settled for a loan from me. As his father-in-law is one of the wealthier members of society, I believed he was good for it, and that indeed was the case as he repaid that loan in full within a year.

Havenstone returned to my hell a month or so again, inebriated once more, losing once more. The loan I provided to him on this occasion wasn't for quite so great a sum. I don't make it a habit to inquire for what my patrons need funds, and I didn't alter my habit on these occasions. I can only say that Havenstone needed money, and I provided it. I do hope whatever you are involved in won't impede his ability to repay me on this second loan. For his sake, as well as my own.

And as to your brother-in-law, Lord Perrin, to whose home I am now sending this letter, even though you didn't ask me about him, I will tell you that he is not allowed within any of my hells. I suspect he cheats at cards, and that is something I will not tolerate.

For purely altruistic reasons, I must caution you against pursuing whatever scheme in which you have now involved yourself. Desperate men are dangerous men, and I have seen Lord Havenstone at his most desperate. I would not want you to see that side of him.

Take care. I look forward to the time when I can ask you to return the favor which you now owe me.

Yours truly,
E.C.

I sagged back in my chair. I decided it did no good to worry over what London's foremost crime lord would want from me for repayment of a debt. I could do nothing about that situation now. So I turned my thoughts back to the investigation.

Two years ago. Was that when the money Havenstone had invested with Perrin had been lost? And what had happened a month ago? Was Perrin involved in yet another financial loss for the baron? And if so, why would Havenstone come to Perrin Manor for a party?

I laid the letter on the desk, frowning. Mr. Cooke had provided me with more information than I had hoped for, but all it did was leave me with more questions.

And it was time I got some answers.

Chapter Twenty-Seven

Henry

SUNLIGHT STREAMED THROUGH the empty window into Perrin's study. Henry had removed the boards on one of the windows and dragged Perrin's desk beneath it so he could finish reading through Perrin's documents in the light. Today, all the clouds had dispersed and it was once again a beautiful spring day. The recent rains had made the green in the grass and trees just a bit brighter, made the birds sing all the louder now that they were free.

And Henry could enjoy none of it. He planted his elbows on the desk and rested his chin on his enlaced fingers. Another man was dead. The only things of import he'd discovered in Perrin's office were letters he hoped would never see the light of day. He was starting to develop feelings for a woman not of his station. And even if her father would deign to allow him to court her, said father might be guilty of murder, a circumstance that would devastate Miss Smith.

Katherine. It had been almost a shock when he'd heard Lady Mary call her such. He'd known Miss Smith's Christian name before, of course. He'd written it onto the marriage contract. But he hadn't known *her* before. Hadn't felt the warmth of her smile or tasted the sweetness of her lips. Lady Mary had taken the liberty to address her on a first name basis, and Henry wanted the same liberty. Truly, he'd taken so many others, what was one more?

If Katherine's father had killed Perrin and Taylor, what would become of her? He slouched back into the chair. He couldn't see it. Not the man he'd spent a pleasant afternoon with, exclaiming over his youthful exploits, laughing at his ribald jokes. In the anger of a moment, Mr. Smith might bloody a man's nose, but he wouldn't plot, and scheme, and lie in wait. At least, Henry hoped not.

A shout had him turning his head to look out the window. Two men were working on repairs to the axle of a carriage, one yelling directions, the other following them, face red. The roads would be well rutted from the drying mud, and strengthening the guests' conveyances was a sensible task. But the one servant looked ready to punch the other in the face.

Henry clenched his hands. Anger made men do foolish things. He'd only landed one punch to Taylor's face, but he'd made many more to the man's body. And worse, he'd enjoyed it. He'd thought he could shake some sense, or at least some penitence, from the secretary for almost shooting Katherine.

Taylor had no penitence in him. Or sense. Perhaps it was because Henry was generally a peaceful man that Taylor had thought he could escape punishment for his remarks. That he could insult Katherine so vilely and suffer no consequences.

He'd been wrong. But Henry had been wrong, as well. Violence to Mr. Taylor's person hadn't been the answer. Had he weakened Taylor to the point where hours later he'd been unable to defend himself? Was Henry partly to blame for the secretary's death?

Limbs dragging, Henry gathered up the many drafts of a letter Perrin had written, folded them, and slid them into his pocket. He wouldn't want anyone else to come across them. The rest of the documents Henry returned to their cabinets, replaced the boards on the window, and departed from the gloom of the office.

He made for the rear sitting room, surprised when he found only Mr. Withers and Mr. Ryder occupying it. "Where is everyone?"

Mr. Ryder rested a book on his knee. "The sun's reappearance has tempted most everyone out-of-doors. I believe the Havenstones have gone riding, and the rest have taken to the trails around the estate to exercise their legs. I have myself just come back from a walk about the gardens."

"And Lady Mary?" Henry fingered the papers in his pocket. "Is she also taking a walk?"

Mr. Ryder's eyebrows drew together. "I didn't see her, but as she isn't here, I assume so. Perhaps she is in her room."

"Mary isn't one to stay in her rooms." Mr. Withers turned from his station at the window, a small smile on his face. "That woman loathes inaction."

Mr. Ryder rubbed his thumb over his book's spine. "You know her well?"

Withers's smile faded. "She and my wife and my sister used to have a grand time when we'd come together for the holidays. She is the only one still living of the three." He faced out the window once more.

"I understand your sister died after a fall." Henry gentled his voice. Something about Withers seemed breakable if one spoke too firmly. Henry suspected it had been a long time since the man had had anyone to talk to. "How did your wife die?"

Withers clasped his hands behind his back. "My wife died of scrofula, a disorder of the lymphatic system. I'm not certain the account of my sister's death is accurate, however. She had been feeling poorly before she fell. Which makes little sense. She was a talented herbalist. I trusted my health to her more than any apothecary."

Henry glanced at Mr. Ryder, but the other man looked as confused as Henry felt. "You believe your sister's stated cause of death was in error?"

Withers frowned. "It hardly matters. This storm hasn't been

good for her garden. Her *pulsatilla vulgaris* look half drowned. I gave that plant to her. It was her favorite."

Henry's one and only brother had died young, before Henry had much memory of him. Every once in a while he would still ache from the loss of something he could never know. How much worse the pain must be to lose a beloved sibling, one with whom you shared a childhood, who knew you better than most anyone else?

Mr. Ryder beat him to the condolences. "I'm sorry, Withers." He stood and crossed to the window. Ryder took a small silver case from his pocket and removed a card. He handed it to Withers. "This is my club in London. If you ever want to talk, you can find me there. And it is a fine club to join, if you're looking. Good conversation."

Withers took the card, staring blankly at it. He rolled it between his fingers like it was one of his playing cards, a small tremble in his hands, then excused himself from the room.

An uncomfortable silence settled between Ryder and himself. Ryder returned to his seat, and it was Henry who went to the window to stare out. Someone else's grief was almost as hard to carry as one's own. It was sad for Perrin that no one deeply mourned his passing, but it made it easier for the rest of them.

A glimpse of snowy white hair caught his attention. "If you'll excuse me." Henry nodded to Ryder, then left the sitting room for the back garden. He trotted around the edge of it and toward a path that wandered into a wooded copse. He met Lady Mary halfway between the house and the trees.

"Lady Mary." He inclined his head. "A fine day."

She squinted up at him, the rim of her bonnet far too shallow to block the sun's rays. "I suppose."

He shifted his weight from his left foot to his right. "And your walk? Has it been enjoyable?"

Lady Mary leaned on her walking stick. "Oh, quite. Now why don't you tell me why you sought me out instead of boring me with these inane pleasantries?"

Henry sighed. He had been delaying. As a solicitor, he was accustomed to speaking of indelicate matters, but this conversation seemed harder than most. He drew his shoulders back. "Yes. Well, I found some letters in Perrin's study."

The lady's blue eyes glowed. "Something to point to our killer?"

"Er, not exactly." Not unless Lady Mary was the killer, but after coming to know the woman, that was an idea he could no longer credit. Especially after the death of Mr. Taylor. He pulled the bundle from his inside coat pocket. He'd wrapped the mass with a bit of string he'd found in Perrin's desk drawer. "These were letters Perrin had intended to send to several different papers. For their gossip pages."

Her hand paused reaching for the letters, trembled just the slightest bit, before taking ahold of them. "The letters are regarding me. My marriage to Perrin's brother."

It hadn't been a question, but Henry nodded nonetheless. "I don't believe anyone other than Perrin has seen them, and he can no longer tell tales. And, of course, you can rely on my complete discretion."

The letters were a nasty business. Henry didn't know whether what Perrin had written had been the truth, and he didn't want to know. It wasn't his, or anyone else's, concern. But the fact that Lord Perrin had felt the need to harm Lady Mary's reputation, that he would delight in sullying her name, left a bad taste in Henry's mouth.

"I thank you." She stared down at the letters, her gaze vacant. "The sun is becoming a bit too warm for me. I think I'll go inside."

"Of course." He watched her go, his chest heavy. He should return to the house, as well. Continue examining Perrin's documents. But he couldn't make his feet move toward the manor. He closed his eyes and lifted his face to the sun instead, feeling like the rays washing over his skin helped to cleanse him from the filth Perrin had produced.

A bird sang. Footsteps crunched over gravel. Henry opened his eyes and saw Miss Walker winding her way around the central feature in the garden, a basket half full of cut flowers on her arm. Her bonnet had a much larger brim than Lady Mary's, a gardener's hat that would easily keep the sun off her face. It unfortunately also had the effect of pressing the curls that framed her face more tightly to her cheeks and forehead with a most unbecoming effect.

Movement over the chest-high hedge that encompassed the garden's interior drew Henry's eye. A pale green ruffle ducked behind the hedge, a head of honey-brown hair reflecting the sun.

Henry drew his eyebrows together. What was Katherine up to now?

Chapter Twenty-Eight

Katherine

S HE SHOULD HAVE brought something with her to write notes, but when Katherine had left her room this afternoon, she hadn't known she'd be following Miss Walker. The woman made Katherine suspicious. How long could a love go unrequited before it turned bitter and twisted?

The woman bent out of sight, rising up a few moments later with a new bloom in her hand. Miss Walker had been puttering about Perrin's gardens for the better part of two hours, giving her ample time to hide, or harvest, any poisonous flower she wanted.

The large problem that faced Katherine was that she didn't know anything about horticulture. Miss Walker could feed her a salad full of death and Katherine would never know. She wanted to compare the flowers Miss Walker picked with sketches from that book on herbalism she'd found in Perrin's library, but she was having trouble remembering what they all looked like.

"Purple flower with a stalk full of blossoms. Yellow tulip-looking flower. Small white buds." She muttered the descriptions on a loop, trying to imprint them to memory. "Purple flower with a stalk full of blossoms. Yellow—"

"What are you doing?" He whispered the question near her ear, causing Katherine to jump.

She covered her mouth with her gloved hand, smothering her squawk. Frowning, she glared at Mr. Evans. "You shouldn't sneak up on a person," she said, after raising her hand to shield her eyes from the sun. "It isn't polite."

He shifted, his shadow blocking the sun's rays. "And here I thought we'd moved past the forced politeness stage of our relationship. How disappointing."

Katherine's stomach fluttered. She always forgot just how tall and broad he was until he stood next to her. His wide shoulders tested the strength of the fabric of his jacket. His buckskins molded across muscular thighs.

Flustered, she gave him her back. "And here I thought we didn't have a relationship."

His chuckle sent a shiver skittering down her spine.

She frowned, not quite sure she liked the feeling and searched for her quarry. "Drat. She's gone."

Reaching around her, Mr. Evans plucked a leaf from the hedge that stuck up out of place. "Why are you following Miss Walker?"

"I've told you I think she is the most likely suspect in Perrin's murder." She turned back to face him. "You and Lady Mary seem biased against her guilt, I'm guessing because of her sex. Women can be just as vicious as any man."

"I have no doubt." His whiskey brown eyes twinkled. "I'm certain you've left many a man devastated in your wake, with little regard for his heart."

She knew it was a jest, that Mr. Evans found pleasure in teasing her, but her chest tightened. "I don't have the luxury of breaking hearts. It is known that my father will choose my husband, with little regard for my wishes. And most men who choose to flirt with me do so with an eye to their financial gain. Their hearts aren't involved."

Mr. Evans sobered. "I apologize. I shouldn't have teased you so soon after both Lord Perrin's and Mr. Taylor's deaths. I'm certain, however, that if you had married Perrin, even if it were from mercenary reasons on his part, he would have quickly grown fond of you. Anyone would."

Her cheeks heated. "Mr. Evans—"

"Henry."

She rocked back on her heels.

"My Christian name is Henry. I wish for you to call me that, at least when we are alone. And may I call you Katherine?"

She hesitated, her heart pounding unnaturally loudly for such a small request. "Henry." The name suited him. Strong and practical, just like he was. She said it again. "Henry. I noticed you and my father were quite friendly the other day."

"He seemed most appreciative of my actions toward Mr. Taylor after he nearly shot you." A shadow crossed his face. "Contrary to what you may think, your father loves you very much."

Yes, but he loved other things, too. "I feel I must give you a word of caution." She hesitated, thinking how best to phrase this. "My father is most agreeable when it comes to his friendships and with those with whom he is acquainted, but do not expect that amiability to translate to anything further."

"Are you trying to warn me not to expect your father to give me your hand in marriage?" His eyebrows shot up.

The back of her neck tingling, Katherine turned and started walking away.

He followed.

"I don't mean to imply that is something you would wish for." She grabbed a purple flower and yanked it from its bush. Another man would try to ingratiate himself with her father, hoping to profit from the relationship, but she didn't believe it of Mr. Evans. Henry. He didn't strike her as a social climber.

He did strike her as someone who wanted to pursue a deeper relationship with her, however. And that would need her father's approval. Which he wouldn't receive. It was best to nip whatever this was in the bud now rather than let more feelings develop. It was best if she tried to forget about Henry altogether. "I only mean to say that my father would see no benefit to pursuing a friendship with you."

He grasped her shoulder, halting her progress and turning her to face him. "Katherine." His hand lingered, his thumb resting on the curve of her neck. "Right now I am unconcerned about your father's wishes. Yours interest me much more. Do... do you regret what has happened between us?"

She touched her mouth, the silk of her gloves a poor substitute for his lips. No, she didn't regret it. That memory would sustain her for years to come. It didn't seem possible that a kiss could have felt as good as she remembered.

She swayed forward, her chest almost touching his. Perhaps if they tried again, perhaps then—

"Hallo there." Miss Walker's cheery voice startled Katherine from her preoccupation. "Are you enjoying Perrin's gardens as much as I am?"

Henry gave the intruder what Katherine had come to think of as his professional smile. "Very much so. Though it was my understanding that these gardens are due to Lady Perrin. After her death, Lord Perrin merely maintained them."

Miss Walker's face tightened. The edges of her smile turned brittle. "Yes, Lady Perrin took great pleasure in her work here. It is to her husband's credit that he indulged her hobby so generously."

Katherine frowned. She didn't doubt Perrin's wife would enjoy working in her garden, but it seemed of little credit to the man himself to encourage something that improved the appearance and value of his estate. And reduced the cost of the labor of his gardeners.

Henry tilted his head. "I thought Mr. Withers mentioned that Lord Perrin wasn't a great supporter of his sister's hobby. That Withers himself provided the lady with many of her favorite plants here."

Miss Walker tightened her grip on the basket, her knuckles going white. "Mr. Withers? He is hardly one to criticize a man for inattentiveness to his wife. I understand there was a time when he was a most faithless husband."

"You were quite fond of Lord Perrin, were you not?" Katherine's chest burned with sympathy for the late Lady Perrin. She could only imagine this viper's tongue turned on the countess whenever Miss Walker came to call. A woman in love with the countess's husband, and who seemed loath to find any fault in the man. If Katherine had married the earl, how much would this woman's presence have been inflicted upon her?

Miss Walker stiffened. "He was a good neighbor. Kind to me and my father."

"He was more than just a good neighbor, though, wasn't he?" Katherine pressed, ignoring the warning look from Henry. "When I observed the two of you together, you seemed to have developed an interesting...friendship. You felt free to give your thoughts on the management of Perrin Manor, and he seemed to respect your opinions."

That last was more than a stretch. Lord Perrin didn't seem to respect anyone's opinion but his own.

Miss Walker laughed, her chin high. "Well, we had been neighbors for quite some time. Our relationship was one of mutual respect and trust. I sometimes jested that he couldn't get along without me."

"Which made it all the more surprising that Perrin wanted to marry me." Katherine furrowed her brow, pretending to look confused. "I would have thought once the earl had decided upon marriage, he would have looked to his close friend, the woman he relied upon so much. It would have only made sense."

Miss Walker flushed under her bonnet. "Men of a certain rank have other considerations beyond their own desires. My father isn't a wealthy man of business."

That stung more than it should, but Katherine supposed she deserved it. It was her father's money that attracted men to her, not her own qualities. She darted a glance at Henry. He stood with his arms crossed, looking resigned to her interrogation.

When he'd held her, it didn't seem as though he'd wanted her wealth. His desires had seemed much more immediate. Perhaps because he was smart enough to know that her father would never condone a union between the two of them, he knew that immediate desires were all that could be expected from any pursuit of her.

But this wasn't the time to ponder her own relationship troubles. She suspected that Miss Walker hadn't been so composed about Perrin's choice in a future wife when she'd first learned of it. "No. That does limit your options." Katherine gave the woman a sympathetic smile. "It must have been difficult, knowing you and Lord Perrin would make such a good match, and knowing that it would never come about. I wonder that you were able to still accept Perrin's invitations. If it had been me, I would have been too angry to continue the friendship."

"You are not me." Miss Walker pulled the basket tight against her abdomen, crushing a purple bud.

Henry cupped Katherine's elbow. "No. And perhaps it is time—"

Katherine pulled away and laughed lightly. "That is surely true. I, for one, would have been apoplectic with rage had Perrin invited me to a house party along with his current lady friend. It must have burned when you saw Perrin with Mrs. Draper. I heard they weren't discreet with their affections."

Miss Walker's body positively vibrated, the brim of her bonnet trembling. "Mrs. Draper found out that it wasn't wise to toy with a man as she did. That using one's body to seduce only led to trouble. Perrin saw what she was before it was over. A manipulative little trollop. He saw, and she was rewarded for her actions."

Henry straightened. "Yes, her reward was a broken girth on her horse's saddle when last she visited Perrin Manor. She could have been killed."

Miss Walker raised one shoulder. "She took a gamble riding that beast. It didn't work out for her."

"Did you know Perrin invited her back?" Katherine asked. "He still wanted her company. It was the lady who refused."

"That is a lie." Miss Walker's voice was devoid of emotion. Her gaze was so hateful, Katherine fell a step back. "Perrin was a smart man. He didn't repeat his mistakes."

Nothing Katherine knew of Perrin's character supported that assertion. "Where were you before lunch yesterday?"

From the way Miss Walker narrowed her eyes, Katherine knew the woman understood what she was asking. But Miss Walker didn't bother to answer. She turned on her heel and strode for the house.

Even though the sun was warm, a shiver worked its way down Katherine's spine. "Now do you believe me?"

Henry turned to face her, his expression dark. "Believe what? That it is foolish to provoke that woman? Yes, I believe that."

Katherine frowned. "No, that Miss Walker is a good suspect to Perrin's murder."

Henry looked over her head at the path Miss Walker had taken. "I believe she may have wanted to kill Perrin. That she's vicious enough to attempt it. But you're forgetting something."

Katherine pursed her lips, thinking. Finally, she shrugged. "What? What am I forgetting?"

"It wasn't only Perrin the killer murdered. It was Mr. Taylor, as well. And to overcome a man and stab him to death takes a strength even Miss Walker in a rage doesn't possess."

Katherine wasn't so sure about that. How much strength did it take to plunge a knife into a person's chest? She had no way to test it, but there must have been cases where women had stabbed men to death in the past.

No, the question of strength wasn't what bothered Katherine. It was the fact that Mr. Taylor had been killed at all. Perrin, she could understand. He had been an obnoxious bully, one who had toyed with Miss Walker's emotions, at least from Miss Walker's viewpoint. But Mr. Taylor and she had barely spoken two words to each other.

What did the two men have in common that had sentenced them both to death?

Chapter Twenty-Nine

Lady Mary

"I T'S NONE OF your business!" The voice was loud, even through the closed door. I hurried forward, holding my walking stick above the ground until I reached the rear sitting room. "This house isn't a prison," the same voice roared as I opened the door. "I can go where I will."

Lord Havenstone stood by the sideboard, gesturing wildly to Mr. Smith, a bit of his drink sloshing over the rim of his glass.

Mr. Smith crossed his arms over his protruding stomach. "I say it is my business. Two men have been murdered and now you're sneaking about. I want to know why you were on that staircase. Hiding another bit of incriminating evidence?"

"Gentlemen." I gave my voice its most authoritative tone. "What is this argument concerning? We are just about to enjoy another fine meal prepared by Cook Clem. All this fighting isn't conducive to the appetite."

Havenstone flushed. "I beg everyone's pardon." He bowed slightly to the room, which included every guest except Miss Walker. "But I will not allow such insults to my character to go unanswered."

I found a seat that gave me a good view of the action. I sat on the edge of the cushion, resting my hands on the head of my walking stick. "Which insults are those?"

Mr. Ryder sighed. "Mr. Smith is accusing Lord Havenstone of going where he shouldn't in the manor. He seems to think it indicates some guilt on the baron's part."

Havenstone lifted his chin. "It is still quite muddy in parts outside. I need exercise. So I've walked about the house once or twice. What is it to anyone else?"

Mr. Smith poked a finger toward Havenstone's chest, not making contact, I noticed. "It's suspicious, is what it is. And don't think I won't be telling Constable Adams about it next time I see him."

"Tell him what?" Havenstone huffed. "That I've taken a daily constitutional going up and down some staircases? Yes, tell him that. See how much he cares."

Mr. Smith's face reddened. "He'll care if I want him to care."

"Yes, because your money will buy you anything." Miss Walker stood behind a settee, gripping the back.

I frowned, annoyed she had slipped in without my notice.

"You are free with your accusations, Mr. Smith," she said, emphasizing *mister*. "I wonder if it is to divert suspicion from your own behavior."

Mr. Ryder raised a hand. "Ladies and gentlemen, there is no need for acrimony. We are to remain together for the foreseeable future. We should remain pleasant, if possible."

It was almost endearing, the moralist's attempt to civilize this crowd. Fortunately for my purposes, no one paid him any mind.

"Ha!" Havenstone leaned forward, into Mr. Smith's space. "It's about time someone challenged you. Do you think none of us know how you hated Perrin? All you care about is money, and the earl swindled a profit away from you. You are most likely accusing me to deflect from your own guilt."

Mr. Smith clenched his hands into fists.

Katherine jumped to her feet and hurried to her father. She took his arm and tugged him away from Havenstone. "Their words don't matter, Father. Anyone who knows you knows that would be ridiculous."

"The same could be said for me." Havenstone jerked his thumb to his chest. "And for everyone in this room. But someone killed Perrin."

"And Taylor." Henry arched an eyebrow. "Everyone seems to forget about him."

It was a bit sad. I rubbed my finger on the bridge of my nose. Even in death, social status mattered.

"Well, it wasn't me." Mr. Smith patted Katherine's hand. "Perrin was a right sot, and I'll admit I was angry with him, but I was also prepared. A shipping company had previously expressed an interest in my parcel of land. They want to build a dock near the source of the local ores. I'd put them off because I'd already reached an oral agreement with Perrin to exchange the land. Once Perrin died, and after the roads cleared, I sent a note to the company's agent in London. They still want my land. I'll make a tidy profit off the sale."

"But you didn't know that at the time of Perrin's death," Bertram said slowly, his eyebrows drawing together.

"I saw no reason that wouldn't be the case." Mr. Smith poured himself a small glass of wine. "The company's interest wouldn't have evaporated so quickly."

"Of course not." Katherine glared at Miss Walker. "Besides, the fact that someone took the time to gather the poison indicates to me that the killer thought about this murder for some time. It wasn't the action of someone momentarily angered by the earl. It feels more like the action of someone who'd had years of resentment building."

"How dare—"

"Ladies." Mr. Ryder stood. "I realize this is a frightening time, but resorting to insults doesn't help the situation. Let's all of us remember that two men are dead. Our time would be better spent praying for their souls rather than bickering among ourselves."

An uncomfortable silence descended. He was right, of course, but it was hardly something we wanted to be reminded of. I sniffed. And besides, the information I was gathering from the insults of the angry guests was invaluable.

"Dinner is served." The butler stood in the adjoining doorway to the dining room. "Clem has prepared pheasant breast *a l'orange* for tonight's meal."

Regardless of how much I wanted this bickering to continue, the idea of what Cook Clem would do with that dish had me and everyone else hopping to our feet and making for the dining room.

The meal started with a lovely onion soup, surprisingly earthy flavors rolling over my tongue for such a delicate broth. It was difficult not to give all my attention to the bowl before me. But I persevered.

"How was your ride today?" I asked the Havenstones.

Lady Havenstone lifted her chin, her turned-up nose looking judgmental. "Perrin does have some lovely land. We rode along the cliffs. It's hard to believe just days ago a raging storm was coming from the Atlantic Ocean. The channel looked so peaceful today."

"Perrin did keep an adequate stable," Lord Havenstone admitted. "It was an enjoyable afternoon."

"Yes, I've spoken with the stable master." Henry set his spoon in his empty bowl. "He cares for the horses greatly and runs the stables like a tight ship. It's surprising that he let one of the saddles become worn to the point a girth snapped mid-ride at a previous house party."

Katherine beamed at the attorney, his comment obviously meeting with her approval.

From the scowl that appeared on Miss Walker's face, I thought I understood why.

Lady Havenstone sat back. "When did that occur? I noticed no wear on my saddle."

"It was months ago," Miss Walker said tersely. "And I'm certain the stable master learned from his past mistake after that woman fell."

Lady Havenstone blanched. "I thought in that at least we would be safe." She turned to her husband. "You should have checked the equipment before we rode. I have no tonic for a broken neck."

"It was perfectly safe," he assured her.

"Yes, I'm certain it wasn't negligence on the stable master's part." Katherine leaned back so the footman could remove her bowl and replace it with a plate.

The scents of orange and thyme teased my nose. "I agree. You've ridden twice now here. You must have noted how orderly the stables are. You've nothing to worry about."

Lady Havenstone blinked. "Twice? We've only ridden the once, today."

"Oh?" I held my knife poised above the meat. "I thought you and your husband had also ridden yesterday, before lunch."

Mr. Ryder caught my gaze and shook his head. To him, at least, my subterfuge was apparent. But I'd always known the man had a brain behind his handsome face. Unfortunately, he'd used said brain once too often in opposition to me.

"No, we rested before lunch." She shivered. "After nearly being shot by Mr. Taylor, I needed time alone in my room."

"Alone?" I brought a bite of the bird to my lips. My eyes involuntarily closed in appreciation at how succulent the meat was.

"Well, alone with my husband." Lady Havenstone also popped a bit of pheasant in her mouth and paused in appreciation. She patted the baron's hand. "Though I'm afraid I wasn't very good company for him. I fell asleep almost as soon as my head hit the pillow."

"Just being in your presence is company enough, asleep or no." Havenstone met my gaze. "Why the questions?"

"Just making conversation." I busied myself with my meal. So Lord Havenstone had no alibi. A sleeping wife couldn't attest that he'd remained in their room. He could have snuck out to kill Mr. Taylor.

How much blood would have been on the killer's clothes? Would his wife have noticed any stains once she'd awoken? And if the killer had gotten blood on his or her clothes, would they have been foolish enough to leave them out for the servants to clean?

I needed to speak with Marie again, but I couldn't do anything until dinner was over. So I put thoughts of murder out of my mind and enjoyed the meal with everyone else. I would also need to speak with Cook Clem again. I needed him in my kitchen. I'd never tasted a dish so exquisite.

Mr. Ryder must have agreed. "I do hope I'll have a chance to partake of Clem's cooking after we leave. I've never tasted the like."

"Only if I invite you to my house for dinner." I dragged a piece of meat through the sauce pooled on my plate. I chuckled at the thought. "And that is highly unlikely, as you know."

Mr. Ryder dipped his chin. "'Count not thy chickens that unhatched be.'"

I pressed my lips together. I had my own sayings. "'Fortune favors the bold.'" And boldness was something I never lacked.

Lady Havenstone frowned. "It is most unseemly the two of you trying to take Cook Clem. Have you no thought for the next Lord Perrin? How he might wish to keep his father's chef in his employ?"

From what I remembered of Perrin's sons, I liked the boys, but the next earl would have to make his bid for the cook along with the rest of us. However, perhaps that was a point better left unsaid.

The rest of the meal passed pleasantly. The mood of everyone seemed to lift with the intake of the excellent food. Accusatory glances faded and friendly conversations ensued. The power of a well-cooked meal was not to be underestimated. When the last morsel had been devoured and the plates scraped clean, we all stood to retire once again to the sitting room.

Marie stood at the door leading from the dining room into

the hall. She held the end of her apron clenched in her hands, and when she caught my eye, used the hem to wave me over. The rest of my compatriots were filing into the sitting room through the adjoining door. I held back so they might not notice my clandestine meeting with the maid. But before half of the guests had left the room, something caught Marie's notice and she froze. A blush darkened her cheeks and she dropped her gaze to the floor.

I looked over, wondering who could have caused that reaction in the bold young miss. Only the Havenstones, Bertram, and Mr. Ryder lingered by the door, waiting for the slow moving crowd to push through the doorway so they, too, could make their way into the sitting room.

I pushed my spectacles up my nose. How very odd. Yet another question to ask the girl.

But when I turned back toward the outer doorway, I found it empty. Marie had disappeared.

Chapter Thirty

Lady Mary

I HADN'T SLEPT well, and I let the cause of my insomnia know it was her fault. "You said you'd come back to speak with me. I waited up half the night but you never showed."

Jane ran a brush down my ivory locks, pulling a bit harder than necessary at a knot. "I said *if* I learned anything I'd return. I didn't, so I didn't."

I glared at her wrinkled face reflected in the sitting room mirror. It looked to be the start of a glorious day. Birds chirruped outside my window. The rising sun glinted off the pond. The color of the sky was almost an exact match to my eyes.

I appreciated none of it. "You knew I'd wait. What happened? Was there another card game you felt too important to miss?" My tone was snappish. I didn't like it, but couldn't quite find it in myself to moderate it. I needed a large cup of chocolate this morning if my mood was to turn about.

"You'd be surprised at how much I can learn at those card games." Jane laid down the brush and twisted my hair. Years may have bent her fingers, but even rheumatism couldn't stop the expert way she handled my ivory locks. I'd worn my hair in the same style for thirty years. She'd had a lot of experience.

"And?" I tapped my foot against the floor. "Did you learn

something useful?"

Jane stepped back and blew out a breath. "Something strange is going on here. I asked about Marie like you wanted me to, and it was like I'd let Southey do his business on the eating table. No one would tell me anything, only that she's left."

"Left?" I drew my shoulders back, a bad feeling spiraling in my stomach. "She wouldn't have just left. Not when she wanted to speak with me." And not when I needed to speak with her. I didn't need any more barricades in my path. It wasn't fair.

I patted my hair and stood. "Someone must know something. The girl couldn't have just disappeared."

"There's something else." Jane peered about the room, as though expecting the butler to pop up around the corner of the bed. "Another girl is missing, too. Mary, one of the washing maids."

"Two maids gone." I tapped my thumb against my lips. What could it mean? Did it have any connection to the murders? It was hard to see how, but then, what were the odds that two women would go missing in a house with a killer and it wasn't connected?

I went to the wall and plucked my walking stick from its position in the corner. I'd only brought the one with me on this journey, a lovely mahogany stick, with a head made of solid onyx. I brought the round knob down on my palm and nodded approvingly at the sting.

I turned to Jane. "Why wouldn't they talk to you, do you think?"

Jane snorted as she fluffed a pillow. "You think one servant is the same as another? That just because we eat our meals downstairs we're all one family?" She shook her head. "*They* are a family. I might not be as much an outsider as you, but I'm still an outsider. And sometimes family closes ranks."

Indeed. I rubbed my breastbone. My own family had secrets that would burn the ears off the devil. One of them had escaped the family, however. I looked at my trunk. The letters that Henry had found in Perrin's study had been tucked away under some used underthings. Perrin hadn't had it quite right, but he'd known enough. Enough to let me know that Cavindish hadn't kept our secrets just between the two of us. That perhaps one night when he'd had a bit too much to drink, he'd let slip the most private agreement of our life together.

The betrayal burned. Perrin had been his brother, his family, too, but there were some things that happened between husband and wife that should never be known outside the marriage.

I exhaled a long breath. My betrayal had been bigger. Perhaps it was what I deserved.

"Mary…"

I held up a hand. "I'm fine."

Jane gave me a sad smile. "He loved you. Never forget that."

My husband had. I knew it. I also knew that sometimes… sometimes love wasn't enough. I hadn't explained the letters to Henry. I trusted in his discretion. But all of Perrin's cutting remarks, his hatred toward me, they made sense now. He'd thought the worst of me, that I'd betrayed his brother and had an affair. Of course, he'd hated me.

I shook off the sickening feeling like it was a poorly tied cloak. "Best not to dwell on what can't be changed."

Jane nodded agreement.

"There remains a killer to be caught." I strode for the door, ignoring Jane's grumble. Action always cheered my disposition. Dwelling on the maudlin wasn't a habit I tended to engage in. Setting my shoulders, I swung open the door—

—and stumbled over a furry lump.

Southey hopped to his feet and shook. He gave an excited *woof* and danced about my feet.

I will not kick a dog, I repeated to myself as I made my way down to breakfast, the path made more circuitous by the dodging and circling necessary to avoid the terrier. I was one of the first down. Mr. Ryder was in quiet conversation by the far door with the butler. The Havenstones sat at the table, soft-boiled eggs cracked open before them.

I made my way to the sideboard and poured myself a cup of chocolate. I drank half of it where I stood, then refilled the mug. I wandered to the window for a better view as I enjoyed my sweetened brew.

Bertram was in the garden. He stood by the central fountain, his hands in his pockets. He looked somehow like a lost little boy. Who could blame him? With Perrin's and Mr. Taylor's murders, we were all feeling a bit lost.

I stepped over the dog to reach the casement doors, juggled my cup and walking stick while trying to depress the handle. I gave Mr. Ryder a nod of thanks when he hurried over to assist me. I managed to block Southey's egress with my cane and shove the door closed with my hip before he could escape. I smiled at his indignant yip.

A warm breeze greeted me, the day promising some heat. I gave a quick thought to Perrin's body in the ice house, now joined by Mr. Taylor's. The magistrate would need to arrive soon, or the bodies removed to an undertaker in the village. They couldn't remain where they were much longer.

Betram dipped his fingers in the fountain, then brought them to his mouth.

And neither could we. I wanted to discover the killer, but we would all go slowly mad if we stayed here much longer.

"Bertram." I held up my mug in greeting as I made my way about the path to join him. "If you are thirsty, there is drink just in there." I jerked my head toward the dining room with a laugh.

He blinked at me before giving his head a slight shake. "Good morning. How are you?"

"As well as anyone." I leaned on my walking stick. "What are you doing out here?"

"Talking to Miranda."

A shiver slid down my back. Talking to dead sisters wasn't something I usually approved of with my morning chocolate. I paused before trying to make light of the comment. "As long as she doesn't talk back, I suppose there can be no harm."

He strolled to a reedy plant on the side of the path. "Do you never talk to Cavindish? With an empty house, I find myself talking to my wife and sister more and more."

I ran my thumb over the onyx head of my stick. I missed Cavindish something fierce at times, but my house never felt empty. Not with Jane and the other servants there with me. But servants weren't also the friends of most people of my acquaintance. I suppose if they were just anonymous faces who made sure my bed was made and my meals cooked instead of people full of humor and conversation, my house would feel empty, too.

"I don't speak to Cavindish," I said lightly, "but there is one particular fern in my sitting room I sometimes have words with. It always seems to catch at my skirts when I walk past."

Betram chuckled. "I miss having a woman about to speak with."

A heaviness settled on my chest. "We shouldn't have let so many years pass without at least corresponding." After all our spouses had died, the ones connecting us, it had seemed easier to ignore Perrin and Bertram. To not make the effort to stay in touch. I regretted my neglect.

"I have been lonely." He ran his fingers up the shafts of some decorative grass. "I've been thinking of late to remedy that situation."

I squeezed the knob of my walking stick. A dog made a fine companion. Something Bertram could talk to in his empty house. And Southey did need a new master. "Oh? And how would you do that?" I asked, hoping my voice didn't sound too eager. If Bertram wanted the dog, he could start keeping the beast in his rooms now, a way to get better acquainted. And keep the animal from being underfoot.

"By remarrying, of course."

A moment of dread seized me. My heart thudded in my chest. "Any potential candidates in mind?" He couldn't mean me. Betram had always seemed a lovely man, but we didn't know each other all that well, and what I did know wasn't of someone for whom I had any particular inclination.

I buried my face in my drink, hoping the mug would hide my expression of horror when he said my name.

"I'd thought I might try to get to know Miss Walker better." He plucked a flower from a plant and brought the blossom to his nose. He inhaled deeply.

Relief was quickly followed by embarrassment. How highly I must regard myself to think that he would want me for a wife. I couldn't stop my own burst of laughter.

Bertram narrowed his eyes.

"Oh, I'm not laughing at you but at myself. So, Miss Walker has caught your eye, has she? That is to her good fortune."

His shoulders lowered an inch. "She isn't some mindless chit. I couldn't stand the idea of pursuing someone just out in society. And she seems most eager to leave her father's household. Being a caretaker has been hard on her."

I hadn't realized Betram and Miss Walker had spoken in any depth, but there had been many hours trapped inside from the rain where two people might cozy up by a fire for a private chat. "I'd thought her feelings lay in a different direction." And feelings didn't disappear the moment the object of one's affection died.

Unless she'd caused that death. Unless she was one of those people devoid of natural affections, a person who could show tenderness to a person one moment and loathing the next.

I'd met a few people like that in my life. Thankfully, they had been few, but I'd learned never to turn my back on them.

Moral insanity, I believe was the terminology for such a person. I finished my chocolate, but even the heat streaming down my throat couldn't warm the rest of my body. A physician had once given a lecture at The Minerva Club about the research of Phillipe Pinel. How he'd described some individuals as suffering from a type of insanity without the symptoms of delusion. That a person could appear ordinary and rational but suffer from a madness consisting of the perversion of natural feelings, impulses, and affections. How a mother could feed and care for her child and then hold its head under the bath water if the child's crying became too irritating.

Could Miss Walker be one of those lost individuals? In her mind, could it seem just and reasonable to kill the man who'd spurned her once too often?

I pressed my lips together and considered Bertram. I didn't want him to entwine his life with her if that were the case. If Miss Walker was the killer, I needed to discover that, and soon. "Don't be in a hurry to make any big decisions. Miss Walker had some attachment to Perrin. I'm sure she needs some time to properly mourn."

Bertram pulled the blossom from its stalk. "He didn't deserve any attachment. Just as he didn't deserve my sister."

The heat in his voice had me falling back a step. I knew Bertram, felt some natural sympathy for him.

And I'd forgotten that he, too, was a suspect in Perrin's murder.

"Your sister seemed happy in her marriage in my eyes," I said carefully.

Betram tossed the remnants of his flower to the ground and plucked another. "I bought her so many of these plants. Miranda loved to spend her time out here in the sun."

Rather than indoors with her husband, I suppose. "I was looking for you on Friday before lunch. I'd hoped to ask if you wanted to include a note in the letters I'm planning on sending to our nephews. Where were you?"

To anyone with a devious mind, my unsubtle question would have been recognized for the attempt at ascertaining an alibi for Taylor's death that it was. Bertram merely smiled. "Those dear boys. Without any parent now. We shall have to be there for them, of course. Give them any guidance and assistance they might need."

"Of course." I shifted my weight. "And Friday? You were….?"

"Practicing my corner shot in the billiards room. I find I play better when there is no one about to distract me."

My shoulders drooped. Practicing alone. Not an alibi. I'd ask some of the others if they'd seen or heard him playing but I didn't hold out much hope. I turned for the house. "I think I've gotten enough sun. Let's eat some breakfast."

He tucked the blossom into his jacket's lapel. "You go ahead. I'm going to wander a bit more."

Nodding, I made my way along the gravel path, my stride not as sure as when I'd come out. Bits of crushed shell interspersed with the stones beneath my feet, reflecting the sun's rays and making me wince. I didn't believe Bertram was a killer. He didn't try to hide his dislike for Perrin. He would have been a liar if he'd said he thought Perrin was a good man. But not liking your sister's husband was hardly grounds for murder.

Southey greeted me at the door, his little behind wriggling. For once I didn't mind when he jumped at me, resting his paws on my leg.

One thought weighed on my heart. Was I putting little account into the possibility that Bertram was the killer because the evidence wasn't there?

Or was I letting my natural affection for the man cloud my judgment?

⊰ ━━━━━ ◦◦◦ ━━━━━ ⊱

Chapter Thirty-One

Henry

S HE WAS IN the folly in the small copse of trees behind the lake. Henry took the two steps at a jog and glared down at her seated form. "Your father told me you'd gone out for a walk."

Katherine rested one shoulder on a faux Greek column. She sighed. "It sounds as though there is an accusation in that statement."

"Damn right." He crossed his arms over his chest. "There is a killer at this house. You cannot go wandering about alone."

It was miraculous that he'd found her. Perrin Manor had miles of paths looping about the property. His anxiety had increased with each step he'd taken in his search.

She traced the outlines of one of the flowers embroidered on her gown. "I didn't know where I was going so how could anyone know where to find me? If anyone wanted to find me," she muttered.

He bit his tongue, deciding not to point out she could have been followed. He wanted her to take precautions, but he didn't want her frightened. He tilted his head. "What's wrong?"

"There is nothing wrong."

"Liar." Frowning, he stepped close, forcing her to raise her head to look at him. "Tell me."

"There is nothing wrong that wasn't wrong yesterday, the day before, or all my life." She raised one shoulder, her shawl slipping down her back. "Father informed me he has a new husband in mind for me. He is going to write to ask for introductions when we return home. Not an industrialist, as he previously threatened. Even though he won't admit it, I think he does like his daughters having titles. At least this one is younger." Her smile was bitter. "The son of a viscount."

His stomach rolled. "So soon?" It did appear that Mr. Smith was eager to marry his youngest daughter off, though from speaking to him, Henry knew the man cared for Katherine very much. He probably thought getting Katherine settled was the best thing for her.

She picked a leaf off the seat beside her and threw it into the air. "You should give my father your direction. You're already familiar with one party in question. You can write the new marriage contract."

"I don't want to write your marriage contract," he growled. Not unless...unless he was the other party. But he wasn't of sufficient wealth or status to make a contract necessary to any woman he married. And her father would likely laugh him out of the room, or punch him in the nose, if he asked for her hand.

And why the hell was he putting marriage and Katherine Smith into the same sentence at all?

He scraped his fingers through his hair. "We should get back to the house."

"He'll pay you well for your services."

Heat flushed through his body. "I don't care about your father's money," he gritted out.

She smiled then, and a weight he hadn't even realized he'd worn lifted off his chest. "You don't, do you? You're content with what you earn and don't waste your time grasping for more."

Giving up on a quick return to Perrin Manor, Henry sighed and sat next to her. Her thigh pressed against his, and the light scent of flowers rose from her skin. "I appreciate money as much as the next fellow, but I have enough wealthy clients to know it isn't what brings you happiness. I have enough to be comfortable, and that's more than enough." But could it be enough for her? For someone who'd been raised with every luxury? If he lost his senses and asked for her, could she be content merely being an attorney's wife?

"And you decide which clients to take, where to live, how you live." She stared down at her slippers. "I envy you that."

"Katherine...."

She held up a hand. "Ignore me. I'm feeling dispirited today. I know I'm fortunate. If I feel trapped, at least it is in a lovely cage. There are so many trapped in much worse. In poverty. Sickness. They would exchange their cage for mine in an instant."

She was right, of course. Life was misery for so many. That didn't diminish the pain she felt, though. When she turned and gave him a watery smile, he could restrain himself no more.

Wrapping his arm around her, he pulled her into his side.

She stiffened for a moment, then buried her face in his shoulder and wrapped both of her arms around his waist. A soft sob escaped her lips.

Henry kissed the crown of her head. "I'm sorry, Katherine." Instead of comforting her, some of her despair seeped into him. She would be married off to a person of quality, and he would live the rest of his life wondering about what could have been. It was the way of the world. And for the first time, he resented it.

And when she raised her face, her breath caressing his jaw, it seemed the most natural thing in the world to lower his head and press his lips to hers.

It started out as a kiss of comfort. An acknowledgement of all the things that must remain unsaid between them. A goodbye.

It didn't last that way.

The kiss was salty from her tears, her despair clawing into his body, raising his ire. His body tensed, his fingers digging into her flesh. It wasn't fair. Some other man would get to hold her like this. Taste her. If he ever met the man, Henry didn't know that he would be able to stop himself from thrashing the bloke.

She opened for him, sweetly, her fingers clinging to his shoulders. Her eagerness cooled some of his anger, but made him no less demanding.

He was losing his mind. He knew it, but seemed unable to stop his actions. Not his tongue from tasting every inch of her mouth, not his hand from skimming up under her skirts.

His body knew. In another time, in other circumstances, this woman would be his. His mind mocked his body. They weren't in other circumstances. They lived in a society, one that wouldn't condone their union.

Katherine tentatively lapped her tongue against his, and his mind lost the battle. Rational thought abandoned him, leaving only sensation. He reveled in his mindlessness. If he only allowed himself to feel, to act, he might just be able to forget that she would marry another man.

IT WAS MOST unfair. She should have never met Henry. Never have known what true passion felt like in the arms of someone she loved. Not before marrying an earl or viscount's son. If she had entered into her marriage without knowing, she might have been able to find a sort of contentment.

Now all she could hope for was that these memories would sustain her.

Henry gripped the back of her thigh, tugged, and she gladly followed his direction and straddled his lap.

This was better. Knowing what it was like to be touched by the man she loved, it had to be better than going her whole life without ever experiencing this feeling. So when Henry released his falls and guided her hand to his member, she let him, reveling in the pleasure she saw etched on his face.

When he tore at the opening of her pantalets, his fingers

starting a fire as they moved against her, she let him do that, too.

And when he guided her to seat herself upon him, God help her, she let him do that, too.

They moved as one, staring into each other's eyes, and Katherine thought nothing in the world could ever feel so good.

And then it got better.

Chapter Thirty-Two

Lady Mary

"IT IS A sad commentary that we are always able to find ourselves alone in this room." I took my usual seat by the fire and examined the rows of books in the library. How many had Perrin read? How many had his wife? The books had a lonely feel to them now, as though they were abandoned, never to be opened again.

"Dinner will be served soon." Katherine tugged at the edge of her fichu. "I should go clean up beforehand."

"Yes, Lady Mary," Henry said. He rocked up onto his toes. "Pouncing on us right as we came through the door is hardly the thing."

"It was hardly pouncing." I narrowed my eyes. "And how much cleaning up do you need to do? It isn't as though you were rolling around in the dirt."

Katherine burst out in a fit of coughing. "Excuse me." She cleared her throat. "Yes, you are right. Now what did you want to speak to us about?"

"The new tariffs being imposed on goods from the East In-dies." I jabbed my finger at the chair across from me. "Sit. Please."

Katherine sat.

Henry leaned against the mantel. "Have you learned something new about the murders?"

"I spoke with Betram." I stabbed at a blue swirl on the cream rug with the tip of my walking stick. "He says he was practicing his skill at billiards when Taylor was killed. Alone. I asked around. No one saw him, although the butler did hear billiards balls clacking at some point before lunch."

"So not much of an alibi," Henry said.

"Not much of a motive, either." I pressed my lips together. If not liking someone was grounds for murder, there would be a trail of bodies in my wake.

"At least my father is no longer a suspect." Katherine patted her hair. A small, wrinkled brown leaf fell out and drifted to the floor.

Henry hesitated. "Why do you say that?"

Katherine frowned. "Because he didn't lose money when Perrin changed the terms of the contract. He already had a buyer waiting. He might have been angry at Perrin's deceit, but he had no real motive."

"Anger has been a sufficient motive for many a murder," he said carefully.

I tapped my thumb on the armrest. "I agree with Katherine. Her father is a man of business. He must have had many deals fall through, and I doubt he went about killing everyone who crossed him. No, I think Mr. Smith is no longer on the suspect list."

Henry inclined his head. "That is a relief."

"Miss Walker had motive, and she knows her plants." Katherine scooted forward in her seat. "She could well know what to use to poison a man. And, with the element of surprise, I believe she'd have the strength to stab someone, too." She sent a look toward Henry, eyebrow raised.

"There were no bruises on Taylor. No signs of any struggle." I tilted my head. "He must have been surprised by his killer, which takes strength out of the equation. A woman could have done it."

"She did refuse to tell us where she was when Taylor was

killed," Henry conceded. "But I still wonder, why Taylor? What's the connection between him and Perrin?"

"He must have known something." Southey trotted into the room and made straight for me. I sighed, resigned. "All those hints about him coming into money, that he'd be able to support Katherine. I'd guess that he knew who the killer was and attempted to extort money from him."

Katherine loosed a low whistle. "I don't want to think so badly of the man, but it makes sense."

"I have no problem thinking badly of him." Henry grimaced. "I must say I find it irritating that Taylor discovered the killer's identity while our efforts have been fruitless."

I agreed. I didn't like to contemplate that the sniveling secretary might have been smarter than me.

"I'm sure he must have witnessed something," Katherine said soothingly. "He didn't deduce the knowledge, only observed it."

That appeased me somewhat, and from the look Henry sent in Katherine's direction, he felt the same. "And that leaves Lord Havenstone," I said. "What have we learned about him?"

"We all heard the argument between Katherine's father and Havenstone." Henry ran his hand up the back of his head. "A sleeping wife doesn't make a sound alibi for the time of Mr. Taylor's murder."

"And he has been sneaking about," Katherine added. "Why?"

None of us had an answer to that. I scratched Southey behind the ear before standing. "Let's ask him."

Katherine and Henry gave each other arch looks but followed after me obediently enough. We found him in the front sitting room, puffing on a cigar, yesterday's paper on his lap.

"Good afternoon, Lord Havenstone," I said briskly. "I hope we aren't interrupting."

He laid the paper aside. "The sunlight is fading and I am too lazy to light a lamp. Conversation is welcome."

"Good." I settled myself on the settee across from him. Katherine sat at my side and Henry took another armchair.

I inhaled the sweet scent of the smoke. "One of Perrin's cigars?"

"There were a few things he had good taste in." Havenstone's lips quirked. "That includes you, my dear." He inclined his head to Katherine.

Henry sat up straight, one vertebrae at a time.

Not wanting to be put off topic, I leaned forward and tugged my skirts from Southey's mouth. "As you know, someone here killed Perrin and Taylor."

"I am aware," Havenstone said dryly.

"Then I won't waste time." I folded my hands over the top of my walking stick. "We are trying to ascertain everyone's whereabouts from when we returned from the shooting field until lunch on Friday."

A muscle ticced in his jaw. "My wife already told you."

"No, she told us where she was and where she assumed you were." I arched an eyebrow. "Where do you say you were?"

He crushed his cigar onto the side table. "I was with my wife in our room."

"And you wouldn't want to contradict your wife." Henry tapped his fingers on his knee.

"What does that mean?" Havenstone asked, voice sharp.

"You lost a great deal of money when Perrin's investment went sour a couple years ago." Henry pinned him with a look. "I had heard that you almost lost your home because of it. It was only through your wife's intervention that you were saved."

I controlled my expression, trying not to show my surprise. Henry had left out a few details he'd learned during our discussions.

Havenstone's face mottled. "You heard wrong."

"That's possible," I agreed. "I'd heard that you went to Mr. Edric Cooke, first hoping to win a large sum in his hells, and next for a loan. A loan that you paid off in a short amount of time. Are you denying you acquired the funds to repay the loan from your wife's father?"

Havenstone jerked his head back. "How did you…?"

"I have my sources," I said and left it at that. I didn't want Mr. Cooke to gain a reputation for being indiscreet, especially as that might limit the information he could provide to me in the future.

He slumped back in his chair. "All right. Yes. You're right. Do you know how humiliating it is to beg your father-in-law in order to save your ancestral home?"

I did not, but I could imagine. "And this last time you needed funds? This second loan you've taken from Mr. Cooke. Was that also the fault of Perrin?"

His face paled. "How do you know this?"

I sniffed. "That is neither here nor there. Please answer the question."

Havenstone gave a harsh chuckle. "Indirectly. Can you believe he asked me to invest with him again? That he had the gall to think I'd give him more money?"

Katherine leaned forward. "But if you didn't give him money, why did you need funds?"

The baron scratched at an invisible mark on his trousers and mumbled.

I put my hand to my ear. "What was that?"

He sighed, all the air seeming to leave his body. "I thought to give Perrin a taste of his own medicine. There was a competing venture which I funded, hoping…."

"That Perrin's investment would fail." Henry frowned. "I take it that didn't happen."

"No." Whatever was on Havenstone's trousers had fully captured his attention. "Perrin's venture bankrupted mine. Had I invested with him this time, I would have made back my previous loss in full."

It was all very Shakespearean. The quest for vengeance doubling back and trapping Havenstone instead. Perrin finally having a successful investment but dying before he could enjoy the fruits.

I didn't admit this to many, but I didn't enjoy the works of our national pride as much as many. The melodrama and histrionics. The overwrought plots. There were moments of inspiration, an understanding of important truths in Shakespeare's plays, but all too often it felt as though I was watching or reading overly emotional children behaving badly, and that never held my interest.

But perhaps we were destined to always remain emotional children and behave badly. Perhaps Shakespeare had understood human nature on a deeper level than me.

"And the letter you received a few nights past?" I asked. "The one that had you marching out of the sitting room in anger?"

He slouched deeper into his chair, seeming almost to become one with it. "That was from my wife's father. He has refused to repay my loan at this time."

"I see." I stared at him over the top of my walking stick. "Why did you accept Perrin's invitation to this party? You'd lost money because of him a second time. Being in his presence couldn't have been a pleasure." Unless he'd come for a purpose. His plans for financial revenge having failed, had Havenstone decided to enact the ultimate vengeance?

"My wife saw the invitation," he said. "She wanted to come."

And with his wife's father controlling the purse strings, Havenstone was hardly in a position to refuse. Still, it showed a lack of awareness on his wife's part, inflicting Perrin on her husband. Or a lack of compassion. Or maybe this was her idea of revenge, forcing her fiscally irresponsible husband to face the instrument of his folly.

"Where were you when Mr. Taylor was killed?" I asked.

"With Lady Havenstone." His jaw set. His stare hardened. I knew I wouldn't get a different answer, no matter how much I pressed.

My problem was I couldn't determine if it was the honest answer or not.

Chapter Thirty-Three

Lady Mary

"**B**UT WHERE HAS she gone?" It was after yet another succulent dinner, and I had cornered my quarry at the top of the stairs leading down to the kitchens. "And why? She didn't seem the sort of girl to go larking about."

The butler ran his fingers through his thinning hair. "Marie had a family matter to attend to. She won't be far when the magistrate comes, if he wants to ask her some questions."

I wanted to ask her some questions. "And where is her family?" The roads should be passable for my carriage by now. Or at least a cart.

Mr. Ryder joined us, a small glass of cordial in his hand. "Leave the poor man be. There are some goings-on around here that aren't related to the murders. And aren't our business, either." The corners of his eyes crinkled, but his tone was firm.

I eyed him with suspicion. Why did it feel as though Ryder knew something that I didn't? It was a feeling I didn't appreciate. And I didn't like this business of a maid disappearing. I drew my eyebrows together. Two maids. "And what of the other girl? Did she also have a family matter to attend to? The odds of two maids each leaving on family emergencies seems too great to countenance."

Ryder and the butler shared a look, and the back of my neck heated. The moralist definitely knew something I didn't.

"As you say, it is a great coincidence." Ryder hooked his thumb in the pocket of his waistcoat. The motion emphasized how flat the man's abdomen remained, and I sucked in my own, just a little. "The girls are friends. Could not one have left to aid the other?"

The problem with Mr. Ryder was he always managed to sound so reasonable. It made me unreasonably irritated. "It is possible," I conceded. "But I—"

A clatter of pots and pans hitting stone rose up from the kitchen.

"Excuse me, milady." The butler inclined his head. "I must attend to that." And he disappeared down the stairs, looking more relieved than he should for the mess that awaited him.

I turned on Mr. Ryder. "What do you know?"

"That it is abominably rude for a gentleman to keep a lady standing when a comfortable chair is nearby." He crooked his elbow, inviting me to take it. "Shall we join the others in the sitting room?"

Scowling, I took his arm. "Marie wanted to tell me something, and now she's disappeared. I want to know why."

His warm chocolate eyes glinted down at me. "And do you always get what you want?"

"In general, yes." For the small things, at least. Being the daughter of an earl and the aunt to a duke guaranteed me some power. But for other things, the things that really mattered, I was as susceptible to the vagaries of life as anyone else.

They stopped at the open door to the sitting room. A harried-looking Lord Havenstone stood in the center of the room, waving his arms about in an attempt at pantomime.

I fell back a step. "And right now I wish not to join this game," I whispered.

With a nod, Ryder pivoted and led us quickly away. I hurried, shoulders bunched, expecting Miss Walker to chase after us, but we made our escape without interruption.

We went to the library. A small fire was dwindling in the grate, and Ryder went over to add more coal.

I settled myself in what I was coming to think of as my chair and leaned my walking stick against the armrest. I examined Ryder as heat from the fire crept past my clothes and warmed my body. "Why are you privy to information about Perrin's servants and I am not? Until Perrin's sons arrive, the butler has looked to me for direction."

Ryder sank into a chair across from mine and stretched out his long legs, crossing them at the ankles. "I am not attempting a mutiny, if that is your concern."

It hadn't been, not until now.

He continued. "I overheard some sensitive information last time I was in the kitchen." He held up a hand. "It has nothing to do with your murders. Since learning of the situation, however, I have tried to assist the parties as best I can."

"What information?" And had he met with any success in the kitchen? I knew he must have been there in an attempt to woo Cook Clem. He'd best not have succeeded.

He laced his fingers together and rested his hands on his abdomen. "It is not my secret to tell."

"Balderdash." Southey trotted into the room, apparently finished with his evening meal, and plopped down by my feet. "You have no way of knowing what is, or isn't, pertinent to the killings." I sniffed. "And they're not *my* murders."

He tilted his head. "Aren't they? You seem to have taken ownership of them, or at least in trying to find the killer."

"And you are trying to divert my attention from the matter at hand." I heaved a breath. "I do have some skill at discretion. If it is truly unrelated to the murders, I won't repeat one word that you tell me."

He smiled. "I believe you. All I will say is that the other maid, Mary, got herself into a spot of trouble. I knew of a home not too far from here for girls who have gotten themselves in the same trouble and wrote a letter of introduction. Marie accompanied the girl to help her get settled."

"Ah." That seemed oddly decent of Ryder, considering he must abhor the activities that led to the maid's 'trouble.' My heart sank. "Could Perrin have been the source of the trouble?" That opened up a whole other motive for his murder if he'd fathered a child with his maid. An angry father or beau. The girl herself feeling the earl wasn't taking care of the situation properly.

I rubbed my forehead. I was getting a megrim.

"He was not," Ryder said.

"You're certain?"

"The girl was." He rubbed his jaw. "She named a young man who works in the stables. Someone who has no desire to marry, even when I and the butler pressed him most severely. If I controlled the management of this estate, I would release him from employment."

I rubbed the tip of my boot along Southey's spine. "It takes two to make that kind of trouble." It struck me anew the unfairness of it. How two people, in a happy, secure marriage, could try and try and never conceive, yet a baby could be blessed on those who didn't want it. "You seem to have saved the girl from your condemnation and given it all to the boy."

"I don't condone either of their actions, but the girl wants to make the best of it. And she has the larger cross to bear." He tipped his head to rest on the back of the chair and stared at the ceiling. "The boy is unrepentant."

Repentance was always the key. An acknowledgement of one's sins and an attempt to do better. The trouble came when one wasn't certain if he or she had sinned.

The back of my throat went thick, loneliness swamping me. It had been so long since I'd had anyone to confide in, someone to help me find my way in this world. I usually had no trouble knowing right from wrong, but there were some days....

"You must have wondered what Mr. Taylor was referring to when he said Perrin voiced accusations against me," I said quietly.

"His words must have confirmed what you already think of me. A woman of low virtue."

He turned his head, his eyes meeting mine. "That is not what I think. Even though you fail to appreciate the dangers your club presents to society, I hold you in high esteem."

I smothered a laugh. "That I find difficult to believe."

He returned his gaze to the ceiling. "I can't control what you believe, only my own actions."

I pushed up from my chair. Stepping over Southey, I went to the fireplace and stared at the flames. "Yet you must be curious what Perrin knew about me. Or thought he knew." From the drafts of the letters he'd intended to send to the papers, it was clear that he hadn't known everything.

"Who can know what all goes on inside another's marriage? No one should even try. Some things are only meant to be known between husband and wife."

There he went sounding reasonable again. I turned to glare at the man. "That hardly sounds like the words of the president of the London Society for Morality and Decency."

"Do you want me to judge you?" Southey got up and sniffed the cuff of his trousers. Ryder bent and picked up the terrier, putting him on his lap. "We all err. None of us go through life blameless, least of all me. That doesn't mean I won't continue to push for a better world."

I gripped the mantel, wondering just what sort of sins might lurk in Mr. Ryder's past. He did have a surprising acquaintance with the crime lord Mr. Cooke, one he seemed loath to acknowledge. In his youth, had Ryder worshipped one of Aquinas's four false idols? And which one was the greatest temptation for him: wealth, pleasure, power, or honor?

My curiosity piqued, and so did my suspicions. "You don't want to know what Perrin intended to write to the papers about me? Even if it would help you in your quest to shut down my club?"

His look was kind and just a bit chiding. "Your personal life is your own. What I learn about it will be from that which you wish to tell me."

My throat went thick. "There are some stories I'll never wish to tell. But I do want you to know I loved my husband. I would never have turned to another man for base pleasure."

There had been another reason. A reason I'd thought Cavindish had supported. He'd even introduced me to the man in question, given his silent consent, and left us alone.

Cavindish had sanctioned it, he'd understood, but perhaps, deep in his heart, it wasn't something he could forget. And in the end, it had all been for naught. I still hadn't conceived a child. We'd always thought the defect had been on Cavindish's part. He'd been married before me, and no children had come from that union. Perhaps his first wife had been just as barren as it turned out I had been.

Ryder nodded. "I never would have believed otherwise."

That only increased the ball of guilt in my stomach. A part of me would have preferred if he'd pointed his finger, called me 'Jezebel', turned his back on me. Such actions would have accorded more with what I wanted his character to be. It was harder to understand someone who targeted one's business, deemed it immoral, but was also kind.

I toed the grate of the fireplace. "You must regret accepting Perrin's invitation. All you've accomplished is to become entangled in gossip and intrigue. You won't even get a cook out of it."

He arched a salt and pepper eyebrow. "You're certain of that?"

I wasn't, but there was nothing wrong with a good bluff. "I've engaged in further negotiations with Cook Clem. I believe I've made my case." Clem had seemed ready to leave the country for London. And I could pay significantly more than Ryder's club.

A throat cleared at the door. "Excuse me, milady, Mr. Ryder." The butler inclined his head. "I thought you'd want to know that Constable Adams sent the household a message."

He paused, whether waiting for permission to continue or for dramatic effect, I didn't know.

"And?" I asked, trying to keep the irritation from my voice.

"He says the guests can prepare for departure soon. The magistrate arrives tomorrow."

⸙ ❧ ⸙

Chapter Thirty-Four

Henry

" A ND THOSE ARE all the motives you know for why someone might want Lord Perrin dead?" The magistrate, the Right Honorable Lord Preston, rubbed his eyes. The skin beneath them was bruised and puffy, speaking to many sleepless nights. Henry couldn't help but wonder just how many miners he and the other men were able to pull from the collapsed mine. And how many bodies.

"Yes, my lord, although I do want to point out that Mr. Smith was easily able to recoup his losses." Henry leaned forward on his seat in the front sitting room. The morning sun was streaming directly into his eyes. "I no longer feel his motive to be strong."

Preston closed his notebook. "Thank you for your opinion. You've given Constable Adams your direction if I need to contact you again?"

Henry nodded.

"Then you are free to leave Perrin Manor," Preston said. "Please send in Lord and Lady Havenstone."

Henry nodded and stood, his chest oddly tight. He went to the rear sitting room and told the Havenstones it was their turn with the magistrate.

Katherine jumped from her seat. She took a step toward him,

paused and looked about the room, then made her way to him at a moderate pace. "What did you say? How did it fare?" she said in a low voice.

"I told him what I knew."

Her eyebrows arched. "Everything?"

"Well, I didn't mention we had been looking into the murders ourselves." He made sure no one was looking their way and dragged his finger across the back of her hand. "Or anything else that is none of his concern."

His chest tightened. And tomorrow he would be gone back to Exeter and she to London.

She swayed closer. "Does he—"

"So what did the magistrate say to you?" Lady Mary stood behind them, a cup of tea in her hand. She took a small sip. "He was most closed-mouthed with his thoughts when we spoke."

"Imagine that," Henry murmured. He shrugged at the older woman's glare. "He has only just arrived. I would not expect to be privy to his opinions on the matter."

Lady Mary sniffed. "Yet he is allowing everyone to return home on the morrow. He seems a bit rash."

"How long can he expect everyone to remain?" Katherine asked. She rubbed her arm. "Constable Adams is removing the bodies to town. He said the magistrate has a physician he wishes to examine them and then he will release them to be buried. Life moves on."

Without him.

Henry pressed his lips flat. Did she have to sound so resolved to that fact? Would their separation mean so little to her? Or was she only being smart, resigning herself to what neither of them could change?

He looked to her father. Or could they?

"There is still the matter of the killer to be caught." Lady Mary stabbed her walking stick into the carpet. "I, for one, will not be leaving until this has been solved."

Henry grimaced. "You have a reason to stay, as the nearest

relation. I, however, can think of no excuse to explain my remaining. And even if I did, everyone else will have left, including all of our suspects. What would be the point?"

Lady Mary's shoulders curved. "That does present a problem."

The Havenstones returned. "Miss Smith, Lord Preston has asked to speak to you," Lord Havenstone said.

Katherine chewed on her lower lip and gave Henry a worried look.

"If you aren't guilty, you have nothing to worry about." Lady Havenstone looked down her nose at Katherine. "The magistrate seems a most civilized man."

"Of course." Katherine straightened. "I will go to him at once." And with chin high, she strode from the room.

Henry's gaze lingered on the empty doorway.

"…tonight."

"Hmm." He blinked and turned to Lady Mary. "What was that?"

She stepped closer. "I said if everyone is to leave tomorrow, we need to think of a way to trap the killer tonight."

He squinted at her. "Might one ask exactly how we are to do that?"

She stared into her cup. "I'll think of something."

Silence fell between them. Mr. Smith laughed uproariously at something Mr. Ryder said. Miss Walker attempted to rally others to another game. Mr. Withers tried to explain the curative effects of colchicine on gout to Lord Havenstone.

Henry tried to think of the most polite way to phrase his question. "If it were such a simple matter to contrive a trap for our killer, would we not have thought of it already?"

Lady Mary glared at him over her spectacles. "Before, we were not properly motivated." She turned and made her way to one end of a settee.

Henry went to the window and looked out over the gardens. They had feared for their lives before. He thought that was more than enough motivation. But right now, his thoughts were more concerned with another consequence of everyone leaving tomorrow.

He thought he was sure of Katherine's feelings, but unfortunately they meant little next to her father's. He eyed Mr. Smith. He was a genial man. He cared for his daughter, but like many, thought her welfare best taken care of by a man of wealth. Henry understood his point of view.

But Henry was an attorney. He argued and persuaded for a living. Perhaps it was time he made his argument to the man himself.

He waited until Mr. Ryder had left to sit near Lady Mary before approaching Mr. Smith. "May I speak with you, sir?"

Mr. Smith blinked. "That sounds serious."

"It is to me." Henry gestured toward the casement doors. "May we speak on the terrace?" He ignored the curious looks they were garnering. He had to handle this carefully, like it was the most important negotiation of his career.

Mr. Smith heaved himself up from his chair and led the way outside. Once the doors were closed, he spun on Henry. "You're not going to accuse me of killing Perrin, too, are you?"

Henry fell back a step. "What? No, of course not." And thank God they no longer suspected him. That could make this situation only more awkward.

"Then what is this about?" Mr. Smith asked. Traces of blood still stained the stone floor, and he frowned down at it.

The window by the lily of the valley opened an inch. Henry waited, staring at Lady Mary through the glass until she took the hint and wandered back to her seat. "I wished to speak with you regarding your daughter." He clasped his hands behind his back.

"What about her?" Smith drew his eyebrows together. "Is something amiss?"

"That depends on one's point of view." He inhaled sharply. "You had hoped to marry her to Lord Perrin, and I understand you are now looking at another possible match."

Smith rubbed his jaw. "She has been out in society for several years. I don't want to waste any more of her time."

Henry nodded. "You have been looking for a husband who would not only make her a good match but one who is financially advantageous to you, have you not?"

Smith huffed. "Your tone leads me to believe you think those two goals are mutually exclusive. I can assure you, based on the two happy marriages of my other daughters, that it is not."

"I believe you." Henry wanted to pace, release some of his nervous energy, but he forced himself to remain still. "But what if it did come down between your daughter's happiness and your wealth? Which is the most pressing concern of yours?"

Smith cocked his head. "You're dancing about a question, aren't you, son? I should warn you, in my line of business, I've come to appreciate frankness."

Henry widened his stance. This was it. The moment when he discovered whether he'd been a fool to dream. "I care for your daughter. Greatly. And I believe she feels the same about me. You would gain nothing from our union, except free legal representation whenever you wished. But she would be well taken care of. And well loved."

Smith crossed his arms, resting them on his rounded abdomen. "You're asking for Katherine's hand."

It wasn't a question, but Henry nodded nonetheless. "I am."

"Katherine is my youngest." Smith pursed his lips. "Unlike my older daughters who knew a bit of struggle as I built my business, she has only ever known luxury. You think she would consent to being the wife of a solicitor?"

The back of Henry's neck heated. "I might not be at the top of society, but I am hardly a pauper. I am well-respected in my profession and earn accordingly."

Smith arched an eyebrow. "Even if she were willing to live with less, do you think she should give up the status she could attain? She could be a countess, be the pearl of society."

Henry knew Katherine didn't care about such things. "I believe I heard you say you didn't care about Perrin's rank. As to your daughter's feelings, you should ask her whether being the wife of an attorney would be acceptable."

"How much business do you do in London?" Smith ran his thumb and forefinger along his jaw.

"Quite a bit." Henry's heart pounded faster. Was Smith wondering how much he'd see his daughter if she lived in Exeter? That could only be a good sign.

"And your London clients, many of them are men of business?"

Henry's stomach knotted. He didn't like this turn. "My clients are from varied backgrounds," he said warily.

"And I have various business interests." Smith rubbed his hands together. "It could be most useful having a solicitor in the family."

"Sir, I have to say, I—"

"Yes, yes, nothing comes for free." Smith flapped his hand at Henry. "Any deal you broker between your clients and myself, you will of course receive a commission. And with your inside knowledge of their strengths and weaknesses, we should be able to secure most favorable terms. Perhaps we could set up a sliding scale on Katherine's dowry. If you meet a certain number of goals in bringing me new business, you gain a percentage of said dowry at the end of each year. After, say, ten years, if all goes well, you will have earned the full amount I would pay to any earl or viscount's son. That is more than generous, would you not agree?"

"Exceedingly generous," Henry gritted out. The curtain at the window fluttered, but he ignored it. If Lady Mary wished to eavesdrop, he no longer cared. No doubt Mr. Smith *was* being generous for even considering Henry for the husband of his daughter. And when Henry refused the terms, no doubt said generosity would disappear as fast as one of Cook Clem's cakes. "I must say—"

"You don't have to thank me, my boy," Smith said. "If you

are what my Katherine wants, I can make it work."

"Most kind." Henry drew his shoulders back. "That is not what I was about to say, however. I would do many things for your daughter, but abusing my position isn't one of them. I owe my clients a duty to place their interests above my own. A duty I would show to you had you been one of my clients. If those are your terms, I am afraid I must decline."

Would Katherine consent to an elopement? Would she risk the wrath of her father, the cut direct from her family and friends, just for him?

Smith grabbed his elbow before Henry could leave. "Don't be hasty, Evans. I like an honest man." He lowered his ear toward his shoulder. "To a point. But more importantly, I want a good man for Katherine. That was just the opening volley."

Henry's shoulders lowered an inch, but he still remained tense. "What do you mean?"

Smith gazed heavenward. "There was a benefit in seeking husbands among noblemen. At least they knew the starting point for a negotiation. I would have expected better from an attorney."

A negotiation? Meaning Katherine's father was open to different terms. As long as Henry won Katherine and didn't have to compromise his ethics, he would give just about anything to Smith in return.

But since Henry was a good solicitor, one skilled in negotiation, he kept that knowledge to himself. He crossed his arms over his chest. "All right then. These are my terms."

─────⟨ ⟩─────

Chapter Thirty-Five

Katherine

FOR THE FIRST time since Cook Clem had returned to the kitchen, Katherine couldn't enjoy her dinner. She gave it her full attention, keeping her gaze down on her plate as she cut her roast chicken into ever smaller and smaller pieces, but the bites she finally did put into her mouth were flavorless.

Exceedingly generous.

Henry's words rolled over and over in her mind. He'd bartered for her. Received a liberal offer in return for brokering deals with his clients. She didn't know which hurt more. The fact that Henry had been like all the others, seeing marriage to her as a path to financial prosperity or that he would agree to betray his clients for his own gain.

She'd thought him honorable. Forthright.

She'd thought he'd loved her for her own appeal.

"...isn't that right, dear?"

Katherine looked up to find Lady Havenstone looking at her expectantly. "Umm...yes?"

The woman nodded. "We all are. One never appreciates the comforts of home until sequestered in another's house. But that all ends tomorrow."

"Tomorrow is indeed a happy day." Lady Mary sat two seats

to Katherine's right, at the foot of the table tonight. She must have outmaneuvered Miss Walker for that seat. She waggled her eyebrows at Katherine and gave her a significant look. "Tomorrow everything will be resolved."

Katherine blinked. She turned her head to look behind her, but no one else was there. Whatever cryptic message Lady Mary had was intended for her. Perhaps she should have been paying more attention to the others during dinner instead of nursing her broken heart.

"I am resolved to never again attend a house party." Lord Havenstone swirled his wine in his glass. "Especially during foul weather."

"It hasn't been so bad. If everyone was more willing to engage in the entertainment I suggested, it would have been even better." Miss Walker toyed with her necklace. "I, for one, will be a bit sad on my departure tomorrow. It will well and truly feel like Perrin is gone."

"And good riddance," Havenstone muttered.

Mr. Withers dropped his fork on his plate with a clatter. He leaned back in his chair. "I am most eager to return home, though I'll miss Miranda, of course."

"Miranda?" Lady Mary's forehead wrinkled. "Bertram...."

"Lady Perrin is dead. For many years." Miss Walker slammed her glass down on the table. Wine sloshed over the rim onto the tablecloth. "I don't know why you men can't remember that. She wasn't a saint."

Lady Mary looked at Miss Walker as though she were something unmentionable in the gutter. "Everyone is aware of her passing. I'm certain Betram only meant he'll miss all the memories he has of his sister in this house. A house which she managed so well. A house, and those in it, that loved her." *And not you* was left unspoken but heard by all.

"Of course, that's what I meant." Mr. Withers's face went red. He took a swallow of his drink. "I'm tired of everyone questioning me."

Lord Havenstone leaned over to his wife. "So *very* happy to be leaving on the morrow," he murmured. "To peace and quiet and away from these people."

Lady Havenstone nodded. "Pass the butter. If this is to be our last meal from Cook Clem, I want to enjoy it fully."

Katherine rubbed her nose. The lady's words sounded almost like an accusation, but that made little sense.

Lord Havenstone was quick to comply. "Yes, dear."

Katherine's lips twitched. She raised her gaze to see if Henry had observed the interaction.

Their eyes met. The amusement in hers fled at the intensity in his. She'd forgotten she'd been ignoring him. Forgotten that he was yet another man more interested in an alliance with her father than a happy marriage with her. She looked back at her plate.

"Has everyone finished with their packing?" Mr. Ryder made a valiant attempt for neutral conversation. "The roads are quite rutted, I expect, so if you have anything breakable, be sure to pack it well."

"Yes, a big travel day for all of us." Lady Mary thanked the footman who took her plate and replaced it with a glass dish filled with syllabub. "Well, all but one. One of us won't be leaving in the morning." She gave the table another significant look.

"Uh, you mean yourself?" Mr. Ryder dug his spoon into his own syllabub, lifting it to reveal layers of cream and fruit. "You aren't leaving Perrin Manor tomorrow?"

"Well, no, I'm not leaving tomorrow." She pressed her lips together. "Two of us won't be leaving in the morning, I meant. But, I've said too much."

Katherine couldn't help her glance to Henry. Even in her disappointment, she had to know if he understood Lady Mary any better than she did.

It appeared he didn't. Henry rubbed his jaw. "Is there something you wish to tell us, Lady Mary?"

Lady Mary patted her lips with her napkin. "No, not at all.

What a wonderful dessert to end our time together."

"The last dessert I'll ever taste from Cook Clem," Lady Havenstone muttered.

Her husband's face darkened.

Everyone became too preoccupied with their syllabubs to question Lady Mary further. The hint of sherry and the tang of lemon made the frothy berry and cream concoction a delight. It was almost enough to raise Katherine's spirits.

A few of the men went to the billiards room after dinner, but everyone else made their way to the sitting room. There was packing to be done and early morning travels for some, but no one seemed eager to retire. Even though there weren't many friends among the guests, it did feel as though they were the survivors of some natural disaster. Rescue was imminent, but departing after everything they'd been through together felt like a solemn event. One that should be respected.

Lady Mary took Katherine's elbow and dragged her to the corner of the room. "We need to talk."

"All right." Katherine shook the older woman loose and rubbed her arm. "What is it? And what were all those strange hints at dinner? I didn't understand a one of them."

"It's all a part of my plan." She peered over Katherine's shoulder and lowered her voice. "I'm setting a trap for the killer. I laid the foundation at dinner with my hints about someone not leaving tomorrow. Now we must be overheard saying the magistrate told me he will be making an arrest in the morning."

"Did he tell you that?"

Lady Mary sighed. "Of course not. It wouldn't be much of a trap then. It would only be the truth."

Katherine crossed her arms over her chest. "To what end? How, exactly, do you expect this trap to spring?"

Lady Mary spoke to her slowly, as though she were a particularly dull-witted child. "When the killer hears he or she is to be arrested in the morning, he will take a runner tonight. I've put the stable master on alert, and we'll be staying up to watch who tries to leave."

"What will we be doing?" Henry strolled up to them, a cup of steaming tea in his hand. He gave it to Katherine. "Have you finally devised a way to discover the murderer?"

"I have," Lady Mary said.

While the lady repeated her plan, Katherine took a sip of the tea. It was sweetened just to her liking, with the smallest dollop of cream.

Her shoulders drooped. The man had observed how she took her tea and made it exactly to her specifications. Was even this a ruse, a manipulative attempt to win her affections in order to obtain her father's money? Or was he a decent enough sort of man who would try to keep any wife of his happy?

Neither of those options appealed.

"It seems highly unlikely that your ploy will work." Henry ran his hand up the back of his head. "The magistrate seemed an intelligent enough fellow. I say we let him do his job and stop playing at detectives."

"Playing?" Lady Mary sounded insulted. "I can assure you this is no game to me."

In her heart, Katherine agreed with Henry's assessment, but pride had her siding with Lady Mary. She lifted her chin. "It's a brilliant plan. Shall we deploy it now? I can speak just loud enough to be overheard."

Lady Mary glanced over Katherine's shoulder again. "Yes. And sound shocked, like you can't believe it."

That would be easy enough. Raising her voice just enough, she exclaimed, "The magistrate told you he would be making an arrest in the morning? If he knows, why wait?" Even though Lady Mary hadn't told her to include that last bit, Katherine thought it added a dash of authenticity.

She'd expected loud gasps. Perhaps an oath or two. But there was only a brief pause in conversation behind her, a slight hush, and then everything resumed as it was before. Miss Walker attempted to convince the others to engage in one last entertainment, Mr. Withers made some nonsensical comment to the

Havenstones, and Mr. Ryder sighed heavily.

"Was that all right?" Katherine asked. "Did they hear?"

"They heard." Lady Mary adjusted her spectacles. "Now we wait."

"For how long?" Katherine had her belongings to pack. A letter to write, letting Mr. Evans know his schemes toward her had failed.

She swallowed. Well, perhaps it would be best if she just left quietly. Let him think that her heart had only been but lightly touched, that their parting was of little consequence.

"All night if necessary," Lady Mary said.

"You may choose to stay awake all night, but Katherine and I won't be joining you." Henry took her cup of tea and set it down on a side table. "She and I need to talk."

"We certainly do not." Katherine felt a grim sort of satisfaction at the surprise on his face. "I heard enough this afternoon. I have packing to do. I, for one, cannot wait to return to London."

He grabbed her elbow, halting her retreat. "What is the matter?" His forehead wrinkled. "I have good news to tell you. Will you not listen?"

"No." She jerked her arm away. She was tired. Tired of being a chess piece her father moved about his board. Tired of looking over her shoulder in this house, suspecting decent people of being killers. Most of all, she was tired of herself, for succumbing to a silly hope that she could control her future. She should accept her position, be grateful for all that she did have, and never again surrender to silly feelings like love.

Henry darted a glance at Lady Mary. "Let's go somewhere where we can speak privately."

Lady Mary tsked, her gaze bright, flitting between her and Henry. "That wouldn't look proper. You can pretend I'm not here. I will be the soul of discretion."

Katherine was glad someone was finding this situation amusing. "No discretion is needed. I am going to my room." With a quick good night to her father, she fled.

Only to find Henry barring her way up the stairs. "What has happened between when we were last together and now? Why are you angry?"

She'd hoped to avoid this, but perhaps it was better to air everything out. Let her start fresh with no regrets. "After my interview with the magistrate, I came back to the sitting room. I heard you and Father on the terrace through the window."

Henry rubbed his temple. "And? Shouldn't you be happy? Your father gave his permission for us to marry."

"You think that's what I wanted?" Katherine made an effort to lower her voice. She'd thought he knew her better. Knew that she didn't want a man who saw her as an acquisition. It seemed even the best of men, when presented with an opportunity for wealth, didn't have the strength to refuse.

He slowly straightened, a mask dropping over his face. "Yes. When you let me inside your body, that was the impression I was under." He stepped aside, and waved his arm toward the steps. "Forgive me for being but a roadblock in your path. I should have remembered my place."

She clenched her fists. She wanted to pull out her hair, tear at his clothes. Why was he so frustrating? He was the one in the wrong. He knew she didn't care about things like status. Was he trying to make her the villain in order to protect his own ego? Or had he actually been hurt by her words?

She blew out a breath. This was too important to run from. She needed to be explicit. "Did you, or did you not, negotiate with my father on what terms you would accept for marrying me?"

"I did." A muscle ticced in his jaw. "Do you want to hear said terms?"

The backs of her eyes burned. At least he'd had the honesty to admit it. No, Henry wasn't the sort of man to dance around the facts, to wheedle or whine when he was caught out. Even when he broke her heart, he made her fall for him a little bit more.

She blinked rapidly, not wanting to let him see her cry. "I do not. Goodbye, Henry." She darted past him and raced up the steps. She waited for him to call out, chase after her, try to stop her in some way.

He did nothing.

Chapter Thirty-Six

Lady Mary

T HE *HOOT HOOT* of the tawny owl jerked me back to wakefulness. Or perhaps it was a barn owl. I wasn't an expert on bird calls. I was only certain it was an owl that had kept me company on my hours' long vigil.

I checked the mantel clock. I had placed it on the table in front of me in the front sitting room so the light of the waxing moon illuminated its face. Only six minutes had passed since last I checked. Not enough time for my brief nap to allow anyone to escape this house unnoticed.

I pushed out of the settee and stretched. My back popped, making the tendrils of regret I'd had about forgoing my bed that night resurface. I shoved them down. I had a killer to catch. Any fatigue or minor aches and pains could hardly measure against that.

I dug my knuckles into a sore muscle in my lower back. And these aches and pains definitely didn't need to be mentioned to Jane. Instead of supporting my idea, she'd had the temerity to laugh in my face as she'd made her way to her comfortable bed. Told me I'd regret it.

I sniffed. I might, but I'd never admit it.

The killer must have heard Katherine. Why wasn't he running?

She and the owl watched black melt into Prussian blue and that turn into a mercury-gray morning. The house started to awaken with the sounds of the servants moving about. Southey hunted her down, seeming most excited to find her boot available for a good chew instead of locked behind her bedroom door. He was a warm lump on her lap until the first of the guests called their carriage to the front doors. Southey wasn't overly fond of horses and carriages, apparently, so he opted for greener pastures. The kitchen I suspected, begging for a bigger breakfast.

The Havenstones seemed the most eager to leave. As they had the farthest distance to travel, their early start made sense. The sun had barely broken the horizon when their trunks were secured to the back of their carriage and Lord Havenstone was handing his wife into the conveyance.

She leaned forward from her seat and stared at Perrin Manor. "Good riddance to a house of sadness. I hope the new Lord Perrin can make a better go of it."

As Perrin's eldest son had taken on a profession that preferred to manage relationships with God instead of earldoms, I somehow doubted it. I expected the new earl to sort through his father's matters and then turn the running of the estate over to his younger brother.

"Why do you call it a house of sadness?" I asked. "I'd always found gatherings here to be most merry." Especially when Perrin absented himself from the group.

Lady Havenstone shrugged. "Just something Cook Clem said. About the manor ghost now having two more to keep her company."

Lord Havenstone sighed. "Sarah...."

"My husband doesn't believe in ghosts." Lady Havenstone sniffed, her nose turning up. "I, however, have always enjoyed a good horror story."

"Who is supposed to haunt these halls?" I, also, didn't believe in ghosts. But there had been those shadows and that face in the window Katherine had seen. A shiver raced down my spine.

"The Lady Perrin." Lord Havenstone trundled past me and climbed into the carriage, sitting across from his wife. He also leaned forward, both of their heads framed by the carriage doorway. "It's a story the servants apparently use to scare the new hires. That Perrin killed his wife and now her spirit haunts the manor, getting up to mischief. Why any fool would believe that." He shook his head.

Lady Havenstone straightened. "Are you calling your wife a fool?"

He patted her knee. "Never, my dear. Good day, Lady Mary. I wish you safe travels back to London." He tapped the ceiling of the carriage and shut the door. He lowered the carriage window and gave Perrin Manor one last look.

"This has been a most trying ordeal." Lord Havenstone frowned. "Trapped with a killer, suspected of inhuman actions. The only good consequence is that Perrin can no longer cheat anyone else. He will not be missed."

And without even a nod of his head, he raised the window and they were off.

"We won't be inviting him to speak at Perrin's funeral," I said to the butler who stood next to me.

His lips twitched. "No, milady."

Mr. Ryder left next. "Will you be all right here by yourself?"

"Perrin's eldest should be arriving within a few weeks. And I won't be alone." I nodded to the butler.

Ryder took my hand and bent over it. "There is never a dull moment with you, is there?" He set his hat on his head, his eyes warm. "I look forward to furthering our acquaintance in London."

I had no answer to that. Ryder was an irritant, a threat to my business. Yet a part of me would look forward to sparring with him again. I must be perverse to feel the slightest twinge of regret at my foe's departure.

I had no such feelings at Miss Walker's egress, and she was not as efficient at the taking of her leave as Mr. Ryder.

She wandered down the hall of Perrin Manor, a scone in her hand, poking her head into each room she passed and sighing deeply. "Poor Perrin. Such a tragedy."

"Regardless of the size of one's home, being murdered usually is."

Miss Walker glared at me. "His boys, dear as they are, won't know how to manage all this. I hope they know they can always depend on—"

"Your father must be most anxious to have you home." I put my hand on the woman's lower back and guided her toward the open front door. "You are his rock, as I understand it."

"Yes." She turned on the front terrace, looking up at the manor house. Regret flashed across her face. "So much wealth here when my father and I have so little. I had hoped—" She pressed her lips together. "Well. I must be off. Be sure to tell—"

"I will." I tapped the tip of my walking stick against the top step of the front terrace until the woman was safely away. That only left Betram and my fellow conspirators.

Bertram I was sad to see leave. The loss of his wife and sister seemed to have wounded him more than I'd realized. He was paler and thinner than I remembered. Even his hair was thinner. I wondered if I would ever see him again.

I clasped his hand. "Even though this party turned to disaster, it was good to visit with you once more, Betram. If you should ever come to London, please call on me."

"Of course, of course." He turned and looked back at the house. "Same goes for you."

My heart ached. It was another connection lost for the both of us. We might not have liked Perrin, but he had been the brother to both our spouses, and with him gone, there was one less memory, one less string connecting me to Cavindish and Betram to Miranda.

I squeezed his hand. "Don't you worry. I'll see to it that Miranda's gardens are maintained. She so loved her primrose and foxgloves, her cornflowers and monkshood." I tried to remember the names of the plants in the Perrin gardens but could come up with no more. "I will make sure her sons know how important it is to maintain them."

"Yes." Bertram pulled a handkerchief from his pocket and coughed into it. "Very well. 'Til we meet again." And then he was gone, as well.

I found the rest of our group in the dining room. Mr. Smith had piled his plate high with bacon and cakes. Katherine and Henry only had cups of tea and sat across from each other at the table, studiously avoiding eye contact.

"Everyone else has gone," Katherine said. "We should be going, too."

"I am going to fully enjoy Cook Clem's last meal." Mr. Smith licked a dab of icing off of his thumb. "Besides, we are only traveling to Exeter today. There is no great hurry to leave."

"Why Exeter?" Katherine sounded suspicious. "We stayed at that lovely public house in Ilminster on our way here."

"Exeter also has *lovely public houses*." Henry directed his words to the father. "I will give you the names of a few I know to be quite comfortable."

I made my own cup of tea and sat with them. I felt weighed down. Not only had all my suspects left the house, now Katherine and her beau were at cross-purposes. Perhaps the house *was* cursed, a sad phantom wandering the halls ensuring no one else could find happiness.

All too soon, Katherine managed to convince her father to make their departure. She gave me a fierce hug, ignored Henry's attempt to assist her into the carriage, and left Perrin Manor with her father without even a backward glance.

A groom held the reins to Henry's horse. "We sent your trunk ahead this morning, sir."

"Thank you." Henry took the reins. He waited for the groom to leave before turning to me. "I am only thirty miles away, but a half a day's ride. If you or Perrin's sons need any assistance with the disposition of the estate, let me know."

"I'm sure they will be contacting you." I raised my hand, shading my eyes from the sun. "So is that it then? You're giving up?"

He raised one eyebrow. "The magistrate has taken over the case. Hopefully, his physician will be able to narrow down the poison, giving him a better idea of who murdered Perrin. It isn't *giving up* to leave the matter with the proper authorities."

I wholeheartedly disagreed with that sentiment, but at the moment, that wasn't the point. "I meant are you giving up your intentions regarding Katherine? I had thought you were made of sterner stuff than that."

He blinked. "You knew that Katherine, Miss Smith, and I were…."

"Courting?" I snorted. "If you were trying to be subtle about it, I regret to inform you that you didn't succeed."

He turned the brim of his hat about in his hands. "And you aren't shocked that an attorney would be fool enough to try to pursue an heiress?"

"At my age, there is very little that can shock me." I thought of the attorney's calm and kind demeanor when he'd given me Perrin's letters. Apparently very little shocked Henry, either. "Your match would definitely make the gossip circles. Katherine might lose the company of some who had pretended to be her friends. But if your intentions are noble, there is nothing immoral about your pursuit. Who cares about wagging tongues? If, that is, you haven't given up." Katherine deserved better than a man who turned tail at the first trial.

His lips curved. He truly was a handsome man when he smiled. "I have not given up." He slapped his hat on his head, making his horse skitter to the side. Henry placed a calming hand on the animal's neck. "The Smiths and I are meeting for dinner tonight. Katherine and I have much to discuss."

"An apology for whatever you did that raised her feathers

wouldn't go amiss."

A muscle ticced in his jaw. "She misconstrued a situation."

A laugh burbled out of me. How much he had to learn. "I wish you luck."

Henry nodded and mounted his horse. "I will send you an invitation to the wedding when it is announced."

"You're that certain of success?"

"I am a skilled negotiator." The horse pranced backwards, kicking up dust. "Besides, there are also practical concerns for why we must marry. She will see reason."

I waved him off, then turned back to the house. Henry's optimism had buoyed my spirits for a couple of minutes, but the reality of the situation quickly deflated them.

The servants should be directed to put black crepe in the windows before Perrin's sons arrived. I would let Perrin's boys go through his personal belongings, but I needed to determine if any bills needed paying. What purchases needed to be made to keep the estate running.

I had a moment of envy for my brother-in-law. Dying was easy; it was the cleaning up after that was hard.

My chest tightened. That was a detestable thought. What were a few hardships to the joy of waking up to a new day?

I grabbed my skirts and raised them an inch as I climbed the stairs back to the house. My steps dragged, each foot seeming a mile. I didn't want to face the fact.

Perrin was dead. Murdered. And whoever had killed him had returned home to his or her warm bed.

I had failed.

Chapter Thirty-Seven

Lady Mary

I DIDN'T LET my foul spirits keep me from working. The house needed a good cleaning and airing out after all the guests had left. The windows were finally being replaced in Perrin's study, and as the workmen attended to that matter, I went through his desk and collected the few bills that had accumulated.

I consulted with the butler on the immediate needs of the house, sent a note to the parish clergyman that as soon as Perrin's body was released, it would need a burial, followed by a service when his sons returned home. It was mid-afternoon before I had a moment to myself.

I sat in my chair in the library. It was a grand chair and would look quite well in my parlor. I wondered if the boys would be willing to part with it.

Instead of laying down at my feet as he had done all day whenever I'd paused, Southey paced back and forth, occasionally nipping at my skirts.

"For once, you might have the right idea," I told him. I was rather peckish, as well. A nip down to the kitchens wouldn't go amiss. Neither would another attempt at convincing Cook Clem to come work for me. I'd sensed he'd been warming to the prospect. I wanted at least one good thing to come from my trip to Perrin Manor.

Heaving myself upright, I made for the stairs down. I leaned on my walking stick more than usual. The day would come when it might be a necessity instead of an affectation. I frowned at the idea.

The aroma of freshly baked bread made my pique disappear. "That smells heavenly," I told Clem when I entered the kitchen. "I don't suppose I could get a bit of an advance on that before dinner? With some butter and jam?"

"Of course, Lady Mary." He cut off two large wedges from the loaf and put them on a plate before me. The butter and jam quickly followed.

"Won't you join me?" I indicated the spot across from me at the wide wooden table.

"Don't mind if I do." He fixed his own plate and sat. "I hope the syllabub was to everyone's liking last night. I wanted to make a more exotic dessert, but couldn't get the needed spices in Modbury. That will be one benefit to living in London."

I paused, a bit of jam trickling down onto my fingers from the slice of bread I held. "So you've decided? You'll be leaving Perrin Manor?"

He nodded. "I will be moving to London, but—"

"Splendid." My empty stomach fluttered, most likely looking forward to all the delicious food it would soon be enjoying. "Absolutely splendid. You won't regret it. And London is a much more suitable place to live for an unmarried man such as yourself. Many more prospects for potential matches."

He nodded again. "I expect that too, but—"

I loosed a chuckle. "And to think Ryder thought he could get you for his club. It isn't even White's but some small, bookish affair over on Brown Street. It would be an absolute monotony cooking for those members."

"No, a club doesn't interest me." He sucked in a deep breath. "I do feel I should tell you—"

"Oh, we can work out all the details later." I hummed a happy tune as I bit into the bread. I loved being the victor, especially over Mr. Ryder. "He shall be so disappointed."

"He's not the only one," Clem muttered before savagely biting off the crusty bit of his bread.

"Hmm?" I flapped a hand. "Oh, yes, I'm sure the vultures were circling. You've made quite a reputation for yourself. Who else asked for you?" I couldn't imagine enjoying a victory over anyone else as much as I did over Ryder, but I was open to being surprised.

He hesitated. "Well, Lord Havenstone pressed his case most avidly. He and his wife even cornered me in my bed chamber, trying to make the case that their servants' quarters were more comfortable than any that I'd slept in before. Havenstone tried to make that sound as though it compensated for the salary he offered, which was significantly less than what I make now."

I inhaled sharply. The nerve of Lady Havenstone. She'd tried to make me feel guilty going for Clem when she and her husband had set their sights on him, as well. She was a most unpleasant woman. The baron's failure to acquire Clem's services partly explained his wife's sour countenance, however.

It also explained something else. My heart sank. As macabre as it sounded, I'd hoped Havenstone had been the killer. If he'd been sneaking about only to bargain with the cook, then that left only two other options. "The night they went to your chambers, was it last Tuesday?"

He nodded. "The night the windows were broken. When we heard the commotion, the baron and baroness flew from my room faster than a winning racehorse."

"And last Friday before lunch, did he find you then?"

"He did." Clem twisted his lips. "I was trying to take a nap before I had to begin dinner. I'm still not feeling all there since my illness. I think that was when I definitively knew I wouldn't be accepting his offer. He also found me again after lunch. He was relentless."

I made a note to myself. Don't pester the cook. Now that I'd managed to lure him away, I didn't want to aggravate him into leaving my service.

I finished my snack and brushed the crumbs from my hands. "Thank you for the treat. I think I'll have dinner in my room tonight. If you could send up a plate?"

"Of course, milady. And...."

I stood. "Yes?"

He gave me a tight smile. "You'll be here for a bit longer. We'll have time to talk further."

I hoped he wouldn't try to negotiate for a higher salary. I'd pay it, of course, but I didn't want to feel taken advantage of. "Goodbye for now."

I climbed the stairs, exhaustion pulling at every step. I had one more letter I needed to write today. I only hoped the magistrate would believe it.

Chapter Thirty-Eight

Henry

S HE WAS A most frustrating woman, his Katherine. And with a
most nimble tongue. Whenever Henry tried to steer the
conversation in the direction he wanted, she twisted it to an
entirely different matter. He understood that she didn't want to
be at this tavern eating dinner with him, but she needed some
understanding, as well. She should understand it was only natural
for her father to want something in return for agreeing to his
proposal. And she damn well should understand Henry would
sacrifice almost anything to marry her.

"And that's when I had to put my foot down." Mr. Smith
mopped up the last of his stew with a torn piece of bread. "She
could find as many costumes as she wanted in that attic. I wasn't
going to perform any scenes for the entertainment of that lot."

"I believe Miss Walker thought you would find it entertaining, as well." Katherine tapped her thumb against the rim of her
wineglass and peered over her father's shoulder at the small clock
that rested on a shelf over the bar. It was the fourth time that
she'd done that. Henry wondered what she thought was an
appropriate hour for her to make her excuses and retire.

Mr. Smith snorted. "Not hardly. I was almost glad when that
Taylor fellow was found dead. It put a stop to that idea of hers."

"Father!"

"I said almost." He sniffed. "No need to get superior. You know you also would have detested her latest entertainment."

Katherine flushed and slid a side-long glance at Henry before staring back into her wine.

That flush was the same one that had heated her cheeks when he'd brought her to crisis in the folly. She must know there could be consequences for their actions. She must understand they had to marry. He pushed his empty bowl away. "I feel like taking a turn about the room. Miss Smith, might I—"

"Speaking of poor Mr. Taylor, do you think the murderer will ever be caught?" Katherine asked her father. "It is gruesome to think that it is someone we know."

Mr. Smith leaned over the table and patted her hand. "Justice has a way of coming for everyone, my dear. In this world or the next." He patted his breast pocket, then pulled open his jacket and dug about in the pockets of his waistcoat. "Drat. I hope I haven't left it behind."

"What did you forget to pack now?" Katherine gave her father an indulgent smile. A smile Henry hoped she would turn on him if only she'd give him a moment to explain.

"My pipe." Mr. Smith frowned. He muttered as he searched every possible pocket. "…not the only one. But I'm not turning back for it."

Henry jerked his glance from Katherine's face. "What was that? What did you say?"

Smith rubbed his jaw. "You must have seen it, too. It's a distinctive carriage. It had that worn panel over the left front wheel. We passed it coming here. The driver must have turned back to Perrin Manor on instruction from the occupant."

Henry tapped his fingers on the table. Why would any guest return to Perrin Manor? Yes, an item could have been forgotten in packing, but it could have been sent for. Everyone had been most eager to leave that cursed house. It would take a strong reason to make someone return.

Not unless they had to. Not unless whatever had been left had been incriminating.

He jolted upright, his hip knocking into the table.

Katherine grabbed for her glass.

"I must leave." Henry threw some coin down, enough to cover all their meals.

"Good gad, man," Smith said. "Where's the fire?"

"Back at Perrin Manor." He strode for the coat rack and shrugged on his overcoat. "No time to explain. We'll speak later." He hurried from the tavern at a veritable run. The stables where he kept his horse was three blocks away. And Perrin Manor was over thirty miles. He'd push his horse as fast as he could, but it was night and there were limits.

He wouldn't get there in time.

But he had to try.

⎯⎯⎯◦∞◦⎯⎯⎯

Chapter Thirty-Nine

Katherine

HE'D LEFT. KATHERINE rubbed her breastbone. Not only had he left, he'd done so at a sprint. Like he couldn't wait to be out of her presence.

She scowled down at the table. Of course, he'd fled, the coward. Katherine ignored the fact that she had been preparing her own escape from the moment she'd seen him at the dining table. He'd left, and without even making another try for her.

She was unreasonable. She knew this, but she couldn't help but feel hurt that he had given up on her so easily. Perhaps, deep down, she'd hoped he'd have some excuse to explain his actions. Something to prove to her that she hadn't put her faith in the wrong person.

She gave the barmaid a tight smile as she cleared their table. "Shall we retire?" she asked her father.

He swiveled his head about. "I want a smoke. I wonder if anyone here has a spare pipe?"

"You should make that one of your requirements in the next marriage contract." A sour taste filled her mouth, and she took a large swallow of wine. "My future husband must always have a spare pipe on his person."

Her father stopped looking about and focused on her. "What

are you going on about?"

Her shoulders dropped. "You know, in addition to providing you with confidential client information, or a good land deal, anything to make you more money, my husband must always be ready to lend you a pipe. I'm sure that could be added to any sale contract for me."

"Sale contract?" His bushy eyebrows drew together. "Truly, what *are* you going on about?"

"It isn't exactly a secret, Father." She shrugged. "Your daughters are a commodity. You did quite well with my sisters, though you do seem to be having a bit of trouble bartering for me if you've had to drop your standards to an attorney. A man without wealth of his own but only useful for his contacts."

His face blanched. "Is that what you think? That I want you married only to profit myself?"

"It's what I know." She rested her hand on his and squeezed. "It is what society expects. You are not alone in your actions. It's just what is done. But you can't expect me to be happy to be seen as nothing more than an asset."

He turned his hand and grasped hers tightly. "My dear, nothing is further from the truth. I want you, all my daughters, to be settled happily to good men. And good men will have the intelligence and resources to take care of you. I don't deny your matches should strengthen our family, but how reckless would it be of me to give you to someone who hasn't the means to provide for you?"

"Father, I love you, but I also heard you." She blinked, the backs of her eyes burning. "You traded me to Mr. Evans for access to his clients. He bartered his ethics away for a chance at your money. That does not make him a good man."

"Where did you hear this?" He narrowed his eyes.

"You and he were having a discussion on the terrace at Perrin Manor." She'd heard them, clear as day. "Please don't deny it."

"I have no intention of denying it. I learned much about your beau in that conversation." He huffed. "You stopped eavesdropping too early, however."

Katherine straightened. "I wasn't eavesdropping, only standing by an open window." She patted her hair. "I wanted the breeze."

"Of course." He arched an eyebrow. "Well, you must have developed a chill and left your breezy window before your Mr. Evans declined my terms. Most strenuously. He said he wanted you but wouldn't abandon his morals." He slapped his palm on the table. "I only argued for an agreement that would benefit all sides," he muttered. "You and he would be happily married, and his clients and I would enter into mutually profitable business deals. Nothing wrong with that."

Her breath caught in her throat. "What did he agree to?"

"That he would give me free legal services, as any good son-in-law would." He dipped his chin and gave her a look. "The dowry I was willing to give him he would only accept in your and your future children's names. None for himself."

Her chest went tight. If that were true…. "And you agreed to that? You'd allow me to marry Mr. Evans?"

"I did and I will." He shook his head. "You won't have the same dress allowance as you would with an earl, or the fancy jewels, but if you can live without that, I can live with a son-in-law who is an attorney."

Her heart leapt. Henry hadn't negotiated to increase his purse. And her father would accede to her wishes. She popped up and leant over the table, her arm bumping into a candlestick. She kissed his bristly cheek. "Thank you, Father."

He slapped at her sleeve and shook his head, his lips curling. "Well, don't set yourself on fire over it. Mr. Evans is going to have his hands full with you. If I were a better man, I'd warn him away."

"You will do no such thing." Katherine plopped back down and glared at the tavern's door. Why had the confounded man left, now when she wanted to talk with him? Could he…could he have given up on her? Considered her more trouble than she was worth? She almost couldn't blame him.

But she'd been troublesome before and hadn't scared Henry away. And he'd arranged for them to have dinner together. So if he did care about her, he wouldn't have run out of here without a very good reason.

But all they had been talking about before he'd left was that ratty old carriage....

"Oh my Lord," she breathed. Lady Mary was at the house, as good as alone. What did Henry think he could do, all by himself?

Images of him hurt and worse flashed through her head. Not now. Not when they finally had an open path to happiness. She couldn't let anything happen to him. "Father, call the carriage. We need to leave. Immediately."

Chapter Forty

Lady Mary

THE SOUND OF breaking glass roused me from my slumber.

Not that I had been sleeping deeply. I'd tossed and turned for hours before finally succumbing to fatigue. I glanced at the clock, waiting for my eyes to adjust to the dark before I could read it. Two eighteen.

I could just close my eyes again. Wait until morning to see what had broken. A servant had probably gone down to the kitchen for a glass of milk and dropped it.

I blinked at the ceiling. Drummed my fingers on the counterpane. And, finally, threw my covers off of me and rolled out of bed. My feet rooted around the floor for their slippers. I grabbed a wrapper and my walking stick and stepped out into the hallway.

All was now silent. I looked back at my bed. A beam of moonlight pierced the gap in the window's curtains and crossed the counterpane, marking the spot where I should be lying. I set my shoulders and closed my door behind me. It wouldn't take long to search for the source of the noise. And perhaps when I was done, a nice cup of milk of my own would be my reward.

I first went to Perrin's study, but the newly installed windows remained whole. I heaved a sigh of relief. The rest of the windows on the ground floor were similarly unscathed.

I paused at the steps down to the kitchen but decided to search the bottom floor last. That cup of milk was supposed to be a reward for finishing the search, after all. I climbed to the first floor and peeked my head in the now empty guest rooms. The staircase up to the servants' quarters was illuminated by the nearly full moon, but even I didn't have the gumption to go knocking on the servants' bedroom doors to ask if they'd heard anything. All that remained on this floor was the ballroom, and with all the glass and mirrors in that room, it seemed probable that might be the source of the disturbance.

If there were any ghosts, they would be here. It was the room Katherine had seen the face in when coming back from the ice house. But no phantasm met me. Only my own reflection, bouncing from the mirrors to the floor-to-ceiling windows. The white of my wrapper nearly glowed in the moonlight. If someone saw me now, they would think I was the ghost.

A muffled whine halted my step. My eyes searched the shadows in the corners of the room. It was the dog. It had to be. He'd knocked over something, broken it, and now would cut his paws on his own mess.

I was tempted to leave him to it. I grimaced. "You dratted dog. Where are you?"

For once, Southey didn't come running when he heard me. The beast must actually be hurt.

My mouth went dry. "Southey." I clapped my hands softly. "Let me know where you are, boy."

The shadows shifted in the far corner, and I heaved a breath of relief. I started forward. "Don't move. I'll come get...."

My feet froze. The movement from the corner was much larger than any dog. The darkness curled, transformed, until Bertram emerged to stand in the moonlight. Southey was clamped in his arms, his snout held in Bertram's hand.

I faltered back a step. "Bertram? What are you doing here?" My question didn't even sound convincing to my ears. I knew why he was here. And he knew that I knew. Or else, why would he come back?

"Do you remember dancing in this room?" He swayed back and forth, his gaze soft even as he squeezed Southey tighter to stop his wriggling. "What times we had. You and Cavindish. Me and Martha. Miranda and…." His swaying stopped. "Well, it would have been better had it just been Miranda."

I sidestepped, putting a high round table between me and Bertram. "But then, who would she have danced with?" I asked lightly. I should have seen it earlier. There was something wrong with Bertram. Dreadfully wrong. I'd tried to excuse his oddities as a man grieved with loneliness, but there was something more.

"She could have married anyone, lovely as she was." Bertram glided forward, his expression vacant. "Father had to choose the one who would hurt her."

I circled the table as he approached, darting behind a low settee. "I won't deny Perrin was a right sot, but he wasn't violent. He didn't harm her." Not violent, but vicious. He probably did hurt his wife, in a thousand tiny ways, but I had a feeling Bertram was referring to something more than cutting words.

That seemed to snap Bertram out of his dreamlike stupor. "He killed her! She would have wanted me to make him pay. I'm only sorry I took so long."

Southey whimpered.

I held up my hands. "That's only a servants' tale. Something told to frighten newcomers. It isn't real."

"Martha told me you wouldn't believe. She knew you'd betray us."

Arguing with a madman was difficult enough; I didn't think I could persuade a dead wife, too. "Your sister fell from a ladder. She never recovered." There had been witnesses. It had been an accident. And Perrin had seemed genuinely grieved. No, it wasn't Bertram's sister whose death I started to wonder about. It was his wife's.

I remembered her hand tremors. How she couldn't recall that I'd been married the last time I'd seen her. I'd believed Bertram when he'd said she suffered from scrofula. Died from it. Now other possibilities arose. I'd heard the rumors of Bertram's infidelities early in his marriage. His trips to the unmentionable London clubs. The symptoms all fit, and my heart broke.

"He pushed her." Bertram threw his arms out, flinging Southey away from him. The pup hit the mirrored wall and fell to the ground. He didn't move. "But Martha and Miranda told me how to repay him. She told me all about her pretty flower. How I could use the roots, leaves, and petals to avenge her."

"What plant?" I gripped the head of my walking stick, my palms growing slick as I trotted behind a low and long table. Something bit into the heel of my slipper, and I chanced a glance down. The remains of an oil lamp lay shattered on the floor, the fuel making the glass-strewn floor slippery.

My shoulders raised another inch closer to my ears. Bertram had already poisoned and stabbed as methods of execution. I didn't know what he had in mind for me, but now burning to death seemed a possibility.

"Lily of the Valley. It's a lovely flower with white, bell-shaped blossoms. I'll make you a bouquet."

To be lain on my grave, no doubt. "And you made a tisane from the plant? Put it in Perrin's wine?" The cup of hot water he requested each night made sense now. Perhaps he did like to drink it before bed, but he'd used at least one to brew the poison.

"He could never have tasted it over the wormwood flavor." Bertram kicked the settee out of the way, making a clearer path to me.

"And Mr. Taylor? Why did he have to die?"

"Taylor?" Bertram rubbed his jaw. "Oh, yes. The secretary. Grasping, greedy man. He threatened to expose me if I didn't pay him. He saw me holding the wormwood wine the day Perrin died. I told him at the time that I wanted to try it, but after you told everyone it had been poisoned, he knew. Can you believe the audacity of the man? Society has become so fallen."

I almost laughed. Murder was justified but greed was a sin.

But I shouldn't expect logic from the insane. "And locking Mr. Evans and Miss Smith in the ice house? Did you try to kill them, too?"

The moonlight illuminated his cheek but cast his eyes in shadow. He floated toward me, inexorable. "No." He giggled. "I was here, watching."

The face in the window.

"That Taylor shoved the log between the door and the step." He took two steps forward; I took two back. "He was not pleased when Miss Smith rebuffed his advances. I told you he was a venal man. I thought stabbing him appropriate as he'd stabbed Perrin."

It was the matter-of-fact tone of his voice that sent the shiver down my spine. There was no remorse. No acknowledgement of the immorality of his act. No concern even over being caught.

Bertram couldn't distinguish right from wrong. Consequences for his actions probably had never entered his head. And there was no way I was going to reason my way out of this.

"And the windows?" I whispered. "Did you break those or was that Mr. Taylor?"

"Oh, I did that." Bertram mimicked throwing a rock.

"Why?"

He looked confused at my question. "Because I wanted to."

I swallowed. And there was nothing more to it than that. Bertram desired something, so he did it. Without thought or remorse.

Pleasure. That was the false idol Bertram worshipped. He'd killed Perrin because avenging his sister would make him feel good. He'd let his wants overrule rational thought. Though if what I suspected about his health was true, it was hardly his fault.

I circled back to the tall round table, hoping the white sheet draping over it would hide my intent. "Why did you come back here?" I placed my fingers under the rim of the table and tried to lift it. When had my strength left me? It had happened so slowly, year after year, that I hadn't noticed I wasn't the spry woman I once was.

"Because you knew." He tapped his fingers on his thigh. I'd thought it just a nervous habit, but now I saw all his fidgets, the playing with his cards, covered tremors of his own. "You knew, and you were going to inform on us."

Yes, I had known. Once Cook Clem had told me Havenstone had been with him during the time Taylor was killed, Bertram had been the only logical suspect. Despite Katherine's arguments to the contrary, I couldn't credit Miss Walker killing Perrin. She wanted to be lady of the manor and the wealth that came with that. Killing Perrin wouldn't have accomplished her goals. I'd written as much to the magistrate.

The magistrate. I tucked my walking stick under my arm and gripped the table with both hands. "I've already written to Lord Preston. Killing me won't save you from prosecution, it will only add another charge."

"Yes, but—"

I didn't wait to hear his reply. I hefted the table with all my might and turned it over onto his legs. Spinning, I ran for the door.

I was only ten steps away from the exit when he caught me. The blow hit the center of my back and sent me tumbling. My knees slammed into the floor, followed by my palms and jaw. I tasted blood before I felt the first lick of pain. My walking stick had bounced ahead of me, and I reached for it.

Bertram grabbed my hair and yanked me backwards. He dragged me past Southey, a shaking, furry little ball. Past the settee. I clawed at his hands. I knew I broke skin, but he didn't seem to feel the pain. When we reached the floor-to-ceiling windows, he tossed me aside.

"I don't want to stab you." He looked down at me, hands on his hips. "I promise, this will be quick. You won't feel much pain. I wouldn't want a woman to feel pain."

This time, I couldn't hold back my harsh chuckles. It all seemed so terribly amusing. He was happy to kill me, but his chivalry didn't want me to hurt.

Bertram was going to kill me, and I couldn't stop laughing.

He kicked a pane of glass, the window shattering. "I don't suppose you'll jump for me?"

My laughter died. Bertram was going to kill me, but I wouldn't go down alone. I twisted, pulled back my legs, prepared to kick, claw, and hammer his body in any way I could.

He turned his head, his eyes widening. There was the flash of light on a pale face, the shimmer of muted flames. My walking stick made a satisfying crack as Marie struck Bertram across the face with it.

Marie pulled the stick back then jabbed the knob end into Bertram's gut.

He wheezed and fell back. His shoulder hit the jagged window, sending more shards of glass to the terrace below. He hung, half out of the window, his hands clinging to the edge of the window frame.

"Come on." Marie held out her hand and pulled me to my feet. "Let's get out of 'ere."

I had no objections to that idea. The first step sent pain shooting up my bones, but I ignored it. I stopped only long enough to gather up Southey before hurrying after the maid into the hallway.

She took my elbow as we hobbled to the stairs. "Are you injured?"

"No." Yes, but not enough for complaints. Southey shifted, burying his snout at my throat and whining softly. I turned left at the juncture. "We need to get…" I stopped, realizing I was speaking to air.

Marie popped her head back around the corner.

"Come on," I snapped. I limped forward to the stairs.

"We should 'ave gone up to the servants' quarters." Marie trotted after me, looking over her shoulder. "There's a couple of burly footmen who would 'elp us."

I paused on the second step down. I hadn't thought of that.

Bertram's silhouette was lit by the moonlight at the hallway's junction.

And it was too late now. "Hurry," I told Marie. We went down the steps as fast as we could, but I knew Bertram was gaining on us. I'd thought to reach the stables, where I knew the hunting guns were kept and where at least one groom would be sleeping. Now I knew we wouldn't make it. But if we could barricade ourselves in one of the rooms, ring for the servants, we might have a chance.

If they could hear the bell from their bedrooms. If they didn't spend too much time pulling on their wrappers and boots.

Bertram grunted when he reached the bottom of the staircase. There were too many ifs to make survival likely.

We darted into the rear sitting room, my body already reaching for the end table by the door. It was too easy to drag. It wouldn't hold against a child pushing at the door, never mind a grown man. But I started pulling it over.

Marie slammed the door shut, only to be thrown back as Bertram pushed inside. He stepped clear of the door, blood dripping from his arms. He turned toward us, his face wearing an expression that would haunt my dreams, and ran right into Henry's waiting fist.

Chapter Forty-One

Henry

HENRY FLEXED HIS hand. He didn't think any bones were broken, but he might have to punch the arsehole again. He wanted to be prepared. "Is everyone all right?" He looked from Lady Mary to the maid and back again.

Lady Mary patted her hair. It lay in a tangled mess about her shoulders. "Not to sound ungrateful, but what, in the name of all that is holy, are you doing here?"

"Mr. Smith saw Withers's carriage turning about." He toed the man's body, but Withers remained unresponsive. "I realized he must have been the killer and rode as fast as I could back."

"And crawled in through a window?" The maid pointed at the small table he had knocked over when he'd crawled inside the sitting room.

The back of his neck heated. "I didn't want to rouse the whole house if I was wrong. The casement doors were locked, and I know that window has a loose latch. It seemed the thing to do." When he'd heard the commotion and seen bits of the window above fall onto the terrace, he'd kicked himself for his caution. He should have banged on the front door, gotten everyone out of bed.

And speaking of… "Can you wake the butler?" he asked Marie. "We need men to hold Withers until the constable can be called."

She nodded and skirted around the unconscious form before disappearing down the hallway.

Henry drew Lady Mary to the window and examined her in the moonlight. "Are you certain you are all right?" His eyes narrowed. "I believe there is a bruise forming on your chin."

The breath she loosed was a bit wobbly. "A few knocks about, but considering the alternative…."

Henry glared at Withers, wishing the man would awaken so he could plant him another facer.

Unfortunately, the butler and a contingent of strong young men arrived before he had the chance. Oil lamps and candles were lit. A length of rope was produced, and Withers was neatly bound and removed to the stables. Someone was sent to rouse the constable and get a message to the magistrate.

Tea, with a nip of something a bit stronger, was served.

Lady Mary held a saucer of milk up to Southey, who was resting on her lap. The dog eagerly tucked in. Aside from being somewhat subdued, he seemed no worse for wear.

"Marie." Lady Mary dipped her chin to look at the girl. "When did you arrive back to this house, and why did you not come see me? You must know I was worried about you."

Marie stretched her slippered toes out in front of her, the hem of her wrapper falling open. "I arrived late this evening. Yesterday evening now. You'd already gone to bed. I was still unpacking my things when I 'eard the crash."

"Well, you were quite adept with my walking stick," Lady Mary said. "I thank you for saving my life."

Henry waited for his turn to be thanked. And waited. He grimaced. Saving two women from a crazed killer would have to be its own reward.

"I don't understand," Marie said. "Why did 'e do it?"

"Revenge." Lady Mary ran her fingers over Southey's ear. "But for a crime that existed only in his mind. I believe Bertram was quite ill. With a disease that is often treated with mercury, which seems to do more harm than good. I should have realized when you found the calomel in Bertram's room, Marie. It's a form of mercury used for digestive issues, as you thought, but it's also used to treat something worse."

Henry sagged back into his chair. "His rumored infidelity to his wife. That was true?"

"He was quite the scoundrel in his younger days, though became a most attentive husband later on." Lady Mary nodded. "Looking back, I believe he gave the disease to his wife and she died from it."

"Gave it to his wife?" Marie's face cleared. "Oh! Oh…. That kind of disease."

"The symptoms were all there." Lady Mary stared down at the dog. "If only I had paid attention enough to notice."

"So he killed Perrin out of a misguided sense of justice. And Taylor?" Henry asked. "Taylor knew that Withers was the killer? Tried to extort money from him perhaps?"

Lady Mary tapped her finger on her nose. "You have it. Greed was Mr. Taylor's downfall."

Henry rubbed his jaw. "There was an evening, after dinner when the men were conversing. Taylor had said he thought of Katherine as a sister and that 'a brother would do anything for a sister.'" He sighed. "He obviously didn't feel Katherine was like a sister. His words must have been directed to Mr. Withers. Another hint that Taylor knew Withers had taken revenge for Lady Perrin. I missed it at the time."

"We all missed a lot." Lady Mary stroked Southey's back. "Though not one of those blasted herbalist books mentioned lily of the valley as a potential poison. I refuse to take responsibility for not discovering the source of what killed Perrin."

"You were reading books pertaining to home remedies," Henry said. "I believe some people have tried to use that plant to ease the symptoms of gout, but to no effect. Lily of the valley is commonly understood not to have any medicinal value. It wouldn't have been in your books."

Lady Mary sighed, her shoulders rounding. "I didn't want to acknowledge that Bertram was sick. If I did, I would have had to take some action. It was easier to believe he was lonely and eccentric. And now two men are dead."

Perrin's loss would be hard on his sons, no doubt. Henry tried to muster up some sympathy for the secretary but fell short. Not only had the man been willing to allow a killer to roam loose, he'd attempted to coerce Katherine into marriage. No, he would cry no tears over Taylor's death.

Katherine. A small smile tugged at his lips. "She'll be so disheartened to find Miss Walker innocent."

There was a rustle of skirts at the door. "She might not have killed Perrin, but I maintain that woman is far from innocent."

THE SHOCK ON Henry's face did a little to lift Katherine's spirits. As did seeing Lady Mary and the rest of them safe. A bit knocked about, perhaps, but relatively unharmed.

Henry jumped to his feet. "Katherine. What in heaven's name are you doing here?"

"Why do you think?" Lady Mary rolled her eyes. "She came to the same conclusion as you." The older woman tilted her head. "I hope you didn't hare off on a horse like our Mr. Evans here."

Her father stepped next to her. "Of course not. But I do believe we've cracked a wheel bouncing back here at the speed we did. We might have to spend another night at Perrin Manor while it's repaired."

Good. That would give her time to explain her foolishness to Henry. Time to beg him to take her back.

Henry strode up to her, gave one apologetic look to her father, then pulled her into his arms.

All right then. Perhaps she didn't need much time at all. She rested her cheek against his chest and held on to the pockets of his jacket. "I'm sorry. My father told me what you negotiated for. Or more importantly what you didn't. Can you forgive me?"

His hold tightened. "A man almost killed two women here tonight. Could have turned his madness on you at any time in the past weeks. Right now, I can forgive anything."

Katherine burrowed deeper into his hold. She was almost grateful to Mr. Withers. If they hadn't been investigating a murder together, she and Henry most likely never would have fallen in love. And without the threat he posed, Henry might not have accepted her back so readily.

"While I'm here, I'd say we'd best finalize the details of your nuptials." Her father's voice held a bit of warning.

Henry loosened his hold on her, but only a little. "Then it's a good thing there's an attorney in the house."

Chapter Forty-Two

Lady Mary

IT HAD BEEN a week since Henry and Katherine had left. Two days since Michael, Perrin's eldest, had arrived to take over management of Perrin Manor. And on a sunny and warm spring morning, it was finally time for me to take my leave.

I looked back up at the house as Jane clambered into the carriage behind me.

"I'm taking a seat facing forward," Jane called back. "You know I feel ill if I'm moving backwards."

Marie handed her last bag to the driver before scuttling up into the carriage herself. "Ooh, me too. I became positively sick on my last carriage ride."

Leaving the rear facing seat for myself.

The terrier barked as a footman handed him into the carriage.

And Southey.

Tulips burst from their bulbs beneath the windows, dashes of color in front of the black crepe. The mix of cheer and somberness matched my mood. Too much had happened to feel truly happy. But enough good had come out of this party to raise my spirits.

Katherine and Henry becoming engaged was one part of that good. The banns had been read, and the wedding would happen in a month's time in Exeter. I had already decided on the dress I would wear to the event.

I had acquired a new maid, and I thought Marie would make a brilliant addition to my household. I'd have to warn the rest of the servants about her skill at card games, but then, maybe one or two of them could hold their own against her.

I'd acquired a dog.

I glanced down at the hem of my gown. I couldn't see the tiny teeth marks, but I knew they were there. I wasn't quite sure if Southey was more on the tulip side of the equation or the black crepe but it had seemed cruel to leave him.

I shook the butler's hand, accepted a peck on the cheek from Michael, and climbed into the carriage.

The door was shut with finality.

I hadn't acquired a new cook. I blocked Southey from jumping on my lap, and he settled for curling up on the seat, pressed against my thigh. I had half a mind to go to Mr. Cooke's office and give him a piece of my mind. He'd taken the small tidbit of information I'd provided in my letter to him and gone and stolen Cook Clem out from under me. The salary Clem had quoted that the crime lord had offered him was outrageous. Whatever information Cooke had given me was more than paid for by his acquisition of Clem.

"The rotten scoundrel," I muttered, not for the first time.

Jane rolled her eyes. "You were outbid. Accept it."

"I had only added information about Clem in the letter to Mr. Cooke so as the blackguard wouldn't think the only reason I would contact him was to solicit information. I was trying to be *polite*, speaking of the house party before jumping right into my request." I narrowed my eyes. "He used my civility against me."

"Your civility?" Jane smirked. "Well, you don't have to worry about that happening again."

Marie tittered into her glove.

The carriage jostled into motion. I pinned each of my maids with a glare before lowering the window and looking out. The house seemed so forlorn now, but it would only take time for the new master to make his own imprint on it. To have his own parties, start his own family.

Well, perhaps not Michael. That would be up to his younger brother.

My own family was dwindling. Perrin was dead, and Bertram had been removed to an asylum. I didn't think he would last long.

"Gor, do that again." Jane had turned her whole body to watch Marie.

Marie held a playing card up between two fingers, wiggled her hand, and the card disappeared. From Jane's viewpoint, she couldn't see the edge of it sticking up from the girl's sleeve.

Well, a part of my family was dwindling, but another was expanding. Such was life. I had family, friends, and a club that I adored and was anxious to get back to managing. I had much to be grateful for.

Smiling, I turned back to look at the house. A pale oval hovered in one of the second floor windows. No chill ran down my spine. No premonition of otherworldliness. It must be a maid cleaning one of the rooms.

All the ghosts had been in Bertram's head.

The End

About the Author

Alyson Chase lives in Colorado. A former attorney, she happily ditched those suits and now works in her pajamas writing about men's briefs instead of legal briefs. When she's not writing, she's probably engaged in one of her favorite hobbies: napping, eating, or martial arts. (That last one almost makes up for the first two, right?) She also writes humorous, small-town, contemporary romance novels under the name Allyson Charles, and paranormal romances as A. Caprice.

My substack: authorac.substack.com
My website: www.alysonchase.com